AN ABYSMAL SLEEPCATION

A Story By
PAUL TANNEN

ISBN-10: 0-9960061-0-9
ISBN-13: 978-0-9960061-0-1

R.H. WAS HERE.

It'll Go to His Head

A non-emergency ambulance sweeps the damp streets taking full advantage of the dark, early morning pre-rush hour. The driver toggles the knobs and switches within his reach in an attempt to turn on the lights that illuminate the dash. He eventually concludes that the ancient vehicle never had a light to brighten the dash, or maybe it's one of those things that died and the company deemed it a luxury not worth fixing, like the radio. He leans in close, his forehead nearly touching the steering wheel.

He squints at the odometer. "The mileage is 210,344."

"210,344." The passenger scribbles the number on a sheet of paper on his clipboard. "What's your state EMT number?

"I usually just put my name there," the driver says. "Just write, 'Brian R.'"

Brian looks over at his younger counterpart, Chris, a pale young man with an almost freshly-trimmed blond buzz cut.

At the stoplight he reaches to the floor, hand blindly searching.

"What are you looking for?" Chris asks.

"The schedule. Who do we have first?"

"Ms. Mallet," Chris says. "Then we have an hour before we have to pick up Jerry Benson from the nursing home."

"That's what I thought," Brian says. "Just making sure."

"Yeah, we've got a pretty easy day today." Chris looks at the schedule. "No huge people, everybody can at least stand up and get on the stretcher by themselves."

"Yeah." Brian shakes his head. "I don't know about Ms. Mallet though, she's getting pretty bad. We had to lift her the last time we transported her. I think she's on her way out."

"Really? Damn, that sucks. I like her. She's like one of the *only* patients I don't mind taking. I don't mind riding in the back with her either because she doesn't usually talk; she just looks out the back window or sleeps the whole time. I sit in the jump seat behind her and go to sleep."

"She doesn't talk to you?" Brian asks. "Huh, must not like you. She talks to me the whole ride, but I don't mind. She's cool. She knows about all of the reality shows, celebrities, music. You can talk to her about anything, and

2

she knows what you're talking about. I wish I had a grandma like her."

"Speaking of that," Chris says. "Did you know she has a grandson that lives with her?"

"No she doesn't," Brian says. "She lives by herself."

"I thought that, too, but that's what Mitchell told me. He said the other day when they picked her up after treatment, she was talking about her grandson that lives with her."

"Have you seen how tiny that house is?" Brian says. "It's like the size of a trailer. Don't you think if somebody else lived with her we'd know it? We've been transporting her for three years, and I've never heard or seen anybody in that house besides her. Not even a visitor."

Chris shrugs and looks out the window. "I'm just telling you what I heard. Why would she lie about that?"

"I didn't say she was lying. I just think she was probably out of it after her treatment. Or she might be in the beginning stages of Alzheimer's."

"Man," Chris says. "I think she'd be better off living in an assisted living place."

No traffic in sight, Brian rolls past the stop sign through the intersection.

"She wouldn't ever do that though," he says. "She's too independent, and you can tell she's never leaving that house."

"That's true," Chris says. "I wonder how she keeps it so clean. She can barely even walk. I go to my grandma's house and reach in the cabinet to get a glass and I swear every dish in the cabinet has old food stuck to it."

They back into the narrow driveway, remove the

stretcher from the back of the ambulance and wheel it to the door.

* * *

The doorbell rings as Ruth Mallet frantically slides the last sock on her grandson's damp foot. She cringes at the thought of the EMTs having to wait for her to gather her things and answer the door. Every other day, the medics make a trip to transport her to and from her dialysis treatments where she spends four hours being treated for the adverse effects of kidney failure.

Every other day for those four hours, she thinks about her grandson lying at home in bed, helpless. Ruth has cared for her grandson since her daughter brought him to her when he was two years old. Her daughter rarely comes around and spends her days meandering the streets trying to find ways to cop her next hit.

At the time, Ruth wondered how the most beautiful, kind-hearted, selfless and intelligent young woman she had ever known, could find something as pure and innocent as a child so dispensable. Over time she realized that a strong and irresistible love affair with crystal meth could replace the most important of things. That was twenty-six years ago.

Ruth shuffles across the floor to her walker as quickly as possible. Her health is deteriorating swiftly since her diagnosis of end-stage renal disease. That was nearly three years ago, approximately three months after the biking accident left her grandson in a coma. When asked about her grandson's condition, she always remarks she's seen enough crazy things in her 67 years to know that despite what anyone says, he will wake up one day. She won't give up until he does.

She kisses her grandson on the forehead and gives his shaggy brown hair one last stroke before leaving the bedroom. "Grandma loves you, sweetheart, I'll be back in a few hours."

Ruth approaches the two gentlemen. Seeing young men never fails to make her dwell on what her grandson would be like had it not been for his misfortune. She sets her stuffed flowered tote and a large Ziploc bag containing her lunch on her favorite green ottoman near the front door, as is her routine. Ruth notices the layer of grime on the surface of her tote every time she sets it on the ottoman, but never remembers it needs washing until on her way out the door. If there's one thing she takes pride in, it's her knack for cleanliness.

Brian scans the room. "Good morning, Ms. Mallet. How's it going?"

"Oh, just feeling a little weak, that's all. The doctor put me on a new medication, and it just has me feeling so dizzy all of the time."

"Oh, that's not good." Chris looks over at his partner, his voice flat. "Your house always smells so nice. We were talking about that on the way here. Who keeps it so clean? Your grandson?"

Brian raises his eyebrows and smiles as he lets down the railing on the stretcher.

"Thank you, Christopher, you are such a sweetheart, but this house is a mess right now. I try my best to keep it clean myself."

Brian notices she didn't mention her grandson.

"How is that adorable little one of yours, Brian?" Ruth asks.

Brian smiles. It's one of his favorite topics of conversation. "He's getting tall. He just turned three and everybody mistakes him for a five-year-old. He's gonna be taller than me one day, so I have to rough him up now while I still have the chance."

The EMTs effortlessly lift the stretcher and make their way to the rear of the ambulance. Ruth has been steadily shedding weight over the past few months. It seems as if it's easier every time they lift her. The doors on the back of the ambulance slam, and they head out.

Ruth settles in for another five-hour session of bumpy rides, needles, and a cold treatment room.

* * *

Shannon stands in line at the coffee shop waiting to order her daily latte. She scrolls through her phone looking at nothing in particular. She finds that fidgeting with her cell phone seems to make her feel less self-conscious in a room full of people. It figures that the one day she decides to bypass the congested drive-thru, the rest of the free world has decided to join her in line. Shannon has never understood why people like to stare at her. It makes her uncomfortable and she never knows how to react. People have told her she's pretty, not in the traditional way, but in a girl next door type of way. Some have went so far as to compliment her on her long legs and "soul-piercing" brown eyes. Soul-piercing, yeah, right. Certain people have also told her that the intensity in her eyes makes her look mean and seem unapproachable. Well, whatever it is that causes them to openly stare at her, it definitely contributes to her low self-esteem. And that's the official self-diagnosis.

Shannon never felt as if she belonged in the small

town in Virginia where she grew up. She always imagined herself in a high-rise office somewhere in Manhattan, living as a real-life Carrie Bradshaw. How did she wind up on the opposite side of the country in Portland, Oregon, at a nut-and-bolts job as an on-staff hospital psychiatrist? Not so bad as a first stop only seven months after earning her degree at East Carolina University. And besides, it was only a stepping stone toward ultimately having her own behavioral psychiatry practice, and a means to escaping her comfort zone.

Shannon yawns as she struggles to keep herself alert while waiting in line. She's not a morning person, and the schedule of her new job along with her half-hour cross-city commute five days a week have not exactly been convenient for her. The heavy showers, cold weather and four hours of sleep are the culprits of her detached demeanor, disinterested choice of attire, and sadly-neglected ponytail concocted in the rearview mirror of her car before she pulled out of the apartment complex parking lot.

Her coffee is almost ready, so she wanders closer to the counter to prevent the barista from calling out her order. Too late.

"I have a Caramel Latte for Shannon!"

That announcement and the subsequent attention it draws to her may seem minor to some, but it's one of the single most things she hates about her mornings, a close second behind waking up so early. She briskly walks back to her car in the snappy, cold rain and makes her way to the hospital two minutes away.

* * *

A slight breeze produces a blinding sliver of light that

shimmers through the beige curtains across the bedroom where Greg lies. He lets out a soft moan of discomfort and attempts to shift his body to a different position. The house is dead silent with the exception of the birds singing outside. Greg apathetically tries to open his eyes against the wishes of the sunlight. A motorcycle roars down the street, and Greg jerks awake. The burst of adrenaline accelerates his breathing and his heart beats so ferociously it causes chest pain. Thoughts race through his brain. Where is he? Who is here with him? Who is *he?*

Several bags and lines are connected to his body. Why? What? When?

So many questions race through his mind that there's no way to stop and focus on just one. If he knows anything, it's that this environment is unnatural. Dead silence engulfs the room. The quiet ringing of ambient noise contributes to the eeriness of the atmosphere. The warm temperature of the house draws out all of the "old house" smells of the structure. Slightly distracted, he caresses and grasps the linen on the bed, adoring the way it feels against his skin.

Crashing back to reality, he decides to gather information about his surroundings. He shifts his body closer to the edge of the bed and grabs the railing using all of the strength he has to get himself into a sitting position. The next plan of action is getting his legs in position to stand.

Plan A is to use his left leg to forcefully slide his right leg off of the bed. Plan A never comes close to fruition; both legs are extremely too weak to make anything more than slight movements. Plan B is to use his arms to grab both legs and move them to the edge, maneuvering himself into an upright sitting position at the edge of the bed. After four minutes of utilizing virtually all of his adrenaline, sweat, and energy, he accepts that Plan B, though more successful than Plan A, was a failure. Greg rolls over off the side of the bed and crashes violently to the floor—Plan C.

He regains his composure, opens his eyes through the throbbing pain, and peers down the seemingly endless hallway dedicated to photographs of unrecognizable faces and antique paintings.

The ambulance pulls up in front of the old, light gray, ranch home. The tires hug the curb next to the kempt lawn. The driver climbs out of the cab and walks to the rear of the truck and opens the loading doors. Ruth immediately wakes up, impetuously grabs her tote and sits up on the stretcher.

"That was a smooth ride," she tells Chris. "I usually have trouble getting comfortable in the back of these things."

"Don't tell him that, Ms. Mallet," Brian says. "It'll go to his head. It was really my singing you heard that put you to sleep, anyway."

Chris smirks and shakes his head in amusement. Ruth laughs, putting her hand on her forehead. The two men, clad in matching blue bomber jackets and navy blue work pants, roll the stretcher to the landing of her porch. Ruth sighs deeply and grabs both of Brian's hands as Chris places his hand on her back to assist her balance.

"Thank you for the ride, boys," Ruth says, walking toward the front door, key in hand. "Have a good rest of the day."

"You're welcome, Ruth; see you next time," says Chris, as he and his partner both lift the stretcher and walk away.

Ruth inserts the key into the door of her home, which is eerily silent and warm as radiation from a heated oven when compared to the outside weather. This environment is a pleasant one for her as opposed to the bustling, shiver-inducing, and cramped dialysis clinic. She often exaggerates and compares the clinic to a "dressed up" version of the infirmaries for the wounded that you would see in the old war films. Ruth closes the door behind her and retrieves her walker from next to the ottoman where she kept it before she left.

The sound of the front door grabs Greg's attention, and he instinctively looks for a place to hide. He tenses up and his eyes get significantly wider at the thought of being defenseless against whatever or whoever it is bound to discover him in this foreign environment. The noise of cabinets and drawers being shut resonate through the halls. He hears the clashing of metal silverware being sorted through in the distance. Greg's efforts to go into hiding are pointless, as there is no way he could move fast enough to get anywhere anyway; he must await his fate. Slow footsteps are are evident through the creaking floors of the hall. He sighs deeply and stares at the door wide-eyed with apprehension. The steps get louder and a shadow closes in.

A frail, old woman enters the room with a food tray containing a tuna salad, a two-pack of graham crackers, and a small glass of water; her eyes are fixed on the tray making sure to keep it steady. She raises her head and looks at the bed. Realizing that the bed is empty, she looks down at the floor. Ruth and her grandson's eyes meet. The stare lasts about five seconds before Ruth blindly attempts to set the food tray on a stack of folded hand towels on the edge of the dresser. The tray crashes to the beige carpet. Against her natural instincts, she shows no regard to the mess left behind. Covering her mouth with her right hand, she extends her left arm in front of her like a person navigating themselves through a dark room. She walks to her grandson and whimpers as tears uncontrollably run down her face. Ruth wraps her arms around the back of his neck and buries her head into the chest of his gown, soaking it with tears of joy.

Greg is overcome with relief to discover that he is in the company of someone who seems as genuinely concerned about his well-being as he is. Ruth stands above him and clutches both of his forearms, resting them on her shoulders. She uses about as much energy and strength than she typically uses in a full day to get him upright and into the bed. Empathizing with the struggle of the old woman, Greg does his best to keep his feet flat on the floor. His weak body collapses to the bed, the side of his face re-uniting with the soft, plush sheets. Ruth uses the balance of her energy to lean over and grasp his legs and place them on the bed. Greg's body, now completely on the bed diagonally, allows just enough room for Ruth to take a spot beside him. She climbs into the bed, leans her back against the headboard, and rests his head on her shoulder, combing her fingers through his hair.

"It's ok sweetheart, don't be afraid. Grandma is here with you," Ruth assures him in a slight whisper.

The old woman's words provide him with a considerable amount of serenity.

Taco Bell Grande

Fred Jenkins, 38, a diminutive, gaunt black male, leans forward in his plastic school chair disclosing all of his inner feelings to the psychiatrist.

"I don't control what I do. I can't even eat the food I like no more. I'm talkin' bout things I been eatin' for years. The little Taco Bell Grande from Taco Bell—I been eating them things for yeeears. He told me to stop. He said he don't like Taco Bell Grandes. He wake me up at night talkin' bout go get him some cigarettes, I tell em 'I don't *want* no mothafuckin cigarettes.' I don't even smoke you know, that shit kill you. I ain't even smoked no crack since 2007. When I did it...that shit don't even—I'm sorry, baby girl, excuse my French."

"No worries, Mr. Jenkins, go ahead," Shannon says as she glances at him from the top of her legal pad with a smile, waving her hand for him to continue.

"I was just gonna say it don't even make me act like myself, ya know what I'm sayin'? It just make me feel like a different person. Ya know? I got grandkids. I don't want 'em to see they grandaddy like this."

"So who is the man you're referring to when you say 'he?'"

"What man?" asks Fred, one eyebrow raised.

"The man who tells you to buy him cigarettes and not to eat the Nacho Bell Grandes."

"Ohhh. He ain't a man. He a robot," says Fred, as a matter of factly.

"Oh? A robot, robot?" she says in an unintentionally condescending tone.

"Yes! A robot, ro-BOT!" Fred bellows. "What other kind of robot you know about?"

Fred's jaundiced eyes are now staring Shannon down like a raging bull ready to charge upon the slightest provocation. The room is dead silent.

"I'm sorry, I was just making sure. Ok, sort of like Robocop," she says as she continues to make notes on her writing pad.

"No, no, no," states Fred, with a shake of his head for each *no*. "Robocop was half-man, half-robot, and half-cop. I'm talkin' bout a real mothafuckin' robot."

"Ok, that's cool. A real robot. Is this robot with us right now, Mr. Jenkins?"

Fred's expression changes from frustration to that of

disbelief and anger, as evidenced through his wide-eyed frown.

"Bitch, do you see a mothafuckin' robot?!"

"No, I just didn't know if you meant..." she closes her eyes, smiles and shakes her head. "Never mind, go ahead."

"What's so *got*-damned funny?"

"Nothing's funny, it was just that—"

Fred leaps from his chair as if it instantly heated to 400 degrees. "Bitch you think I'm crazy! Don't you?" he says. "You wanna see a crazy ass mothafucka'? I'll show you a crazy ass mothafucka'!"

"Fred! I'm only gonna tell you once to please, sit down."

Fred grabs the chair with one hand and hurls it at the wall next to her and looks her directly in the eyes.

"Keep on fucking with me, ya' hear? And you won't ever fuck with nobody again in your life," he says with his index finger pointing two inches away from her face.

The clamor heard through the closed doors attracts several onlookers, including the nurses and mental health techs on duty. One of the techs, a clean-cut, Hispanic male with a goatee in his mid-thirties, calmly approaches Fred and places his hand on his shoulder. "Hey, Fred, what's up?" he asks in his light Spanish accent. "What did we talk about, when was it? Two days ago? You can't be doing that, man. How would you like it if somebody disrespected you like that, huh? You'd be ready to throw down wouldn't you?"

Fred puts his head down and begins to smile.

"You know you would! Wouldn't you? Don't lie!" shouts the tech as he smiles and firmly grabs Fred's shoulder, giving it a playful shake.

Fred eagerly exits the room to congregate with the other residents. The crowd of onlookers also disperse to tend to their previous activities. The tech, Jimmy, and a nurse are the only ones left in the room with Shannon. The nurse looks at the both of them and raises her eyebrows signaling that she has nothing to say, and leaves the room.

Jimmy approaches Shannon. "You ok, Dr. Brewster?"

"Yeah, Jimmy, I'm fine," she says. "Thank you."

"Don't worry about things like that. It was the same way when I started. You'll get used to it. Some patients just have to be talked to a different way than others."

"Yeah, I know, thank you. It's no big deal."

"Ok, good. You know if you ever need anything I'm here." He walks toward the door.

"As you always are," she smiles, her mood now lighter.

"You sure you don't need anything?" Jimmy asks as he turns around. "How about a refill on that coffee?" He smiles as he points to her coffee mug.

"No! Get out of here!" she exclaims, laughing as she pretends to hurl her legal pad in his direction. Jimmy exits the room, closing the door behind him.

Most would chalk up an episode such as this one as insignificant, however, to Shannon it may as well have been broadcast over the hospital P.A. system. She lets out a sigh of relaxation, which for that second feels like a release of all of the encumbrances of her stressful day. She is now certain that she won't be able to concentrate for the rest of the day with the thoughts of her gradually crumbling credibility as a leader lingering in her mind. It's almost as if not a day can go by without an incident that portrays her as incompetent. She is well aware of her deficiencies but isn't one to reveal the insecurities that she keeps locked inside of her. As a psychiatrist, who could she confide in and feel free to expose her social issues, emotional sensitivity, and mild depression without being deemed as a fraud?

Shannon rests her temple on her fist and looks at the clock above the door. The glance soon becomes a gaze. Amid the drama, repetition and seemingly endless days of her job, she sometimes feels as if she's stuck in an episode of *The Twilight Zone*. Shannon grabs her coffee cup and savors the last sip of her now cooler than lukewarm coffee. She has preferred her coffee at that temperature since she started drinking it in college to keep herself awake during late nights of studying. Since she didn't particularly like coffee, it would take her hours to finish a cup, hence, the cool temperature; after years of drinking it that way, she acquired a taste for it. She fastens the buttons on her blazer and stands to make her way to the break room for a refill.

Shannon walks past the nurses' station and overhears the chatter of gossip between the three women behind the desk. She can sense the stares of the women as she passes by them through her peripheral, and they resemble the glares of ravenous wolves plotting on their prey. She can't help but at times wonder what they say about her. However, despite the curiosity, she would rather not know. Their chronicles of the previous doctor were admirable but occasionally smeared with disapproval. The doctor who held the position before her was a psychiatrist of 38 years who had extensive experience in various aspects of the field, which included specialized treatment of Vietnam War veterans who suffered from PTSD. The fact that the motherly, veteran nurses that comfort and coddle her when things go awry could be the same ones backstabbing her couldn't possibly be helpful to her current psyche. She reaches the door to the break room and grabs her ID keycard clamped to her lapel and scans it to gain entry.

Before she walks in, a patient approaches her from behind. "Excuse me, Miss Dr. Brewster. Can I ask you a question?" asks the woman in a very quiet tone, displaying the apprehensiveness of that of a small child asking for a piece of candy. The fact that she holds a naked and dilapidated cabbage patch doll adds to the comparison.

Madeline Richards, a stout Caucasian woman in her mid-thirties with red, frizzy and slightly barbarous hair had repeatedly been in and out of this institution for several years, like the majority of the other patients. She was born with mental deficiencies and alcohol dependencies passed down from her mother. Her cheeks are smeared with makeshift blush and lips with red lipstick created with a red, washable marker taken from the whiteboard in the activities room. In the past, the nurses were able to successfully hide the red markers because of this, until they became aware of her uncanny ability of finding black Sharpies; they found that red, washable markers make much higher quality cosmetics than black Sharpies.

"Hey, Madeline, yes you can. What's up?" asks Shannon, her eyes lit up incredulously.

It's a rare occasion that patients approach her for anything, triggering the impromptu reaction.

"I'm sorry for bothering you," says Madeline, bowing her head apologetically.

"No, no, you're fine," Shannon turns toward her and lets the break room door that she just slightly opened close.

"Is there something wrong?"

"Yeah, kind of," Madeline admits, with a distressed expression on her face. "They always wanna watch sports, and I hate sports. They're being selfish and they won't let anybody else watch TV. Girls don't like *sports*. Can you tell them to change the channel?"

"You're right, we need to find a way to share the TV time so that we can make it fair for everyone. What do you think we can do to resolve this situation?"

"I don't know," Madeline answers with her head down, dragging her words in a whiny tone, obviously more frustrated.

"Ok. Let me start out by asking you what you would like to watch."

"I don't wanna watch anything; I just don't want them to watch sports."

"Ohhh," Shannon says, unable to conjure up a more appropriate response.

Madeline stares, eager to hear what is a nonexistent resolution. The shabby doll, also facing Shannon, seems to stare in similar fashion. Well aware that the patient won't recall this conversation minutes from now, Shannon chooses to casually avert the situation.

"That is such a pretty little girl you have there," Shannon beams, as she fondles the doll's ponytail. "What's her name?"

Madeline blushes. "Her name is Anne, and she's sad because she's hungry right now. I have to go feed her."

Madeline abruptly ends the conversation and walks down the bright, sunlit hallway to her room. Shannon enters the break room to get another cup of coffee to help her through the rest of her grueling day.

* * *

Greg has been immersed in his thoughts for hours trying to recoup even the smallest clues as to who he is and how he ended up here. The bright sun has rapidly faded into a dim sliver of light on the wall. The old woman has been resting her head on his chest and hasn't moved for at least three hours. Greg has been too shy to awaken her from her peaceful sleep. The previous warmth of the perspiration on his gown from the old woman's head is now cold against his skin. He softly taps the old woman's arm with two fingers.

"Ma'am," Greg says in a loud whisper.

No response.

"Excuse me, ma'am," he says in a normal tone, softly shaking her frail bicep.

Still no response.

After slightly shifting his leg in a final attempt to provoke a response, he grasps the woman's flimsy shoulders and props her into an upright sitting position. Ruth's body slumps back down. He grabs her again and notices that her skin is frigid and her color is a cyanotic blue. Her mouth is open, and the top dentures noticeably protrude from her mouth. He then realizes that the soggy spot on his chest wasn't the woman's sweat, but her saliva.

A rush of anger, despair, and nausea succeed the moment he discovers that the old woman is dead.

Greg, now feeling utterly defeated, clenches the sheets with his left hand and repeatedly strikes his forehead with his open right palm in a violent effort to release his frustration. Why didn't he didn't ask her questions as soon as he saw her? Why didn't he attempt to wake her sooner?

19

The thoughts and self-inflicted mental abuse prevent him from calming down. His hopelessness can be compared to that of an author who was on his way to finishing a book only to lose it all and have to start again from scratch.

Greg turns to the old woman again, observing her chest one last time in a desperate attempt at discovering the slightest sign of life. After confirming what he already knew, he covers the woman with the top sheet, which he feels would help him block out the thoughts of a possibly inauspicious fate. His mouth is dry and pasty; and his stomach feels as if it's being tightly clenched by an enormous hand, unsure whether its derivation is from hunger or nerves. The IV bags on the pole next to the bed that held his normal saline and parenteral nutrition have been completely desiccated since the morning.

The time is six minutes past 8 p.m, and Greg feels a sense of urgency. If anything constructive were to happen, it would most likely be done by way of being proactive. His vulnerability and the impending nightfall doesn't exactly commingle well in his imagination. He sits upright and inches his way to the edge of the bed and cogitates different ways to deliberately fall off the bed without it being so painful this time around.

Greg successfully plants his feet on the floor, leans forward, and places his hands on the floor in front of his feet. Because of his body weight being supported on his hands and the relative inability to control his muscles, his weak arms fail, causing his chest and shoulders to fall ungracefully to the floor. The light switch is above the dresser several feet away from his landing, and he immediately exerts himself across the floor in its direction.

His arms and elbows burn on the floor each time they drag against the dry hardwood. Fortunately, for the sake of his manhood, being able to relieve himself without a toilet isn't the only protection his diaper provides him.

Looking at the floor for the duration of the crawl, he looks overhead when he gets below the light switch. Covered in sweat, panting and thirsty, he closes his eyes for a few moments to rest. He then eases himself into a sitting position and raises his arm to try to grasp the dresser in an attempt to use it to help him stand to reach the light switch. Lethargy, vertigo and his weak limbs prevent him from doing so. His IV catheter shifts around in his arm every time he lackadaisically reaches for the drawers.

Physically spent, Greg slouches against the dresser awaiting a second wind. He removes the tape covering the IV catheter and slowly draws it out of his arm; a stream of blood incessantly flows from the antecubital vein. He grabs a handful of his hospital gown and presses it firmly against his arm. The bleeding slows and he listlessly dabs away at it as he stares at the lump on the bed of what was quite possibly the shortest tenured "best friend" in human history. He looks at the IV pole and the line stretching from the pole to his arm. He lightly yanks at the line. The pole wobbles. He yanks at it harder, causing it to crash to the floor. He weakly drags the pole across the floor toward him with the line. He raises the pole, and with it, easily flips the light switch to the "ON" position.

No light.

Greg raises his eyes to the ceiling; there is no light fixture on the ceiling. The switch is connected to an outlet in the room that was meant for a light. He scans the room in search of a light source and notices an old ceramic lamp on the nightstand on the right side of the bed next the old woman. Darkness closing in, with no choice but to wait until sunrise to make progress, he closes his eyes in abjection.

* * *

Shannon walks down the deep, drab eighth-floor hallway of her condominium building, arms full of groceries. The padded, velvet benches placed sporadically down the walls is an attestation to the length of the halls. She approaches her condo, sets her bags on the floor and opens the door. She gathers the paper bags and places them on the counter. Her groceries include potato chips, French onion dip, Oreos, strawberry ice cream, a frozen pizza, hard lemonade, and root beer. Shannon's health conscious tendencies tend to go out the window on her most stressful days. Tonight, the aim is to eat as much of the food as possible before tomorrow when her guilt resurfaces.

Shannon removes her hat and rain-dampened pea coat and drapes it across the arm of the sofa. She kicks off her shoes and removes the rest of her clothing as she peers out of her large panoramic window. The view from this particular window, which extols the beauty of a bridge over the water and the city skyline, was the deciding factor in her purchase of the condominium. It offers little in terms of space, which is why the love seat that matches the sofa is absent. She makes it a daily custom to stand in front of the window and gaze at the city atmosphere that never fails to fascinate her. Watching pedestrians and the rush hour traffic from her ideal vantage point is one of her favorite pastimes. The thoughts of the lives, history and agendas of the thousands of people that pass through each day seizes her curiosity and lets her imagination fly free. She doesn't consider this pastime as bizarre, instead, chalking it up as a means of mental exercise applicable to her profession. Her childhood dream of living the city life has been realized but she feels her time is being wasted as a spectator, an outsider. Television and the lives of others manage to somehow maintain a facade that makes things look so much more appealing.

Shannon sets the oven to 425 degrees before making her way to the bathroom to draw a bath. She pours a generous amount of bubble bath, dips her toes into the water, eases into the tub, and slouches her back against the cold ceramic. Her eyes close in gratification with the sensation of the hot water against her cold toes as the water quickly fills the tub. She opens her eyes and extends her torso and right arm from the tub and reaches for a handle on the cabinet beneath the sink. Seemingly hidden, yet strategically stashed behind beauty products, cleaning solutions, and a large package of toilet paper lies a purple, waterproof vibrator. After frantically fumbling through all of the clutter, she finds her trusty friend. Shannon then submerges her body, shoulders deep, into the heated water and slowly closes her eyes as the toy meets the apex of her amply spread thighs. The sensation of the steady pulsation moving across her labia and clitoral region diminishes her stress and quickly evolves into relaxation and pleasure as she slowly slides her finger inside of herself, simultaneously reaching climax. She drops the vibrator from the side of the bathtub and lets her arm hang over the edge, absorbing the serenity of the moment. The oven beeps signaling the 425 degree temperature.

You ready?

Greg stands in an elevator examining his reflection on the mirror-sheeted ceiling. He adjusts his necktie and combs his hair with his fingers trying his best to minimize his disheveled appearance. He tightly tucks in his shirt as the elevator door opens to an expanse of cubicles, office equipment and the socializing of men and women dressed in business casual attire. Almost immediately after stepping foot on the office floor, all activity ceases and attention is drawn to his entrance. Greg nonchalantly walks to his desk, completely oblivious to the change in atmosphere. He enters his cubicle and hangs his bag on the back of the chair.

A short, overweight, young, yet balding man eagerly

approaches his desk. "What's up man? Where ya been? We thought you were dead or something."

"Good morning to you too, Sid," Greg snaps back sarcastically, smirking, "What are you talking about? I'm not *that* late, am I?" Greg raises his left forearm to look at the large black analog watch fastened tightly around his wrist. The hour and minute hands are motionless.

Before long, a mob of co-workers encompass the opening of his cubicle, with Greg resembling an athlete sitting at his locker after the loss of an important game being crowded by the press.

"What do you mean what's he talking about? You've been gone two weeks without telling anyone anything. We almost put an AMBER alert out for your ass," exclaims a young black male bystander dressed in an Atlanta Braves baseball cap, jeans, and a plain black tee shirt.

Several people in the crowd laugh in agreement. The man turns to the crowd and chuckles in satisfaction from the unexpected feedback of his verbal gem. A beautiful woman overbearingly parts the crowd encircling Greg, apparently delivering an important message. The beautiful, tall, dark-haired woman clad in a navy blue mini dress so tight that the chance of it randomly busting at the seams is a very real possibility, does nothing to improve the situation. "Greg! Long time no see, buddy," the woman exclaims through a wide smile and large green eyes that could invoke shyness in even the most confident of men. "Bill wants to see you in his office. And the rest of you guys might wanna go back to your desks before he comes out here. I think he's on the rag; he's in one of his moods today."

The crowd surrounding the cubicle disperse before

Greg can get up from his chair. He leaves his work area and walks to his left, admiring the woman's stunningly exquisite, curved figure as he follows her down the hall.

The woman abruptly stops and turns to him. "Where are you going?" she asks with raised eyebrows, smiling and pointing in the opposite direction, "His office is over there."

Greg glances ahead and catches sight of the restrooms. "I know. I just wanted to go to the restroom first, but only if that's okay with you...Boss. Maybe I *should* be coming over here to your office," he condescendingly quips, shocked and pleased with his quick-witted retaliation.

"You think you're funny don't you? Don't patronize me," the woman says, flashing a grin as she shoves him lightly in the chest. "I was just making sure you knew. I mean, can you blame me?" Her skin is now much more fair and hair more of a reddish tint than Greg perceived it as being before.

Greg waits for the woman to turn the corner and heads in the opposite direction toward the boss's office. He passes the employee lounge and several smaller offices until he reaches the largest office at the end of the hall. The brass nameplate beneath the frosted glass window on the door reads: *Bill Elson.* Greg grabs the lever knob and turns it, opening the door. His boss, with a telephone wedged between his ear and shoulder, looks up at Greg as he slowly walks in. He stares at Greg intimidatingly for several moments; his expression is of obvious stress and disappointment. Greg stands at the door staring down at his shoes, then at nothing in particular.

Bill snaps his finger to get Greg's attention and gestures for him to take a seat; he continues his telephone conversation.

"Oh yeah, and then we're in the middle of the lake and the motherfucker tells me to pull the boat off to the side so he can talk to his wife...Yeah, I shit you not. I told him 'Yeah she's really gonna believe you got that wife beater-shaped farmers tan sitting in meetings in Seattle all weekend'...I don't know, you know Elaine's not too sharp anyway; she won't figure it out until Larry posts the pictures on the Internet of that hot waitress practically on his lap when he was passed out at the cove...I can't wait, but yeah, buddy, let me give you a call later on I got a lot on my plate right now...Ok...Take care."

Bill hangs up the telephone, leans back in his chair, crosses his fingers and rests them on his beer belly. They exchange stares for a few seconds before speaking; they stare so long that Greg starts to notice characteristics of his boss's face that he's never noticed before, such as the droopy bags under his eyes that would make him a perfect candidate for an advertisement of cold medicine or sleeping pills. Bill's demeanor is now in stark contrast to the gregarious person Greg saw talking on the telephone just moments ago.

"So what's going on?" Bill asks in a mild, yet intimidating tone.

Greg opens his mouth hoping it will help him muster up something, any decent response to the question; he wasn't expecting such an open-ended question. As a matter of fact, that was probably the *worst* possible question that he could have been asked. Greg raises his eyebrows and shrugs slowly and comes up with the only appropriate response.

"I don't know."

"Well you're gonna have to give me something, Greg. You've been AWOL; no call, no show for over two weeks. There are some things I can help you out of, but this...This isn't like you, man. I've got people I have to answer to just like you do. If you've got anything outside of work going on, maybe we can figure something out, but you gotta help me."

"I honestly don't know what's going on. I came in this morning with everyone asking me where I've been. It's just been a really odd morning for me." Greg stops talking mid-sentence, squints his eyes, smiles and hops out of his chair. "Hold on. You guys are fucking with me!" Greg put his hands on his head and does a complete 360 turn overcome with relief.

"Let's try this again," says Bill, as his voice escalates to a roar, "Close that fucking door and sit your ass down! Do you think this is a game?"

Greg's facial expression immediately becomes grim as he takes a seat. Bill's face gradually turns red, going from flushed pink skin to a vibrant shade of reddish-purple. Steam blows out of his ears consorted with the whistling of a tea kettle and his eyes roll into the back of his head. Astonished and stupefied by the events happening before his eyes, Greg can't do anything but watch. After fairly regaining some composure, he dashes to the side of his boss's chair. Greg moves to touch him but the sheer terror of the situation and the man's condition promptly changes his mind.

"Bill! Bill! Can you hear me?" Greg says. "Calm down. I'm gonna get you some help. Just stay with me."

Bill's body begins to violently shake, shirt soaked with sweat. Greg snatches the telephone from the desk and dials 911. The telephone rings once, followed by silence. The dead silence is followed by the song "Nights in White Satin" by *The Moody Blues*.

Greg frantically presses down on the plunger of the phone repeatedly trying to hang up to redial, but the effort is in vain. Bill's eyeballs protrude almost completely out of the sockets, and his head suddenly explodes. Oozing brain matter, blood, and fragments of his head run down the wall behind the desk. Greg stands motionless and in shock, his face and body drenched in his boss's bodily fluids.

A series of forceful and continuous knocks at the door startle him.

* * *

Greg wakes up slumped against the dresser in the bedroom, drenched in sweat. "Nights in White Satin" plays on the alarm clock on the nightstand as the knocking continues at the front door. Two men in suits with satchels containing religious literature wait for an answer on the other side. One of the men is approximately in his mid-thirties and mildly rugged, hairy, with an average height. The other man in his early twenties, is slim, clean-cut, and tall with a somewhat nervous demeanor. Hungry, thirsty, exhausted, and in wretched pain, Greg realizes that this is his chance to summon help.

"Come in!" he exclaims in his loudest possible outcry, his voice weak, due to the abeyance of his speech.

Although standing at the door for several moments, neither of the men hear the cry for help. They turn to walk away.

"Hello!" Greg calls again, mustering as much force from his lungs as possible. He extends his body as far as possible toward the window.

"Did you hear that?" the younger man asks his partner, frowning.

"Hear what?" says the older guy, stopping in his tracks.

"I think I heard somebody say something."

The older guy shakes his head. "I didn't hear anything."

"Hey!" Greg screams again. They both hear it and walk briskly back toward the door.

Still lethargic and slumped against the dresser, Greg observes the bustle of the paramedics, police, a neighbor, and the men who discovered him. A paramedic kneeling to his level pokes and prods at him, asking a series of redundant questions.

"I always told her that she needed to put that boy in a nursing home or something; she could barely take care of herself, let alone someone else," says a female bystander, who has been a prying neighbor of Ruth for a number of years.

The back of the woman's muumuu sweeps across the back of the paramedic's head with every animated movement of her body. The paramedic turns to the woman as she continues to provide her useless testimony to anyone who cares to listen as she unknowingly irritates him to the point of being unable to focus on his job. Meanwhile, a young firefighter standing at the bedside is having a difficult time moving the corpse from the mattress and into the body bag.

"Hey, rook! Don't be scared of it. It's not that hard,

just grab it and put it in!" says a bald firefighter who bears a striking resemblance to a catfish with his thin, long handlebar mustache.

"Isn't that what that crackhead woman told you last shift when she pulled up her dress for you on the fire scene?" says an older firefighter, laughing, standing by as a spectator in the doorway leading to the hall. The majority of people in the room are amused by the comment but try to conceal it due to the solemn situation.

"Hey Captain, let's be professional. You talk about *me* needing sensitivity training," mumbles the bald firefighter with a grin on his face.

The room goes quiet as they watch the rookie firefighter manhandle the corpse in an effort to keep his ego intact before finally succeeding at placing the old woman's body into the bag.

A police officer chuckles and draws his attention to the two religious men in the room. "I just thought about something," he says, as if he had just come across a revelation, "Did you guys just laugh at that dirty joke?"

"Hey, it caught me off guard!" exclaimed the older religious man, through a huge smile.

"No, it was funny. I just didn't know you guys had a sense of humor," the officer replies.

"Says the cop," the young man sarcastically replies, rolling his eyes and shaking his head. Everyone in the room explodes in laughter, with the exception of Greg.

"Hey, I'm just saying," the officer states.

"I tell jokes, lots of jokes. It's just not real easy to hear them through the sound of a door slamming in your face," says the young man.

"Hey, man. I like you! Gimme one of those things, I'll read it!" says the fire captain from across the room as he reaches to grab a pamphlet.

"Excuse me, ma'am," says the paramedic treating Greg, trying to gain the attention of the woman providing the information; she turns and looks down at him. "I'm sorry, but what's your name?"

"You can call me Helen," she states.

"Ok, thanks, Helen. How long did you say he was in a coma?"

"I would say about three, maybe four years."

The paramedic writes the information on his gloved hand. "Ok, you said his name is Greg Mallet. You happen to know his birthdate?"

"I know his birthday is in November. I've been knowing him since he was a baby. I don't remember a lot of things but I'm good at remembering birthdays. I can't believe I can't remember the actual date right now. I know he's about 27, maybe 28."

"Happen to know any of his medical history?"

"Nothing that I know of, besides the bike accident. The one that caused his brain injury."

"Motorcycle?"

"No, a bicycle. It was raining really hard one day, and he was hit by a kid that was flying around the curve in one of those small, loud, foreign cars they like to drive nowadays. The boy who hit him stopped and called 911. He denied speeding and said that he just happened to see him lying in the embankment when he drove by, but anybody could see the skid marks all over the road. Technically, they didn't find damage on his car to prove that he hit him, so they couldn't charge him with anything. Oh yeah, and since the kid called 911 they made him out to be a hero so, what can you do? I see the kid all the time; he still flies up and down the street to this day. I used to see Greg riding his bike down that road almost every day. He didn't always live here, before the accident he lived about ten or fifteen minutes away but he'd ride here to come see his grandma pretty much every day. I've got 12 grandchildren, and I'd be lucky to see at least one of them once a month."

"I think we've got it, guys," the medic on the floor tells the firemen as his partner and another fireman rolls in a stretcher.

The firemen hastily grab their medical bags as they make their long-awaited retreat from the home. Helen and the religious men follow. The two medics, the coroner, and the police officer are now the only people in the room besides Greg. The medic treating him releases the blood pressure cuff from Greg's arm and stuffs it in a large medical bag. The paramedics hoist him onto the gurney, strapping him down with the belts, and roll him to the ambulance.

Greg is admitted into the hospital, immediately cleaned up, and run through a series of tests after a long wait in the ER examination room. The stupor that is secondary to extreme fatigue deems him a virtually useless asset to those seeking answers about his condition. The blinding lights, periodic visits from hospital personnel, and the constant rolling of his bed across the hospital floor prevent him from sleeping. Somewhere between the whirlwind of activity, a motherly nurse stands over him, grabs his hand and peers into his hollow gaze, not aware as to whether he can understand the words she speaks to him.

"You're gonna be ok, you're doing fine, Greg," the nurse says, sympathetically. "We're going to put you in a room soon in a more comfortable bed. You just woke up from a coma, and you're gonna be very confused and very sleepy for quite a while, it's totally normal. Ok?"

Greg slightly nods his head once; the woman leaves the room.

Sort of Like the Mona Lisa

Shannon rustles through a large plate of lukewarm salad on the hunt for one last crouton in her less than gratifying lunch. The quality of the food doesn't seem to match the appetizing aroma that drew her to the freshly renovated hospital cafeteria. She usually leaves the campus for lunch, but today her workload wouldn't allow her the flexibility. The room is nearly desolate because the lunch hours are nearing their close. She eavesdrops on a conversation held by a small group of hospital nurses within earshot. Their voices drown out the volume of the news program on the large screen in the center of the wall ahead.

"If you need a physical therapist, he's the one you need

to see. If you ever remember anything I tell you, remember I told you this," Kurt implores.

"Is it that serious?" Kendra replies. "Is he really that good? Just because they play his commercials on TV all morning doesn't make him the best; it just makes him the most expensive."

"You've got health benefits, and besides, when have I ever lied to you?" Kurt asks.

"Yesterday when I gave you a $10 bill for my $3 lunch and you brought me back a dollar and some change; I consider that lying," Kendra says. The other female nurse laughs. Shannon smiles and the nurses find the situation even more amusing when they realize that it changed the drab expression on the doctor's face.

"You are not going to let that go, are you? I swear I thought you gave me a five."

"Yeah, whatever," Kendra says. "I'll give you a five to your face."

"Well, ok when have I lied to you purposely? But seriously, after I screwed up my back at the gym about three years ago, I had to go through physical therapy. One day I was there lying flat on my back on the examination bed he came in and stood about three feet away from me. He was facing the opposite direction looking at all the workout equipment and reached his arm back and asked me, 'Hey, would you mind holding my coffee for a second?' It was hard for me to move but it was enough motivation to make me sit up without help for the first time in over a month. I didn't think I could do it. It was like magic. Mind you, I had only seen him for a week and I had been seeing some other physical therapist Dr. Radja referred me to for about three and saw no progress. He's the real deal."

"Sounds to me like he was trying to figure out whether you were faking or not," Kendra quips.

"Hold on, hold on; shut up Kurt, this is the guy," says Erica, the other nurse, as she emphatically points at the news program on the television screen.

"I wasn't even talking anymore, Kendra was," Kurt replies.

"Shhh!" Erica commands as she tries to cover his mouth as he tilts his head back to avoid her small hand.

All of them, including Shannon go silent to watch the news story:

A young man from Northeast Portland experienced a "rude awakening" Tuesday morning when he arose from a three-year coma surrounded by police, paramedics and firefighters responding to a call at the residence of his grandmother, 67-year-old Ruth Mallet, who was found deceased from causes of unknown origin. No foul play is suspected. The young man is in stable condition at Cascade-Columbia Medical Center. News 13 Portland will provide you with the latest details on this story as it unfolds. Stay tuned as News 13 delivers the latest top stories, weather, sports, and current events. Visit us on our website, Facebook page, and Twitter on your mobile device for up-to-the-minute news updates, and feel free to leave comments and provide your feedback.

"That's crazy. I couldn't even imagine," Kurt says shaking his head, still looking at the TV as the news program goes to a commercial break.

"I'm confused, Kendra," Erica says, "I thought you said he was still asleep; now the news is saying he's awake."

"He woke up, but he's asleep again. He's in and out. He's asleep most of the day, and every once in a while he wakes up."

"Hold on, Kendra," Kurt interrupts. "Let's break it down in a way Erica will better understand it. He's like a cat. Now do you understand?"

"You're an asshole," Erica says, laughing. "Guys like you are the reason I'm a cat lady. But anyway, that's crazy. You'd think if you were asleep for that long and woke up that you probably wouldn't need to sleep for a while."

"It seems like it, but it's the opposite," Kendra says. "The doctor said it'll take some time for him to fully awaken. It's a little sad, if you ask me. I'll walk in the room sometimes, he'll be awake, and his eyes will follow my every move. He doesn't move an inch; it's almost like his eyes don't even move but they're following you. Sort of like the Mona Lisa, except he's not smiling. It's like he's lost trying to figure out where he is. Just like a baby when it opens its eyes for the first time. But the weird thing about it is he's not like a vegetable like most people who wake up after being in a coma so long, he's very aware. It's odd. It's like he's just *really* sleepy."

"I'm gonna get get him some shades and a cap from the gift shop and me and him are gonna go *Weekend at Bernie's* and have a photo shoot up there in his room. Best profile pic ever," Kurt jokes.

"Yeah, and you'll be on the news just like him for violating HIPAA. Let me know how that works out for you, buddy," Kendra says as she stands and grabs her tray. "I've gotta get back to work, I'll talk to you guys later."

Shannon follows Kendra as she walks to the tray conveyor; they both leave their dishes and head toward the exit door. Kendra walks swiftly down the hall and awaits an elevator. Shannon walks up and stands beside her. Shannon struggles to conjure up a fitting icebreaker to begin conversation, and after a short pause, she speaks.

"Hey, Kendra. This is awkward, and I know you don't know me. I know your name because I heard them say it a few times in the cafeteria. But anyways, I'm Shannon Brewster, the new on-staff psychiatrist," she says, extending her hand; Kendra shakes it.

"*Nooo*, it's not awkward. It's fine. It's nice to meet you. I think I've seen you around."

"Great," Shannon says as she wipes imaginary sweat from her brow. "I know you're probably in a rush to get back to work, but did I overhear you mention something about the guy that came out of the coma? Do you work on the floor he's on?"

"Yeah, I'm headed there now. Did you need something?" Kendra asks.

The elevator approaches and they both enter. Shannon presses the button for the 13th floor and Kendra leans in and presses the button for the 4th floor.

"Yeah, actually. If you happen to be there the next time he wakes up, can you give me a call?" Shannon rummages through her purse for her business cards. "I would really, really appreciate it."

The elevator stops on the 4th floor.

"Sure, I can do that. Of course I don't know *when*

he'll wake up but I'm working a double, so I'm sure I'll be giving you a call at some point today or tomorrow morning. I'm going to text you now so you can have my number."

"Thanks so much again," Shannon replies as she hands the nurse her card and touches her arm in gratitude. "I'll see you later."

"Ok, see ya', Doc," Kendra says as the elevator door closes.

* * *

Shannon dumps half of a jar of salsa in a bowl, grabs a large bag of tortilla chips and takes a seat in front of the computer on her desktop. She opens the Internet browser and in the search bar types the name *Greg Mallet.* Numerous links to news station websites and local newspaper sites offer minute details on his story, but beyond name and age, they provide very little details about his condition. Shannon unconsciously stuffs her face with chips as she sifts through the search results trying to find every pertinent article on comas as possible. Her phone alerts her of a received a text message; she ignores it and continues to read the contents on the screen. The phone goes off again; and once more. Annoyed by the interruptions she silences her phone and reads the received messages, which are all from the same sender:

Im so sorry about the other night, I had a family emergency and I totally forgot about our date. I feel really bad about it. I understand if you're mad and don't wanna talk to me but I promise I'm not an asshole and if its cool I'd love to re-schedule.

What are you up to tonight? If you're not busy, I went to the Redbox and got that movie we talked about the other day and I can bring it over and we can watch it.

Helllooo. You there?

Nevermind. I thought you were pretty cool. Guess I was wrong. I can do wayyy better than you anyway. I can't believe I wasted my time on you. Oh well. Have a nice life. Bitch. LOL

Shannon's dating life has been marred with bad experiences and a myriad of bouts of desperation. The higher her optimism for certain guys, the harder she falls. She has reduced herself to settling for the bare minimum of her standards. From the vainest of men to the bush league of dating material, they have all had the baggage comparable to an airport yet the absence of manners to not help her carry any of it. Wondering whether it's bad luck or if it just means that none of it was meant to be has become a long-suffering personal struggle of her adult life. She cringes at the sight of the last message and begins to reply but decides against it, deleting the thread of text messages.

Shannon focuses her attention back on the computer screen and reads page after page of clinical research and studies pertaining to the condition of being in a comatose state. She gathers information, definitive and inconclusive, and scribbles notes on sheets of copy paper. Shannon has always been fascinated with the workings of the human brain and initially considered a doctorate in neurology, but was significantly more intrigued by the human thought process. She also considered neuropsychiatry as a subspecialty but felt that she would be limiting herself. Aware that this may be a once in a lifetime opportunity, she is eager to be a part of the treatment of such a patient in any way possible. She continues to read as the time rolls by and she begins to nod off. She leaves the computer, lies in bed, and curls up on top of the covers and falls into a hard slumber.

Confused

Greg finds himself standing in the center of Mr. Elson's office; the room is vast and the ceilings lofty. The office is no longer covered in blood, but the remnants of the events that transpired previously still cover the walls behind the desk like abstract artwork; it's a liquid mess of far more than what could possibly be contained within a normal human body. A co-worker walks into the office and gazes at the wall in astonishment as if not to notice the headless body of Mr. Elson in the chair in front of it. The man takes a sip of his coffee. Greg's heart still races as he stares at the man in the same manner that the man stares at the large wall.

"Did you do this?" the man asks Greg, without making eye contact with him.

"I don't know what happened, he was talking to me. He got really upset and—"

"It's amazing," the man interrupts. "It's so beautiful."

Greg, taken aback by the man's statement, looks back at the wall. The grotesque debris that decorated the wall has transformed into a marvelous and breathtaking composition of various shades of coloration similar to those that stained it before. The brilliance of the colors and artistic arrangement are displayed across what seems to be an enormous luminescent backdrop. By the hordes, people wander into the office to admire the wall. A voice from the immediate vicinity of the desk is heard. Greg is the only one who notices the incomprehensible voice as it gradually gets louder and stops. He steps behind the desk and notices a set of lips, which apparently belonged to Bill. They begin to talk again in a voice not similar to that of Bill's.

"Hey, what the hell is wrong with you guys? Can't I get any help over here?" the lips say in a high-pitched, weak, male New Jersey accent.

* * *

Greg wakes up, his eyes focus and the first thing he notices is a thin man, approximately in his early sixties, in the bed across the room. The agitated man sits with his blanket draped over his right leg while he rubs his uncovered left leg, which has been recently amputated above the knee. The man waves his arms in the air to gain the attention of the nurse passing by the hospital room. Kendra nonchalantly walks in.

"I've been pressing this button for the last fifteen

minutes," the man says, in the same voice Greg heard in the dream, as he repeatedly pokes at the nurse call button with the index finger of his bruised and lentiginous hand.

"Please stop pressing that button," Kendra pleads.

"You didn't have a problem with me pressing it for the past twenty minutes while I was waiting for you to come do your job. What do they pay you for? What if I was dying?"

"It has not been twenty minutes, nor has it been fifteen minutes, because I was just here less than," she pauses and looks down at her watch. "Seven minutes ago. But how can I help you, Mr. Shin?"

He raises an empty, clear disposable plastic cup as if ready to propose a toast.

"I need some water. I'm dying over here. It's hotter than two mice fucking in a wool sock."

"Jerry, I just told you the last time I came in that you're on liquid restrictions. You can't have water right now. And when you call me here five minutes from now, I'll tell you the exact same thing. Trust me, as soon as the doctor lets me know that I can give you something to drink, that will be the first thing I do."

"Okay, okay. I get it. I get it," he mumbles, aggressively waving her off.

Kendra leaves the room. Jerry removes a rubber band from his ponytail, releasing his neck length, thinning gray hair, and focuses his attention to the television. Greg rolls over in his bed, facing him. Jerry smiles.

"Well I'll be damned. Look who finally woke up," Jerry says. "Good morning, sunshine."

"Good morning?" Greg says in a quiet, raspy voice. "Where am I?"

"I'll fill you in on what's going on. You're in a hospital where nobody knows how to do their freakin' job. The nurses? These broads are as useless as tits on a bull. If I were you, I wouldn't even let them know I was awake. I'd wait until it was really late at night when they go off and hide somewhere and take their naps or whatever the hell it is they do, and I'd get the hell outta Dodge." Jerry lowers the volume on the small, flat panel television on the wall. "You were on the news last night, people sent you flowers and cards; you're like a celebrity. I wouldn't be surprised if you got letters from some of those desperate cuties out there. That nurse spent a lot of time on you with that bath this morning, if you know what I mean."

Not the least bit amused, nor in a joking mood, Greg cracks a smile through his groggy mug anyway.

"I don't know why you're laughing. I'm serious, man. Even Jeffrey Dahmer had groupies. Hundreds of ladies sending him letters in prison asking to marry him, and this guy was eating other people, forget the fact that he was gayer than a fruit basket hat. You can make some dough off of it. Trust me, I know. I had a lot of 'em chasing me back in my day. I was young, good-looking, and I always had a few bucks in my pocket. It sure as hell didn't hurt that I had a lot of celebrity friends, too. Playing ball in my mom's backyard with Walt Frazier, snorting lines of coke in the back of a limousines with rock stars. Crazy times. I woke up one morning ass naked under a baby grand piano; lots of booze, drugs, and women. That's probably why I'm where I am now. Kidneys don't work, bad liver, no leg. I can't even get a freakin' cup of water for God's sakes."

Jerry looks down at the empty cup, which is now lying

near his groin, and brushes it off his bed with one broad swipe; his eyes wander as he reflects on the past. The catchy jingle of a plumbing commercial from the television is the only break in the complete silence that lasts a few moments.

"How long have I been here?" Greg asks.

Peeved by the obvious disregard Greg shows to the long speech of his, Jerry peeks at him through his peripheral. "Eh. I don't even know how long *I've* been here. I don't have time to keep track of you or anybody else I come across in this place."

Greg's eyes wander the room curiously, ultimately stopping at the windows leading to the dreary climate of the outside world. The meager raindrops creep down the thick glass to form scattered colossal globs of water. After a spell of guilt and a long pause, Jerry reluctantly answers Greg's question.

"Yesterday morning. They brought you here about this time yesterday morning."

"Thank you."

Another awkward silence ensues as an "as seen on TV" commercial advertising a flashy new blender plays in the background. Small talk and the noises of diagnostic machines drift through the hallways. Greg reads the identification band on his left arm.

Mallet, Gregory T. 11/28/85

"What in the hell is going on?" he ponders aloud, rhetorically, vigorously rubbing his eyes with the palms of his hands. As the gravity of the situation at hand presents itself, Greg finds himself increasingly frustrated with his confusion. He grips the sides of the bed rails and and aggressively adjusts himself into a more upright position.

Jerry follows his every move. "You gonna be okay, kid?" Jerry asks.

"No, I'm not okay. I woke up in a strange house wearing a diaper soaked with piss where I spent the night with an old dead lady, went to work the next morning and my boss's head exploded all over me; my face was covered in blood and brain matter. That's all I know." Greg looks straight ahead at the dry erase board that creatively reads: *RN ;-Kendra,* along with other barely legible script. Greg looks over at Jerry. "So if you know anything at all about what's going on, can you please tell me? Seriously! Because I think I deserve to know because this is getting old really fucking quick, man!"

Perturbed by his roommate's outburst, Jerry sits in silence and proceeds to flip through channels on the television aimlessly. Kendra walks in the room heading directly to Jerry's bedside, her eyelids fluttering in agitation.

"Why are you looking at me?!" Jerry directs his eyes and motions his head in Greg's direction.

Kendra looks at Greg for a brief moment, noticing that he is fully alert. She immediately darts out of the room in excitement. Almost immediately, a group of hospital personnel flood the room. The expressions on the faces of the group of spectators range from smiles similar to prideful parents admiring their beautiful daughter on prom night, to a group of people animal watching at a zoo, along with some who just seem to join the crowd because it seems like the place to be. Kendra goes through her phone contacts and dials Shannon. The phone rings until it sends her to voicemail. A doctor approaches the head of the crowd and removes a penlight from a pocket of his lab coat. Greg's eyes alternate between the doctor and the dozen of other people in the room.

"Good morning, Gregory. I'm Dr. Vankman, the neurologist," he says, shining a pen light into the patient's eyes. "I know everything might be a little overwhelming for you, but we're gonna get you squared away in the quickest and best way possible. How are you feeling?"

The doctor looks at the electrocardiogram monitor. The heart rate is accelerated and the rhythm tachycardic.

"Confused," Greg responds.

Quiet conversations being held in the room make for a slightly noisy environment. Kendra's phone vibrates. It's Shannon returning her phone call. She quietly answers.

"Hello, Dr. Brewster. I was just calling you to tell you that he's fully awake now," Kendra whispers. "The neurologist is here talking to him now. I'll see you when you get here."

The doctor continues checking Greg's sensory neuron and motor responses as he asks simple questions to assess his mental status.

"Okay, press your feet against my hands as hard as you can," Doctor Vankman says. "Very good. Can you tell me what year it is?"

Greg frowns, mulling over the question, knowing very well that there is no possible way for him to come up with the answer.

"Do you know your name?"

"Greg Mallet," he answers, recalling the name on his wristband.

"Good," the doctor nods.

The quiet chatter escalates to the point that it's not so

much as loud, but irritating for the doctor; he mumbles quietly to the charge nurse standing across the bed from him. Unable to make out the words, she makes her way around the bed to his side. He repeats himself.

"I'm going to have to ask everyone standing around to leave the room right now," the nurse announces, gesturing toward the door in a sweeping motion. The majority of people exit the room as Shannon enters. Kendra, along with three of the bystanders remain. Shannon finds a spot beside them.

"That means everybody," the charge nurse says emphatically in a grating, smoker's voice. Kendra lightly frowns at the charge nurse as if speaking through expressions.

"Not you, Kendra, you stay. But everyone else needs to leave."

"Nancy, Dr. V, this is Dr. Brewster. She's the new psychiatrist in the Behavioral and Mental Health Unit," Kendra says, pointing at Shannon as the rest of the bystanders head for the door.

The doctor takes a quick glance at Shannon before turning attention back to his patient.

"I'm sorry Dr. Brewster, I had no idea. I was just trying to keep the crowd to a minimum," whispers Nancy, smiling, placing her hand on Shannon's arm.

"No worries, you're fine. I totally understand," Shannon assures her.

Shannon moves closer to the bed and looks down at Greg; he looks back at her. Meanwhile, Dr. Vankman glances at Jerry, who is uncharacteristically quiet as he intently watches the doctor's assessment. The doctor again focuses his attention on Greg.

"Do you know where you are?" the doctor asks.

"I'm at the hospital," Greg quickly responds.

"Okay. Do you have any idea why you're here?"

Greg hesitates, trying to gather his thoughts. "Not really."

"How much do you know about why you're here?"

The raised brows and fixed eyes of the watchers in the room resemble the audience of a trivia show hoping for him to answer a question they all know the answer to.

Greg ponders hard, to the point of frustration. "I don't know, ok? I don't know at all. Can you please just tell me what the hell is going on?"

"Mr. Mallet, I'm going to be patient with you, and you're going to have to be patient with me. That's the only way we're gonna get through this. It's a process. Okay? Do you know what year it is?"

"I don't know what year it is," Greg says. "Can you tell *me* what year it is?"

"It's a yes or no question, Greg," the doctor says.

"Oh, you don't like it when I ask you questions. It's no fun wanting answers and not getting them, is it? Just bypass the bullshit and tell me what's going on."

"It ain't no fun when the rabbit's got the gun!" Jerry chimes in, getting enjoyment from the ongoing drama.

The nurses both scowl at Jerry. "You shush," says Nancy, emphatically pointing in his direction, one of her trademark motherly gestures.

The doctor, seemingly unfazed by the situation, continues to write in his memo pad. Shannon, however, feels as though she is the only one fascinated by Greg's ability to not only gather his thoughts and make appropriate responses, but to actually form sentences after such a long period of mental inactivity.

Dr. Vankman slides his pen and memo pad into his coat pocket and takes one last glance at Greg's baseline vital signs. "I'll see you later on, Greg. Again, I'm Dr. Vankman. If you need anything just let these nice ladies know."

Greg, still desperate to piece together the puzzle of his mind, comes to terms with the fact that he has to rely on himself to do so. The nurses leave the room followed by Dr. Vankman. Shannon stays behind for a few seconds longer before leaving to catch up with the doctor as he walks down the hall.

"Doc, are you thinking what I'm thinking?" Shannon asks as she quickly catches up. "It's not common for someone in his condition that's been dormant that long to be as reactive as he is. Neurologically and intellectually."

"You can say that," the doctor says.

"Why'd you leave the room? Why didn't you let him know what was going on? I'm not second-guessing you. Just curious to see what—"

"Who are you?" Dr. Vankman interjects.

"I'm sorry. I didn't introduce myself. I'm Dr. Shannon Brewster, Behavioral and Mental Health."

"Oh yes, that was you standing in the room back there. Look, doctor—."

"Shannon. Just call me Shannon."

"Before we get ahead of ourselves we've gotta figure out what we're dealing with. I want to allow the patient to get his thoughts together. He just woke up; sometimes it takes me hours to get my thoughts together after a *nap*, let alone someone who's been asleep for three years. We'd be there all day trying to fill him in on what's going on, who won the last three Super Bowls and so on and so forth. And you're right, I agree, this is a unique case, but first things first, we have a lot to deal with before we even *begin* to think about cognitive therapy at this point. Neurological evaluations, brain scans, CT's, EEG's, EMG's, ENG's, evoked potentials, a polysomnogram, just to name a few."

"But wouldn't cognitive therapy be a part of his evaluation?" Shannon debates. "How can we really gauge his mental condition without it?"

"Correct. Ideally, they would go hand in hand, but that's not realistic at this point. We can assist in his recovery but this is a hospital, we only deal with the short-term aspect of his rehabilitation. We do what we can do and we transition him to a long-term care facility where they do what they can to make him a functional member of society. Even by saying that, we're getting ahead of ourselves. The prognosis for those who wake up that long after a coma or a minimally conscious state is bleak."

"Which is my point, Dr. V.," Shannon says. "He could fall asleep tonight and never wake up again, which is why I think we should take a precipitated approach with his treatment. There are plenty of documented patients that have been awakened from sleep states as long as his but none similar to what I've seen from him so far; we have something interesting on our hands. Do you know how many people would love to be in our shoes right now?"

"How long do you typically keep your patients?" Dr. Vankman asks. "No longer than a week? Not only that, but with the budget cuts they probably have you working a ridiculous amount of hours for your salary, and Dr. Andrews can't be of much help. He's probably one of the smartest and quite possibly the best psychiatrist I've ever known, but he's got one foot here and one foot out of the door, and his mind is in Florida drinking pina coladas and cruise hopping with his wife."

Shannon nods, unsure of how to respond to the brutal truth that was just laid upon her.

"Okay, Shannon, I'll tell you what. As soon as my people finish what we have to do we'll send him to you and you can do whatever you deem necessary. But until I medically clear him, I don't see a point in your interference. In the meantime, if you can find time in your busy schedule, figure out a game plan and get some control over the patients you *do* have because he'll probably be a difficult one."

"I guess I'll be hearing from you," Shannon says, disheartened.

Dr. Vankman walks away and turns the corner headed toward the elevators.

Shannon turns around and walks back into the hospital room. Greg's face is planted firmly on its side against a fluffy, bright white pillow; his eyes shut, mouth open wide as if he wasn't fully awake only ten minutes ago. Jerry peeks over the top of a pair of blue reading glasses at the doctor, then at his snoring roommate, and goes back to flipping through an old, rumpled issue of *People* magazine. Kendra lightly knocks on the door and steps in the room with an ingenuous smile on her face.

"Told ya," Kendra says. "He's like my grandpa. Narcoleptic. I was surprised he was still awake when you got here."

"Yeah, I figured he probably wouldn't be awake for long," says Shannon, monotonously.

"Well, I've had my excitement for the day. It's almost time for me to go home and get some sleep," Kendra says, looking at her watch. "Standing here watching him sleep is making me jealous. I've been up for about 19 hours straight."

"Must be nice," Shannon says. "I have a lot to do before I get to leave."

"It seems like you're always working," says Kendra.

"Yup. Pretty much all the time. Or at least it seems like it."

"That sucks."

"Tell me about it." Shannon rolls her eyes.

"Do you ever have time to do anything? What do you do when you're not working? It must be stressful working with crazy people 24/7, and that includes the people who work here."

"I don't ever do anything really; I've always been kind of a homebody. Sometimes I try out new bars, hit the happy hours, but I usually just stay in. I haven't really been here long, so I haven't met many people yet."

"I see, I'm the same way; just not by choice. I have a very high maintenance little girl, and her dads not in the picture so…" Kendra smiles. "You know how that is."

The room is silent with the exception of the alternating sounds of the snoring patients.

"Hey, look," whispers Kendra, her body language pointing in Jerry's direction. "I swear this old man never sleeps when I'm here. He's always awake, talking just to hear himself talk, complaining."

Jerry quickly opens his eyes as if he was startled by something or like he wasn't supposed to be sleeping. He begins to watch the TV as if he'd been watching all along.

"You shouldn't have said anything," Shannon says exuberantly. "You jinxed yourself."

"I guess I did," Kendra replies, shaking her head. "I guess I'd better get back to work. You have my number. If you get bored or anything and need someone to hang out with I can see if I can get my parents to watch Mandy tonight."

"That works. I'll give you a call when I get off.

Dinner's Ready

Greg is in the passenger seat of a 2003 silver Acura while three male co-workers are packed in the backseat. The heavy rush hour traffic slows to a halt at the red light. Adam, the driver of the vehicle, stops the car below an underpass and begins to nervously tap on his knee to the beat of nothing as the riders in the back hold meaningless conversation. Out of nowhere, Adam grabs his satchel and stainless steel coffee Thermos and opens the door; he proceeds to walk toward the front of traffic where the cars wait for the signal to change. Greg watches the man continue toward the middle of the intersection and remove a manhole cover. The deafening sound of blaring car horns fill the air. Adam climbs into the hole, hangs by the rim of the opening, and drops down into the sewer.

"What the hell is he doing?" Greg asks, exiting the vehicle.

Greg jogs toward the sewer as the traffic light signals green. He considers turning back but quickly changes his mind as vehicles blow past him; following his friend into the sewer appears safer than testing his fate by crossing the busy intersection. Greg sits on the edge of the manhole and blindly drops into the black abyss.

The only noises in the sewer are the sounds of several light streams of water crashing into the much larger reservoir that rests at about the halfway point of his calves. Greg reaches into his pocket and pulls out a cell phone; he raises it eye level to use the light as a lantern. His makeshift navigational tool is not nearly sufficient, but it's suitable enough to make the environment somewhat less ominous. Distant sounds of splashing that are just loud enough to be deceptive.

"Hey man, this isn't even funny! It's just stupid!" Greg calls out, then in a lower voice adds, "But then again, I guess I *am* the idiot that followed you."

Greg continues to trudge the murky waters as it deepens to waist level.

"I swear, man, if I come out of these waters with E. coli I'm gonna fucking kill you!"

Greg's eyes adjust to the darkness and there is nothing in clear view but the damp, rust-stained, shadowy walls. The active water currents echo throughout the large tunnel.

"Ok, I'm getting out of here! And I hope you have a way home because I'm taking your car!"

Greg turns back to retrace the route he came in. He senses that he is being followed, and quickly glances over his shoulder. He wades the water faster as he feels the undercurrent below become increasingly stronger. A beautiful young woman suddenly emerges from the water. Greg backpedals so quickly that he falls on his back into the water; he quickly regains footing as the woman stands over him. Her vibrant, flowing, scarlet hair is visible even through the obscure light. Greg stands at almost eye level to the fairly tall, slim woman; her bright, emerald green eyes are so entrancing that Greg initially fails to realize that she is completely topless.

"Are you Greg?" the woman asks.

Greg looks down, noticing her medium-sized, perky breasts and disproportionately large areolae; he quickly redirects his ogling eyes away from them. "Yeah, I'm Greg. Who are you?" he answers, trying to wipe the water from his dripping face with equally wet hands.

"I'm Arianna and I know where your friend is," she answers.

The vocal tone and look on her face resembles a child bragging to another about what she has and what he doesn't. Their eyes lock for an inelegant moment, as Greg is not caught up in the woman's beauty as much as he is worried about finally making his way out of the conduit of raw waste.

"Ok, well when you see him tell him that he can pick up his car from my house later on," he says. "And why are you swimming in this water? Aren't you aware of all the shit that floats around down here? And by *shit*, I mean that literally."

Greg turns around to walk away. Arianna immerses herself into the water and swims behind him, following him, and raises herself from the water by gripping onto his belt. Greg looks down and notices her head near his waistline as she gazes seductively into his eyes.

"Don't go," she simply says.

Arianna swims away; her supplicant eyes and charmingly callow disposition intrigues Greg, and without a shred of consideration he submerges himself into the water and follows. Arianna pierces through the water as a minnow does, gracefully enough to be difficult for the naked eye to notice how fast she swims. Greg is navigated through the waters that are now delicately illuminated just enough for him to keep a visual on the silhouette of the woman swimming ahead. He loses track of her when a school of catfish the size of automobile engines sail past his face. No longer able to hold his breath, he pops up from the water and clears his eyes. Arianna floats upright in the water a distance away, drying her hair with a towel. Bleary natural light from no particular source reveals the surroundings. A massive waterfall originating directly from an outside source crashes down in the background. Greg keeps his eyes on Arianna as he swims toward her; she grins widely as he approaches. She stands in front of what appears to be an elevated loading dock leading to a standard size rusty brown commercial grade metal door. A set of old, double-pane windows are fixed to the left of the door. The dust and dirt on the surface of the glass has accumulated so long that the glass is too cloudy to be transparent.

"I've never seen anyone swim that fast in my life," Greg says.

The woman looks at him like a child at a pet shop that just spotted the cutest puppy ever. "Awww, you are so cute. I like you." She plants a firm kiss on his lips.

Greg stands silent for a moment, stunned.

Arianna places her towel on the edge of the dock. Greg watches as she pulls herself up on on the ledge. The long, illustrious hair resting between her clavicles could be the main focus of a photo shoot. The rest of her body rises from the water, and at the limit of her tailbone and just before the start of her rear end uncovers something unexpected; instead of bikini bottoms or the lack thereof, emerges a fish tail. The popular representation of a mermaid seems only half true as the tail and caudal fin are far from glamorous; the flaws and unsightliness of the scales are just as those seen on a typical freshwater fish.

"You're a mermaid," Greg says.

"Yes, I'm a mermaid," she answers. "Is that a problem?"

"No, it's not. I just didn't know there was such a thing."

Greg watches in awe as the scaly surface of her tail dries, the color gradually changing to match the color of her skin. Her lower body slowly morphs, revealing the anatomy of a human being. Arianna grabs her towel and heads for the door. She turns the knob while looking back at him, "You coming?"

Greg climbs on the deck and follows the woman through the door; his drenched clothing creates several small puddles on the linoleum floor. Arianna leads him into the living room. Porcelain figurines and tarnished brass knickknacks decorate the room. A large, dated poster-sized photo of a sunset adorns the wall above the sofa. A woman, roughly in her late-forties, sits in an old brown recliner in a corner of the room. The woman immediately closes the recliner, gets up, and approaches Greg to introduce herself. The woman's light blonde hair reaches almost waist-length, covering her bare breasts. A pair of light blue, cotton jogging pants are the only article of clothing that she is wearing.

"Greg, this is my mom. Mom, this is Greg," Arianna says. "This is a friend of Mallory's new boy toy. He was outside swimming, and I just *had* to introduce myself."

"Well, I don't exactly swim in the sewer for fun; I'm looking for my friend."

"What's wrong with swimming in the sewer?" Arianna asks as she flirtatiously slaps him on the chest. "Rude."

"That totally came out wrong," Greg says. "I didn't mean to sound disrespectful."

"It's okay, sweetheart, you're fine. She's just teasing," the mother says, laughing. "I'm Billie, it's nice to meet you."

"See, Mom?" Arianna says. "He is so stinkin' cute."

"Why don't you take a seat, Greg? Make yourself at home," Billie says.

"I would love to, but I really can't stay long. I have a couple friends waiting on me outside, I'm really just here waiting for Adam."

"We're having your friend over for dinner tonight, and you're free to stick around and wait for him if you'd like," Billie says. "I can't make you stay if you have plans, but my cuisine is to die for."

"I'm sure it is. It smells delicious," Greg says.

"Honey, go to Mallory's room and tell Greg's friend

that he's here," Billie demands.

Arianna quickly leaves the room.

"Make yourself comfortable," says Billie.

Greg takes a seat on the old, worn out red sofa that is heavily faded from many years of use. Billie walks through the swinging kitchen door that is attached to the living room. The racket of pots clanking and the delectable aroma of dinner radiate throughout the home. Footsteps coming down the hall get closer and present themselves as Adam and his female companion. They cross the threshold of the doorway embracing one another, smiling like teenage lovebirds. The young woman is a brunette, and more voluptuous in the right places in relation to her kin. She is also nude, with the exception of a pair of boy short panties. Adam is dressed in a button-down shirt with a necktie and gray slacks; he is clean-shaven, and his hair is slicked back.

"What's up, Greg? Did you meet Mallory's sister?" Adam asks.

"Yeah, I met her. What are you doing? And why are you dressed like that?"

"Aren't you gonna introduce me, babe?" Mallory asks.

"Greg, Mallory. Mallory, Greg. Hey, hun, can I talk to him in private for a sec?" Adam asks, rubbing her lower back.

"He's all yours," she tells Greg.

Mallory leaves the room.

"What the hell is wrong with you?" Greg asks, angrily.

"Dude, chill. Didn't I tell you I was meeting my girlfriend's mother tonight?"

"No, you didn't," Greg says. "It sure would have been nice if you had told us before you ditched us in your car in the middle of rush hour."

"My bad, I was sure I mentioned it," Adam replies. "But do you see how these chicks just walk around tits free all day? Even the mom has a nice rack. They sag a little, I like it, though; it gives them *character*. Mallory told me that only human women care about hiding their boobs and that it's really not as big of a deal as they make it out to be."

"Okay, okay," Greg says, chuckling, slightly humored. "One, you're an idiot. Two, I'm leaving. Three, since I don't wanna embarrass you in front of your mermaid girlfriend, I'll hold off on kicking your ass 'til next time I see you."

"Why can't she just be my girlfriend?" Adam asks, smiling. "Why does she have to be my *mermaid* girlfriend, you racist asshole."

"Shut up," Greg says, shaking his head. "I'm outta here."

"Don't leave, stick around for dinner, Mallory's sister really likes you."

"What about the other guys?" Greg says. "They're waiting on us."

"They'll understand. If they were in a house full of hot, half-naked women, they'd do the same thing. Just take a seat, I'll be back."

"Okay, but I'm not gonna be here all night," Greg says as he sits on the couch.

Adam leaves the room.

Arianna comes back into the room, now wearing a pair of running shorts.

"Do you wanna watch some TV?" she asks. "You look so bored."

"Sure. Why not?" Greg says.

An old, woodgrain floor model television set complete with built-in faux drawers sits across from the sofa. Greg scans the area in search of a remote control.

"No remote control, if that's what you're looking for," Arianna says. "You have to change the channels manually; sorry, it sucks. One day when mother lets me get a job that'll be the first thing I buy. Well, not a remote control, but a new TV."

"It's okay, I need the workout," Greg says, springing from the sofa. He powers on the TV and turns the knob, flipping through the channels, most of which are static; he stops at the clearest channel and returns to the sofa. The sitcom *Three's Company* plays on the television.

"Oh my gosh, I love this show," Arianna says, climbing into his lap

Greg is distracted by Arianna's bizarre disposition. It doesn't take him long to conceive that this woman, who is at least in her early twenties, has either been sheltered to a point of childish naive innocence or is proficient in the art of charm that is difficult to resist due to her bold charisma. She continues to watch the program, laughing every time the TV audience laughs.

"I can feel your heart, it's beating so fast," Arianna says, caressing his chest before removing a loose strand of her hair from his shirt.

"Dinner's ready!" Billie yells from the kitchen.

Mallory rushes into the living room en route to the kitchen; Greg and Arianna follow. Billie places the last of the dishes and silverware on the table as they enter the room. The aroma that fills the room is mouthwatering. Greg waits for everyone else to choose their places before picking a seat. Billie stands over the counter mixing a green salad with metal tongs. The girls whisper to each other like schoolgirls, clearly holding a conversation about Greg. Billie comes over and places the large wooden mixing bowl containing the salad in front of him.

"Wow, thanks," Greg says placing a modest amount of the odd-looking salad on his appetizer plate.

"Don't be shy, you can get more," Billie says. "We have plenty."

"Thanks, I'm not really much of a salad guy," Greg uses as an excuse. "I'm not big on vegetables. It looks delicious, though. What is it?"

"It's seaweed salad," Arianna answers as she fills her plate. "You've never had it? It's sooo good."

Greg looks at the empty seat across from him and realizes that it's been well over a few minutes and Adam hasn't showed up yet.

Greg takes a stab at it with his fork. "Nope, this is my first time."

"Well, there's a first time for everything," says Billie. "I'm sure you never thought you'd ever be sharing a meal with mermaids, did you? By the way, your friend will be with us shortly; He was hot and needed to cool off."

"I didn't even know mermaids existed until now. Are the myths true? Where are you from?" Greg asks.

"If you're wondering if we're from Atlantis, we're not," Billie answers. "I'm originally from Vancouver, British Columbia. My family moved to New York City when I was very young. There was a large mermaid population there, and my parents wanted a change. When I got older, I met a man who domesticated me and my family turned on me for marrying outside of the species. We decided to move far away and agreed to live in the Pacific Ocean and moved to the Seattle area. We had two beautiful daughters, but he decided he couldn't take it anymore. He missed his old life and, apparently, human women. We were fighting against nature, and I was too young and dumb to tell."

"Are you the only ones who live down here?"

"We are. The reason we live in the sewer now is because my daughters have needs. They're only half mermaid so they naturally have a burning desire to live above water. They are attracted to human men, whereas I think it was just a phase for me that turned into love. I was always jealous of the glamorous women that I saw frolicking down the streets of New York City in their short skirts, their makeup, beautiful hair, carrying their Bloomingdales bags. I wanted to be a part of it." Billie pauses for a brief moment. "My daughters need to know their heritage on both sides, and I don't want to deprive them of that, hence, the home, the TV, all of this stuff you see around you. They also aren't attracted to mermen, as they are not as smart or as sensitive as human men."

"Hmm, I can understand that. I'm sorry if I'm asking you too many questions," Greg says.

"It's ok, we're getting to know each other," Billie says, getting up from the table.

"Is it ready, Mother?" Mallory asks as Billie slides her hands into a pair of oven mitts and grabs a large roasting pot.

"It's about that *tiiiime*," Billie sings, walking towards the table with the pot.

"So what do you ladies eat besides seaweed?" Greg

asks.

"Guess," suggests Mallory. Arianna sits quietly, closely watching everything through puppy dog eyes.

"Sushi?" says Greg.

"Sometimes," says Mallory.

"Hmmm, lobster, crab, shrimp?" Greg answers.

"Ew, gross. For us, those are like what roaches and rats are for you," Mallory says. "They're pests, and they eat the waste from the bottom of the ocean."

"I think I've heard that before. The food smells delicious," Greg says.

"Why thank you, young man," Billie says as she removes the lid of the large pot. "I hope you like it."

"Oh, I'm sure I will."

"If it makes it any better, the meat and the veggies are so tender you won't have to chew them for long because they'll melt in your mouth," says Mallory.

"Arianna, why are you being antisocial? We have a guest. Don't be rude," Billie says as she glares at her pouting daughter while slicing what appears to be a roast. Tears stream down Arianna's face. She puts her head down and uses her hand as a visor in an attempt to hide her tears and avoid shame.

"Young lady, stop that crying right now!" Billie says, placing a slice of meat and a large spoonful of mashed potatoes on her own plate.

"I changed my mind, mother," Arianna says.

Greg, feeling awkward from the tension in the room, pretends to be oblivious to the drama surrounding him. Mallory passes him the pot of roast. He takes the serving spoon and scoops a generous amount of the meat, carrot, celery, and onion mixture and gently places it on the mountain of mashed potatoes on his plate. He passes the plate over to Arianna, who doesn't reach for it. Mallory stares down her sister like the scum of the earth; the awkwardness in the room reaches an excruciating level. Greg can't decide whether to tell Billie that Arianna's actions don't offend him or whether to comfort the girl; he ultimately chooses not to get involved. Greg scoops up a generous amount of the main course onto his fork.

"Don't eat that," Arianna says softly, without even looking up.

"Why not?" Greg responds. He glances down at his plate and notices a trace of Adam's tattoo on the slab of meat. Greg is frozen from shock for two seconds that, at the least, feel like thirty.

"Run!" Arianna screams.

Immediately the three of the women spring from their seats. Greg leaps from his chair and runs for the swinging door; Billie and Mallory chase him. Arianna grabs the brown, restaurant style pitcher from the center of the table and splashes water on her mother and sister. Just before they make it out of the kitchen, their legs instantly morph into fins, and a loud smack signals their hard falls to the floor. Arianna follows Greg through the hallway, catching up with him near the front door.

"Thank you," Greg says.

"It's nothing," she replies. "Now get out of here!"

She gently shoves him out of the door and slams it. Greg dives into the water and swims toward a ladder that leads to the outside light. He climbs the fifty-foot ladder bolted to the side wall of the sewer. Nearing the top, he looks down and watches Billie and Mallory dive into the water to search for him; they notice their prey making his escape. Their disheartened expressions are then directed at Arianna, who is still standing at the door intently watching Greg's ascension to above ground level. Greg opens the manhole and climbs from the sewer. Rain pours down from the sky. The falling rain has no effect on Greg as he is already soaked from his sewer excursion. He walks toward the sidewalk, and just as he crosses into the bike lane a vehicle traveling at full speed approaches him head on.

* * *

Greg abruptly wakes up from his dream, heart racing and dampened in perspiration. Not a peep is heard in the room. The door is closed. He looks around until his eyes adjust to the darkness and notices Jerry sleeping soundly in the bed to his left.

That's a Turnoff

The residents of the Northwest region, which is normally wet in the fall, appreciate the non-rainy days; this Friday night is no different. The night is warm and dry, and the social scene is alive. Shannon walks past restaurants, bars and night clubs where people chat and relax on the outside tables and benches. She gets the occasional greeting and stares from loiterers who resemble the type that mark their territory by hanging at the same street corner on a daily basis. The parking situation in the area is atrocious and numerous attempts at squeezing into her spot drew the ire of the drivers behind her. The stress of parking and the long, awkward walk alone from her vehicle to the bar has her nervously sweating and ready for a cold, refreshing cocktail. She approaches the bar and begins to make entry before a short, bearded young man seated on a barstool near the door stops her.

"You mind if I check your ID?" the bouncer asks.

"Oh, I'm sorry," Shannon answers as she grabs her driver's license and debit card out of her pocket. She hands him her identification.

"North Carolina, huh? You're a long way from home. What brought you out here?"

"Just work, and it's a nice change," she answers with a smile.

"I hear ya," the man says, returning her driver's license. "Have fun."

"Thank you," she says, walking into the dimly lit bar.

The urbane architecture of the bar has just enough of an unrefined touch to be considered casual. The crowd is a trendy amalgamation of hipsters, young business types, and people dressed ubercasually who only look to unwind with a few drinks. The diversity of the patrons and her ability to blend in puts Shannon more at ease. She stands at the crowded bar waiting to order a drink and pulls her phone from her pocket and texts Kendra: *Where are you?*

The bartender leans toward Shannon and points at her.

"I'll have a whiskey sour," she says.

The bartender nods. Her phone alerts her of a text message. It's Kendra: *Parking. Be there in five.*

The bartender sets the drink in front of her.

"Seven," he says.

Shannon hands him the debit card.

"Open or closed tab?"

"Closed," she says.

Shannon signs her receipt and finds a table in the back corner of the building. She watches the door as more people wander in. She finally spots Kendra at the door, fumbling through a small pocketbook for identification. Kendra walks in, greeting Shannon with a huge smile and hug.

"I'll be right back, I'm gonna get a drink," Kendra says, before rushing to the bar.

Shannon watches as Kendra orders a drink and socializes with a group of people also waiting at the bar. A petite, female server dressed in all black walks past her with a large cheeseburger and French fries. Kendra comes back from the bar and sits across from Shannon.

"The food smells amazing. It's making me hungry," Shannon says.

"It's really good, and pretty cheap. I'm thinking about ordering something myself," says Kendra.

"What's that drink you have?" Shannon asks.

"It's an orange slice martini. It's *soooo* good. Try some."

Shannon carefully lifts the glass and takes a sip.

"That *is* really good," she says. "You wanna try some of mine?"

"What is it?" Kendra asks.

"Whiskey sour."

Kendra grimaces. "Gross. I hate whiskey."

"I do, too, when it's by itself, but for some reason I love this drink," Shannon replies. "I like this place, it's pretty cool. Not too many hipsters but not too pretentious either."

"I'm not gonna lie, when I first saw you I thought *you*

were a snob," Kendra admits.

"Oh my gosh. Why?"

"Because you're a doctor! Almost *all* doctors are arrogant," Kendra says jovially, "and you always look so serious."

"I don't mean to," Shannon says, laughing. "That's just the way I look."

"Well I know that *now*," Kendra says. "Have you spotted any cute guys yet?"

"Nah," Shannon says.

"Why not?" Kendra asks. "You have a boyfriend?"

"No, you?"

"Booty calls, yes. Boyfriend? No."

"Why not?"

"It seems like nobody can accept the fact that I have a child," Kendra says. "Either it runs them off when they find out or they say they're willing to deal with it and they end up not being able to. I can't just go over a guy's house and spend the night when he wants me to, and he can't just come over whenever he wants to. Sometimes I have no choice but to bring my daughter on dates with me when me and a guy spend time together; and a lot of times she's cranky, and I end up apologizing. Then sometimes guys try too hard bonding with her, and I can easily tell when they're doing it for brownie points just trying to impress me; And that's a turn-off. Then you have the guys who think you'll give it up easy just because you had a child out of wedlock. I try to be careful who I let in my life because I don't want my daughter around so many random guys, I don't think it's fair to her. So what's your excuse? You're pretty, good career, you're obviously smart, you make good money."

"I don't know," Shannon says. "Guys just don't approach me. I've met a couple guys, but in the end they all turned out to be douche bags, and the ones I felt like might be pretty cool just never really put forth the effort to keep in contact after we went out. I don't know; maybe I'm too boring. I can't just go up and talk to random people like you can."

"You haven't been here long. Just give it some time." Kendra turns her attention to a rear door leading to the outside. "Hey let's go outside."

"Sure," Shannon says.

They walk outside the back door to a large, semi-crowded gazebo area filled with occupied tables and people standing around chatting over glasses and pitchers of beer. Kendra walks to the minibar located outside and grabs a stack of napkins as Shannon sits down at an empty table. Kendra joins her and frowns in disgust as she wipes the leftovers of spilled beer off the surface of the wooden picnic bench-styled table.

"Do you come here often?" Shannon asks.

"I've been here a few times," she says. "The first time I came here I was with Erica. She got trashed and left with some guy and didn't tell me, so I thought something happened to her. I texted her all night, and she didn't answer. The next morning she showed up at work like nothing happened and had the nerve to be mad at me because I was upset."

"Wow, are you serious?"

"Yes, she always pulls crap like that. I barely even hang out with her outside of work anymore," Kendra says. "She's so wishy-washy, too."

"Oh yeah, I can't stand that," says Shannon.

"For instance, she's going through this phase where she's telling everyone she's vegan when she's not! We'll have a pot luck and everyone will bring something and she'll try to make everyone feel guilty about what they bring. 'I can't eat that, I'm vegan.' And she'll be legit annoyed with everyone who brings meat. I'm like 'Bitch, you're like the worst vegan ever!' The other day she brought crackers and cheese to work. She said it was vegan cheese, and I looked at the wrapper and it said *veggie* cheese, not vegan cheese—it was cheese with vegetables in it!"

"Did you say anything?" Shannon says, hysterically laughing.

"No!" Kendra says, emphatically. "She would have gotten mad at me and accused me of picking on her!"

"Oh my gosh," Shannon says. "That's hilarious."

"But anyway, I get irritated just talking about it. On to the next subject. What's going on with coma guy? Why the interest?" Kendra asks, returning to serious mode.

"I just think it's pretty awesome," Shannon says. "Being able to work 'hands on' with a patient like that."

"Eh, I guess. It *would* look good on a resume."

"Not just that. It's something new and different," Shannon says. "I'd love to be able to delve into his mind and see what's going on in there. Help him get as much of whatever he had there back. You know?"

"Personally," Kendra says. "I view him as just another ass to wipe."

"Stop it! That's not nice," Shannon says through weak laughter and a sympathetic expression.

"I'm *sorry*," Kendra replies. "I guess that part of it is

just out of my pay-grade. No, but seriously, I respect that. You're not just trying to make a paycheck. It's nice to see a doctor that actually *cares* about the patients.

"I really appreciate it, Kendra," Shannon quips, sarcastically. "That's the nicest thing I've heard you say all night. I didn't know you had it in you."

"I can be sweet every once in a while. What did Dr. V say when you guys talked?"

"He basically just told me to forget about it," Shannon says, taking a sip from her straw. "And after that to get in where I fit in; that I can basically have him when he's not using him."

"He sounds like me talking to my daughter's father," Kendra says. "No, I'm totally kidding. But, yeah, that's bull crap; it's really not like that. Dr. V doesn't really call shots like he wants you to think. If you wait on *him*, you'll be waiting forever."

An intoxicated young man in a faded blue V-neck tee stops at the table. "Let me tell you something," he slurs, leaning over the table with a nearly full glass of beer, its contents hovering around the rim threatening to spill over. "You ladies are put together very well tonight," the man says, putting his open palm toward Shannon for a high five. She puts her hand out for a five and they connect. A woman and another man following closely behind the intoxicated man begin pulling him away from the table.

"Come on, Drew. Let's leave these nice ladies alone. We're sorry," the woman apologizes.

"It's fine, there's nothing wrong with having a good time," Kendra says.

The group wanders back into the crowd of people.

Kendra laughs. "That might have been your dream guy right there. Why didn't you give him your number?"

"Yeah, maybe you're right," Shannon says, sarcastically. "The only ones that ever *do* approach me are usually too drunk to have a normal conversation.

"But anyway, back to what I was saying, Dr. V is just bullying you," Kendra says. "You have just as much right to that patient as he does. I know you're nice but with most of these doctors you need to stand up for yourself. Not only are you a woman, but you're young. They're gonna try to walk all over you."

"Yeah, I guess you're right."

Ok, This is Ridiculous

A tech enters the X-ray room, rolls a wheelchair to the examination bed, and locks the wheels. He wraps his arms around Greg, hauls him over to the wheelchair and they travel the floors of the hospital. Greg finds it peculiar how much attention he garners from hospital personnel as if they had never seen anyone in a wheelchair; the fact that he is a celebrity within these walls doesn't factor into his thinking. They take the elevator up to the third floor, and the transporter wheels him into his room. Greg notices a woman standing by the window next to his bed looking outside. She wears a white lab coat, holds a black ink pen, and has a red file folder clenched against her chest.

The woman turns around as she hears footsteps come into the otherwise quiet room

and smiles. "Hi, Mr. Mallet. I'm Dr. Brewster. It's nice to finally get to meet you," she reaches out for a handshake.

Greg obliges. "Hi," he says.

The tech leaves the room and closes the door behind him. Shannon pushes a chair toward Greg's bed, and the grating sound causes Jerry, who is sleeping, to roll over in his bed.

Shannon cringes at the noise, lifts the chair and carries it to the bedside.

"Sorry," she says as she sits down.

"Don't worry about it," Greg replies. "What kind of doctor are you?"

"I'm a psychiatrist."

"Great," Greg says sarcastically, followed by a snicker.

"Can I ask you what it is that's funny?" Shannon asks.

"It's funny because no one has even so much as explained anything to me about what's going on and they expect me to act completely normal. I think anybody would be upset or frustrated in that situation, but I'm now being labeled as crazy. I might be confused as to what's going on, but there is absolutely nothing wrong with me mentally."

"I'm so sorry that you feel that way, Mr. Mallet. If it makes you feel any better, I'm here for you whenever you need me. Whatever you need to talk about and whatever it might be that's on your mind, you can feel free to talk to me about. You haven't been labeled as crazy; we don't like to use the term 'crazy.' Yes, some people have more complex mental and emotional conditions than others but no one should ever be labeled as 'crazy,' I'm here to simply provide a clear picture of your physical and mental state. Nothing more, nothing less."

"Ok, Doc. I know what a psychiatrist is. No need to be politically correct. I might seem a little sensitive right now, but I'm not normally this way. And in this situation, I think it's warranted."

"Totally understandable. I'll be as impolitic as possible. I promise," Shannon says, raising her right hand.

Greg's food tray near the foot of his bed is untouched. The lunch had been waiting while he was out getting his tests done. The food tray near Jerry's bed is devoid of food and spewed with napkins, cracker crumbs, and a small empty plastic juice container.

"Well, Greg, I just wanted to take a few minutes to get acquainted with you," Shannon says. "I'm going to let you finish your lunch. I also have some things I need to get done today but I would like to talk to you more tomorrow afternoon."

"Okay," he answers.

Shannon rolls his tray to the bedside. "Okay," she says, smiling. "I'll let the staff know, and I'll be seeing you tomorrow."

Shannon leaves the room. Jerry is awake.

"I would have told her no," Jerry said.

"No, to what?" Greg answers.

"No to that little meeting she wants to have with you."

"Why?"

"You wanna get out of here, don't you?"

"Yeah, I wanna go home as soon as possible."

"Well if you tell her that stuff you told me about blowing up some guy's head and screwing an old dead lady the other day, you ain't ever leaving here."

"That's not how it went," Greg rebuts. "And they can't keep me here against my will. Can they?"

"They'll say you're an endangerment to yourself and others, then you're stuck," Jerry replies. "But you know everything, so just do whatever you wanna do."

Greg's food tray accommodates a full liquid diet. *The Price is Right* plays on the television as Greg peels the foil covering off of a cup of applesauce as he stares out of the window at the clear horizon. Jerry flips through the channels as usual; he rarely leaves the TV on one program for more than five minutes. He looks over at Greg.

"You gonna eat that cottage cheese?" Jerry asks.

"Huh?"

"The cottage cheese," Jerry says. "You gonna eat it?"

"I am pretty hungry."

"Well it's been sitting there and you haven't touched it, so I figured you didn't want it,"

Jerry replies.

"Oh," Greg answers, scraping the sides of the nearly empty container of applesauce with his spoon.

Jerry gives Greg his "you've gotta be kidding me" stare. "All you had to do was say you were gonna eat it," Jerry states.

Greg squints and shrugs. "I *did* say I was gonna eat it."

"No, you were being a smart ass," Jerry replies. "I might be going blind, but I'm not deaf, and I'm not stupid."

"I said I was hungry. How is that being a smart ass?"

"You didn't say you were hungry. You said 'I *am* pretty hungry," Jerry says wearing a disgusted facial expression exaggeratedly emulating the way he perceived the way Greg looked when he made the statement.

"And I just started eating, I just haven't gotten to the cottage cheese yet."

"I *am* pretty hungry," Jerry repeats. "I fuckin' tell ya."

"This is ridiculous," Greg says. "Are we really arguing about this tiny fucking bowl of cottage cheese? It's like two spoonfuls."

"I'm not arguing," Jerry says. "But what you need to know is that respect is earned, not given."

"Ok," Greg says, extending his arm across the bed to hand Jerry the small plastic bowl.

"If you want the cottage cheese that much, you can have the cottage cheese."

"I don't want your damn cottage cheese," Jerry says, without looking.

"What's wrong with you?" Greg asks. "Do you just try to pick arguments with everybody you come across?"

"I'm done talking about it," Jerry says.

Greg shrugs and proceeds to eat the bowl of cheese.

"You know?" Jerry says. "I should come over there and kick your ass."

"Don't start that shit today. Your threats don't scare me. But they are pretty damn funny, actually. I'd really love to see you try to kick my ass with one leg. But in the meantime, can you please give me a few minutes to enjoy this fresh and delicious cup of creamy cottage cheese?" Greg slowly places a spoonful of cottage cheese in his mouth.

After tasting it, Greg grimaces and looks down into the container.

"Actually, it's really not as good as it looks," Greg says as he places it on his rollaway tray and pushes it toward Jerry's bed. "It tastes like its fat-free or something. You sure you don't want the rest?"

"Fuck you," Jerry says.

"I'm being serious. You can have it."

Jerry looks at the tray through the side of his eye. "Shove it up your ass," he says.

"Just trying to be nice," Greg says as raises his eyebrows and places the cottage cheese back on the tray. A nurse enters the room, pushing an empty wheelchair.

"How's it going in here, gentlemen?" she asks.

Neither man gives a response.

"You guys sure are in a chippy mood today," the nurse says. She lifts a corner of the sheet on Jerry's bed, peeking at his urine drainage bag. The nurse then walks to Greg's bedside and begins moving and untangling lines and wires.

"Me and you are gonna take a trip, Mister," the nurse says. "Can you sit up for me?"

As Greg sits up in bed, the nurse leaves the room and comes back with a male co-worker in blue scrubs. They count to three and move him to the wheelchair. The woman adjusts Greg's gown and rolls the wheelchair as her partner follows with the IV pole.

* * *

After a few hours of testing, a transporter returns him to his room.

"This is going to sound crazy," the young man says. "But would you mind signing your autograph? Me and my girlfriend saw a news story about you last night, and I joked with her and told her I'd get your autograph and she didn't believe me.

"Sure," Greg says. "No problem."

The young man pulls an ink pen and a stack of yellow Post-its from his chest pocket and hands them to Greg.

"Thanks, dude," the young man says. "My girl's gonna be stoked."

"Hey, man," Greg says. "Can you leave me in the chair for a while? I really don't feel like getting back in that bed right now; it hurts my back."

"I really shouldn't let you get out of the wheelchair by yourself " the man said. "It's a liability thing."

"It'll be okay. I'll call somebody whenever I need help getting back in the bed. It's not like I can get back in myself anyway."

"Ok, that's cool. You *did* just give me your autograph."

"Thanks, dude," Greg replies. "You're great. Can you close the door behind you?"

"No problem, bud."

The tech leaves, closing the door behind him. Greg rolls his wheelchair across the room and lowers his bed with a button on the railing. He climbs into bed, closes the wheelchair and slides it behind the headboard. He elevates the head of the bed so that most of the wheelchair is hidden from clear view. Jerry watches the whole time without inquiring about his intentions. Greg leans back on his pillow and rests his eyes.

Are You Crazy?

Greg walks through a set of metal doors entering an interior stairwell. Shoeless and clothed in only a hospital gown, he runs the downward spiral of the stairs; the light dims lower the deeper he descends. He increases his speed in hopes of finally reaching the bottom of the staircase; the stairs are innumerable. He turns back in the opposite direction to return to the door he came in, but when he changes direction, instead of going up, it continues downward. Greg runs his hands across the wall, trying to find an opening. After giving the wall a slight push, a door opens to the foyer of a traditionally decorated, colonial-style home. Now wearing jeans and a faded tee shirt, he walks into the living room and plops down on the sofa.

"Mom!" he yells.

"What's up, son?!" a woman's voice calls from the kitchen.

"I don't smell any food cooking!"

"I know!" the woman responds. "That's because you haven't started cooking it yet!"

"Don't make me come in there, Linda!"

"Bring it on!" she says.

Greg walks into the kitchen. Linda sits at the dining table, eating take-out Chinese food while flipping through a catalog. The woman, of slim to average build, age range in the mid- to late-thirties, has long, curly brown hair.

"You got Chinese food without even asking me if I wanted any? So this is how we do things now?" Greg stands over his mother, checking out her food.

Linda glances at him and smiles. "Aww. I'm sorry, Son. I didn't know you were still coming over."

"It's ok, I'm just teasing. I'm not that hungry. What'd you get?"

"Pepper steak, sesame chicken, and fried rice. You can have some of the sesame chicken and rice if you want. There's no way I can eat all of this by myself."

Greg walks over to the oak cabinet and reaches inside, pulling out a saucer.

"You're gonna need a bigger plate than that," Linda says.

He reaches back inside, grabs a dinner plate and walks back to the table.

"But a smaller plate than that," she says.

Greg sighs forcefully, shakes his head and walks back

to the cabinet.

"I'm just teasing you, come back," she says, laughing. "You're so easy."

The woman scrapes the sesame chicken and a majority of the rice into his plate. A fork appears in the palm of Greg's hand. He pokes at a couple of pieces of pepper steak in the oyster pail. Linda pushes the steak off his fork with her chopsticks.

"Don't even think about it; you can't have my pepper steak. Maybe I'll let you have some if I don't eat all of it," she says.

"You don't mess around when it comes to your food," he says.

"*That* I do not," she answers. "How was your day?"

"Well, I had trouble getting here," Greg utters through a mouthful of food. "For some reason I got lost and totally forgot where I was headed. It was weird."

"That *is* weird," she says. "Why don't you relax? Take a seat."

Greg sits across from her at the small, round, stained-wood table. "How was your day?"

"Ohhh, it was okay I guess," she answers. "Long. Tiring."

Greg tears open a piece of chicken and examines it.

"This does *not* look like chicken breast," he says. "What do you think it is? Dog or cat?

"Neither," his mom says. "It's chicken."

"How much you wanna bet that it's not?" Greg asks.

"Three hundred dollars," she says. "If it's chicken, you owe me. And no backing out."

"And if it's not?"

"You'd still owe me, because you're my son and you love me," she says. "You wouldn't take your own mother's money."

"Ok, let's find out what it is," Greg says.

He gathers all of the remaining chicken from his plate, holds it in both hands and squeezes, as if balling up a sheet of paper; his mother watches in anticipation. He turns his body away from the table and launches the food toward the ceiling. Before it hits the hardwood floor, it transforms into a normal-sized healthy chicken; the chicken runs around the kitchen in a frenzy trying to escape.

"Get him out of here!" Linda screams.

Greg chases the clucking chicken around seemingly every inch of the room. Every time he comes close to catching it, it somehow finds a way to escape his hands. He runs to the back door, opens it and continues to chase the chicken until it runs outside.

They both laugh hysterically.

"You owe me three hundred dollars!" Linda says.

"We didn't shake on anything," Greg responds.

"I would tell you to at least give me my chicken back, but you let him run out of the back door." She sighs.

"What about yours?" Greg asks.

"My what?"

"Your pepper steak."

"This is steak and it's delicious." She says, lifting a piece of it with her chopsticks.

"Wanna bet?"

"I would like to *eat* my food," she answers. "And I'm sorry, but I don't necessarily like the idea of a cow being in my kitchen unless it's in the form of a steak or a hamburger."

"Come on, Mom."

"No."

"I'll buy you dinner tomorrow at any restaurant you choose," Greg says.

"Ok. But if it ruins my kitchen, you're paying for it."

Greg walks over and digs into the container of steak. He walks to the center of the room holding the food between the palms of his hands.

"Not even a scratch," she says.

"Okay," he says. "This time I'll be ready to catch whatever it is."

Greg tosses the steak into the air, and just before it touches the ground it transforms into a large, mangy, brown mutt. The dog is missing a small chunk of meat from its arm, his eyes are a bloodshot red, and he viciously bears his razor-sharp teeth as foam drips from the corners of his mouth. The dog growls in a repulsively deep tone as it stands in the way of the back door. Linda sits at the table, paralyzed in fear as Greg slowly walks toward her. He assists her from her chair, and they slowly back out of the kitchen. Greg reaches back and grabs his mother's hand, leading her into the living room while shielding her from the dog. The dog slowly approaches them, still in attack mode.

"Ok buddy, just calm down," Greg tells the dog. "Everything is ok. Are you hungry?"

The canine lets out a long, agitated growl and begins to bark ferociously. Greg eases back toward the fireplace; Linda is still behind him. The dog closes in. Greg blindly reaches behind him for the fireplace irons.

"Mom," he says, "when I tell you to run, run upstairs

as fast as you can."

"I'm not gonna outrun that dog," she whispers. "Are you crazy?"

"Just do it," he commands. "You ready?"

Linda takes a deep breath. "Ok, I'm ready."

"On the count of three," Greg says. "As soon as I say three, get up the stairs as fast as you can."

"Ok."

"One...two...three!"

Linda darts for the stairs as quickly as possible. The dog chases uncomfortably close behind her. Just as the rabid dog lunges for her calf, Greg extends the hook side of the heavy, iron fireplace poker and gives the dog a forceful blow that fatally pierces it just above the base of it's neck. Greg drags the dog's body down the stairs with the poker and confirms its death.

"I guess I owe you a really nice dinner." Greg says to his mother, still looking down at the bloodied corpse of the dog.

Linda sits on the stairs, productively coughing. Her thin, cotton sweatshirt is saturated in heavy perspiration. Greg is soon aware of her condition and immediately rushes to her aid. He touches her before quickly removing his hand; she has a fever that's quickly reached such a high temperature that extreme heat radiates from her body. Greg's fingers begin to blister. Linda's skin gets hotter by the second until a sound emits from her body similar to a loud continuous buzz of electricity. She begins to seize and a copious amount of foam projects from her mouth.

"I don't know what's happening," she says, struggling to speak through her fluid-filled mouth.

"The dog was sick," he answers, "and you ate some of it."

Greg removes his t-shirt, covers his hands with it for burn protection, and drags her to the landing of the stairs. He places the deathly ill woman on her side to prevent aspiration of the foam and puts the shirt under her head for cushion.

"I'll be back, Mom, I love you! I'll be right back."

Greg runs down the sidewalk until hearing a public transit train heading in his direction. The train rumbles down the street with momentum comparable to a falling meteorite. The explosive noise of the train as it approaches is nearly identical to a continuous boom of thunder. The expeditious train brings with it not just a breeze to accompany its speed, but a breathtakingly frigid draft of wind that causes shivers to anyone standing in its proximity.

People push, scream, argue, and come to blows as the train passes through and they jockey for position to gain entry. The train does not have stopping capabilities. The nearly two dozen prospective passengers must gain access to the train while it's still in motion. One by one, each person who tries to embark is thrown from the train with force like a foul ball from the bat of a power hitter.

Greg is the only person who remains. The train halts to a stop.

* *

Greg suddenly awakens from sleep, covered in sweat, heart racing. The nightmare was interrupted just as he started to make headway in finding help for his mother. He's haunted by the thought of Linda gazing into his eyes, her life seemingly hanging by a thread. Her expression was an expression of trust, faith that he would be able to pull her through her predicament. This crisis, melded with his fears, confusion, and restless mind beseech his brain to seek out answers that cannot be found by sitting idly in a hospital bed. His body screams on the inside, and this frustration is driven by the commotion in his brain of indomitable emotions.

Greg sits up and removes the wheelchair from behind the bed; he unfolds the chair, lowers his bed, and slides into the seat of the wheelchair. He rolls toward the door and stops next to the large cabinet beneath the television; he opens the cabinet and ransacks the closet in search of clothing. The only option is Jerry's wrinkled clothing, which is stuffed deep in the middle shelf. The wardrobe is less than appealing, yet serviceable. Greg quickly grabs the pair of dingy blue jeans, a faded adjustable baseball cap, and an ash gray sweatshirt. He attempts to squeeze into the pair of white tennis shoes over his hospital footie socks, but the shoes are entirely too small; he takes them anyway. He opens the door leading to the hall and peeks out. The halls are quiescent due to the short-handed overnight staff.

A woman stands at the copy machine stapling packets of paper together as another sits at the nurses' station scribbling away in a large gray binder. Greg watches intently for about five minutes waiting for the ideal time to sneak out of the room. The seated woman finally stands and turns around to write something on a large white board on the wall behind her. Greg fully opens the door, turns to his left and with one hard stroke of the wheels quietly rolls past the desk. Neither of the women notice as he passes. He presses the elevator button and waits. He then realizes that the elevators are in clear view of the nurses' station and instead decides to go into the stairwell to hide. In a bind, he must choose between taking his chances and leaving the stairwell or trying to make his way down the stairs in a wheelchair.

Greg rolls to the edge of the stairs and contemplates how to go about making his descent from the stairs as gracefully as possible. He stashes his clothes tightly at his side to keep them from escaping his retention. He rolls down the first flight of stairs recklessly, crashing the wheelchair against the wall upon landing, continuing the rest of the way in the same manner. His body thrashed about and in pain, Greg wheels himself through the stairway door en route to the exit at the main corridor.

The automatic doors slide open and a brisk rush of wind shocks his body as he enters the breezeway. The parking lots are bereft of activity and the roads lonely. He wheels himself out to the sidewalk lining the city street and makes a right turn. Vehicles zip past at relatively long intervals, but there is no shortage of sketchy pedestrians wandering the dark streets and alleyways. Greg, though having a purpose, is also incorporated in the group of aimless wayfarers without a destination. The temperature-controlled hospital, free meals, clean bed, and around-the-clock care was abandoned in favor of the cold, reclusive, and heartless streets in search of elusive answers. He maintains hope that when the sun rises and the city comes to life that he can make some sort of progress. He travels past the homeless people sleeping on the stairs and in the doorways of closed businesses. After two hours of cruising the streets of downtown Portland, he rolls into the lot of a closed gas station.

The interior lights of the gas station are dimly lit, and he decides to park his wheelchair to change clothes. He lifts his gown over his head and struggles with the jeans before finally forcing them above his waist, easily gets into the shirt, and places the cap snugly on his head. He squeezes his feet into the tight sneakers and loosens the strings to ease the restrictiveness. He backs the wheelchair against the building, uses his gown as a blanket and rests his head against the bricks. The uncomfortable wheelchair and a restless mind prevent him from sleeping. He unlocks the wheels of the chair and continues his excursion and crosses a bridge over the water. The sun begins to rise. Greg continues down the sidewalk as foot and vehicular traffic increases by the minute. A young man sitting on a large, plastic paint bucket on the corner of a busy intersection catches his attention.

"What's up, bro?" the man says as Greg passes by.

The young man, of white and Hawaiian decent, appearing to be in his late 20s or early 30s, is clad in a small vintage tee, tattered jeans and a pair of Converse All-Stars that look as if they'd been in service for at least two decades. He has ¾-inch gauges in both earlobes and holds a cardboard sign that reads: *Everybody needs a little help sometimes.*

"Hey, do you happen to know how to get to the train?" Greg asks.

"The what?"

"Public transportation. The train."

"Ohhh, the MAX," the man says.

"Yeah, I guess that's it," Greg says.

"You must not be around here," the man says in a

monotone voice.

The guy walks up to Greg, squinting his eyes through the drizzling, light rain. He points off into the distance of the depressingly dreary horizon. "Go about five blocks in that direction and make a left, then go about two miles until you reach a small convenience store on the right, I can't remember what it's called, but when you see it make another right and go two miles, you'll see what looks like a fork in the road, make a right at that fork and the train should be there. You can't miss it."

"Thanks a lot. Just to be sure, you did say make a left and go two miles until the dead end and what else?"

"Yeah, go straight, a left, a right, another right, and a fork. Oh, yeah and it's on the right. Can't miss it. You get that?"

"Yeah, I got it. Thanks a lot man, take it easy," Greg says, completely confused with the directions.

"No problem," the guy says, walking back to the paint bucket.

Greg wheels himself through the cold, drizzling rain, the light end of the scattered showers that stereotypically beset the city. He follows the directions given to him to the best of his ability, confident that if he could somehow find the train that he took the night he left his mother's home that it would lead him to the answers to all of his questions.

The rain continues to fall and soak Greg's clothes as he approaches a group of people gathered around waiting for the train. He rolls his wheelchair under the bus shelter near the end of the bench to conceal himself from the pouring rain. The majority of those waiting for the train sit and stand quietly, acknowledging none other than cars that pass by;

others are consumed by their cellular phones. Greg awaits the train knowing that he surely can't make it onto a speeding train in his physical condition. However, just the thought of being able to see something that is familiar to him, paired with the possibility of being able to follow its tracks give him some form of hope. He reads the route map posted on the shelter and attempts to decipher it. The group of people also waiting for the train simultaneously move closer to the tracks. Greg follows them, confused; no sound of a train coming, no rumbling of the ground. He parks his wheelchair next to the person who looks the most approachable. A young woman wearing glasses and a thin, waterproof jacket smiles at him as he approaches.

"What are we waiting on?" Greg asks.

The woman looks at Greg, confused.

"I can't hear anything," Greg says.

"I don't understand," she says, pleasantly smiling. "No good English."

"I'm sorry," he says. "Nevermind."

To Greg's surprise, the train approaches slowly and quietly. The people board patiently as he sits back in his wheelchair and watches; this is clearly not the train he was expecting. The doors remain open as he tries to make a decision as to whether to enter the train or not. With no other viable options coming to mind, he decides to board. Greg wheels himself toward the handicapped section and looks around the crowded train. The train takes off as he watches through the window as it coasts through the city. There are some visual similarities outside to the life that he remembers but his thoughts remain obscure like eyes that are unable to focus. The train provides him with refuge from the assiduous rain, but he still has a gut feeling that it isn't leading him any closer to his purpose. He passively listens to an older gentleman holding a conversation with a young man behind him seated next to each other.

"I went to the dollar store—do you go to the dollar store?" the old man asks.

"I never go," the young man with broken English answers in a quiet, Indian accent.

"It is the best place," the old man says as he pulls a small, shiny black cardboard box from a small paper bag. "This is what I found today."

The elderly man hands the Indian man the box, and he examines it.

"Read this, right here," the old man says, pointing at the bottom of the box. "Compare to Drakkar Noir. This is the same thing, same exact smell, just called something else. This stuff is worldwide. A dollar is all I paid for it."

"This is good price," the young man says, nodding his head.

"The store right next to the mall is where I got it; I should have gotten three or four of them. Go and get you some, the ladies will come a knockin."

Greg jealousy believes everyone else around him carries on with their life in a virtually carefree mood while every waking hour he feels subjugated by his own thoughts. He rides the route lines for over five hours, randomly exiting and waiting for other trains in hopes that one of them would lead him to something he is accustomed to. He finally puts an end to his tour of the city and exits the train to find the nearest restroom.

He enters a small 24-hour diner and passes the hostess

booth toward the men's restroom. With the help of the stainless steel support rails he moves himself to the toilet to relieve himself and slides back into his wheelchair. After challenging himself by lifting one of his weak legs to flush the toilet, he exits the stall. As he passes the sink, he catches sight of his reflection through peripheral vision and slowly coasts to the mirror. This is the first time seeing his reflection since being awake. Greg turns his head to look at both side profiles; he takes off his baseball cap and runs his hand against his short hair, which was shaved down at the hospital; he slowly runs one hand down his stubbly face before flashing his teeth in the mirror, inspecting them. It's like seeing his own face for the very first time, and it makes everything else taking place in his life seem so prosaic. Greg slowly wheels himself toward the door, still looking in the mirror until he crosses the door's threshold. The young hostess stops him as he passes her podium.

"Just one?" she asks.

"Excuse me?" Greg asks.

"Is it just you today?"

"Oh, yeah."

"Follow me please," she says.

The hostess is a woman in her early twenties with a long blonde ponytail and a huge artificial smile. The young lady grabs a menu and leads him to a table that is still damp from being freshly wiped down. She moves a chair to make space for his wheelchair and places the menu in front of him.

"Claire will be your server, and she'll be with you shortly," the hostess says. "Enjoy your meal."

Shortly thereafter, Claire approaches the table with a

basket of rolls and a glass of water.

"Hello, Sir," she says. "I'm Claire and I'll be your server today. Can I start you off with an appetizer?

Greg looks down at the menu; the menu is boundless and full of choices and the many photos make it hard for him to decide, which is magnified by his intense hunger.

"Do you need more time to look at the menu?" the waitress asks.

"I'll take the meatloaf and mashed potatoes," Greg says.

"That's a good choice," the waitress says. "Anything else for you?"

"No, that's all."

The waitress walks away.

Greg grabs a roll and stuffs it in his mouth. Before long, he finishes the whole basket. Stuffed and satisfied, he takes one last sip of water and leaves the restaurant. Sunset creeps on the horizon and the rush hour traffic begins to dissipate. Greg leisurely rides his wheelchair down the bike lane and a patrol car pulls up next to him. Distressed by the attention, Greg uncomfortably turns to the officer who then rolls down his window.

"I'm sorry, sir, the sidewalk ended a little ways back, and I planned on getting back on the sidewalk but I wasn't really paying attention," Greg explains.

The officer activates the emergency lights, exits the vehicle and opens the back door on the passenger side. The no-nonsense expression on the officer's face is difficult to read.

"Get in the car," the officer commands, bracing the wheelchair while Greg slides into the back of the patrol car.

The officer helps him get his legs into the very limited amount of leg room.

"Can I ask you what I did, Officer?" Greg asks.

The officer, tall and slightly heavyset, in his mid-thirties, closes the door, walks to the front of the vehicle and gets into the driver's seat. He stares at Greg through the rearview mirror; Greg nervously stares back at him.

"Stop crying like a scared little bitch before I come back there and give you something to really cry about," the officer replies.

Disconcerted, Greg attempts to remain calm.

The officer smiles at him. "What the hell is wrong with you? Do you not recognize me?" he laughs. "It's me, Andy! Andrew Lambere, Paul Lambere's older brother! Sorry, I had to put on a show for that diner back there, they told me you pulled the ol' dine and dash."

"I didn't even eat," Greg says. "I only ate the bread. I thought the bread was free."

"Yeah, yeah, whatever," Andy says, still amused. "Tell someone who's not familiar with your antics. That coma stuff must be crazy, but you *gotta* remember *me*. Don't tell me all those ass kickings I gave you back in the day mean nothing now."

Greg stares hard in an attempt to recall the officer's face, but nothing comes to mind.

"You *really* don't remember me," the officer says.

"Man, I'm really sorry," Greg answers. "I can barely remember myself."

"I can't be mad at you," the officer says. "I can't even imagine. Almost thirty years of memories down the drain."

"Thanks a lot, man," Greg replies sarcastically. "That

made me feel a lot better."

They both laugh.

The police officer's mood changes from cheerful to somber in an instant. "Seriously, man, you're a good guy; we all hated to see that happen to you. If it wasn't for your grandmother, you wouldn't be here. None of us thought you were going to make it, including me. People actually got upset with her when she didn't wanna pull the plug on you. They thought she was being selfish, making you suffer. They thought you'd die or become a vegetable, at best. She was a great woman, so sweet. It just tears me up to think she's not with us anymore."

"I don't remember anything; all I can go off of are my dreams. I'm looking for my mother now. Do you know where she lives?"

"Your mother," the officer answers. "I have a general idea of what area she might be in, but I haven't seen her in a while. I'll let you know."

"Really? How is she doing?" Greg asks.

"I couldn't tell you," Andy says. "I haven't seen her in a while."

"Can you take me there now?" Greg asks.

"I would but it's nowhere near my beat," Andy says. "Plus it'd probably be easier to look for her in the daytime. Why the sudden interest in your mom? You used to get mad if anyone ever even mentioned your mom. But I can totally understand if you want to make amends with her after what happened to your grandmother. Let me get this straight, you don't remember *anything* about your life before?"

"Not a fucking thing," Greg answers.

"Boy, where do I start?" Andy says. "You, my brother,

and your whole crew were slackers, lazy, thieves, and tweakers. I still blame myself sometimes for how you guys turned out. You boys looked up to me, but I was so busy with sports and girls that I always brushed you off. Sometimes I wish I could go back in time; I should have taken more of an interest. You guys didn't care about shit. I used to always joke that all you fuckers cared about were drugs, music and Doritos. No ambition or direction, really. Even up until the accident. About four or five of you guys were living in the back of a convenience store that had been made into an apartment, no jobs; your rent was so cheap you didn't really need jobs, just bummed money from everyone else and stole whatever you could get your hands on. I knew it was going on but I knew it was either you guys would do that or sell drugs, so I turned a blind eye. There was no way in hell I was gonna let either one of you go to prison on a felony conviction. You both were little brothers to me. That and I didn't wanna disappoint your grandma because she was so proud of everything you did, but she didn't know what you guys were really doing."

"Are you sure you're talking to the right person?" Greg asks.

"Oh, yeah," Andy says, "but there was one thing about you, though, you were a good kid back in the day. You used to never get in trouble, but things change."

In deep thought and mired in confused, Greg can do nothing but shake his head.

"So where are you staying? It seems really weird that they'd just let you leave the hospital so soon. It can't be good that you're still in the mental state you're in roaming the streets like this."

"I left," Greg says. "I couldn't take it anymore."

"Take what?"

"The frustration," Greg says. "I couldn't get any answers; they just labeled me as crazy. If I was crazy to begin with, they were only making me even crazier."

"I see," Andy says.

"Do you know where I live?" Greg asks.

"Sure I do."

"Can you take me there?"

"You sure?" Andy says. "I really think it'd be a better idea to take you back to the hospital, you know, until you're ready to take care of yourself."

"I really appreciate you looking out for my best interests, Andy." Greg says. "But I think

I'll be okay."

The officer walks outside and grabs the wheelchair, crams it into the trunk of the patrol car and gets back into the driver's seat; he puts the car in drive and takes off.

Andy pulls into the residential driveway and puts the vehicle in park. He removes the wheelchair from the trunk and assists Greg into it.

Greg wheels himself up the driveway toward the door. The cold rain returns, sprinkling down on their faces.

"Greg," the officer calls out in a loud voice.

Greg stops and turns around.

"I'll never know how you feel, but maybe it's not a bad thing that you get to start over. Take care of yourself, buddy."

"Thanks." Greg looks at Andy for several seconds, mulling over the statement. He opens the door and wheels himself into the dark house.

The patrol car backs out of the driveway, taking off down the puddle-ridden street.

* * *

Mandy, a scrawny ten-year-old girl with strawberry blonde hair and glasses, takes a seat next to Shannon on a large, brown sofa. Shannon is dressed for comfort in a zipper hoodie and cotton jogging pants; she navigates between multiple windows on the screen of her laptop. Kendra paces around the kitchen entertaining a telephone call that she received moments ago; she repeatedly goes back and forth to the counter, compulsively stirring the contents of her crockpot out of apparent frustration. Mandy scoots closer to Shannon and looks over her shoulder at the screen.

"What are you looking at?" Mandy asks.

"Just some stuff for work."

"Oh," Mandy replies. "It looks boring." Mandy's voice is naturally loud, and when she talks it sounds as if she strives to say everything in one breath. At the moment, she is uncharacteristically calm.

"It's not too bad once you get used to it," Shannon laughs.

"Oh," Mandy replies. A few seconds of silence goes by. "Where do you work?"

"I work at the hospital with your mom. I'm a doctor."

"I thought you were gonna be a man," Mandy says.

"Why did you think I was gonna be a man?"

"Duh, because doctors are men, and nurses are women," she explains, getting increasingly louder. "And usually when mom invites a friend over it's usually a man."

Kendra walks to the door leading to the living room

and places her caller on hold.

"Mandy!" she says. "That's enough. Go to your room and watch TV or something until dinner's ready, leave Shannon alone."

"It's ok," Shannon says. "She's fine."

"Right now young lady," Kendra says.

Mandy skips to her bedroom. Kendra ends her telephone conversation and walks into the living room and sits on the sofa next to Shannon.

"Turn that thing off and relax," Kendra says, trying to snatch the computer from Shannon's lap, prompting a game of tug-of war between the two.

"Kendra, stop it," Shannon pleads. "Give me three more minutes. I'm almost done; I promise."

"You need to seriously consider taking some time off to relieve some stress," Kendra says as she walks back into the kitchen, grabs a bottle of red wine off of the counter and two drinking glasses from the cabinet; she returns to the living room and hands Shannon one of the glasses and pours. Shannon closes her laptop.

"No wine glasses?" Shannon asks, smiling.

"Between the dirty ones and the broken ones, I don't have any right now," Kendra jokes. "Lush problems. So what's new with the coma guy? Is that what you were looking at on the computer?"

"No, I was just working on some other things for tomorrow. I've been slacking lately. I have *sooo* much to catch up on."

"I wonder how in the world he left without anyone noticing."

"Who?" Shannon asks. "Left where?"

"Mallet," Kendra answers. "The coma guy."

"Left where? I don't know what you're talking about."

"He left the hospital; they don't know where he went. Don't tell me you didn't hear about that."

"I didn't hear about anything. What happened?" Shannon listens intently.

"Somehow he left the hospital late last night without anyone knowing, and now the big wigs are apparently in panic mode because they think it's gonna bring negative publicity to the hospital. Do you not check your work e-mail account?"

"I check it, but I get hundreds of emails a day, and I skip most of them because most of them are junk. What did it say?"

"They sent a mass e-mail this morning telling everyone not to talk to anyone with the media or any outside sources, for that matter, concerning anything dealing with any patients or internal matters, and to *kindly* tell anyone to direct all questions to the public information officer. Then you know they finished it off with all the HIPAA threats and stuff like that. Basically, they were referring to that incident that happened last night. I kid you not."

"Crazy," Shannon says, her mind drifts off for a few seconds. "Wait a minute. He couldn't even walk, how did he leave?"

"Exactly!" Kendra says. "That's what we were thinking! He had to have some kind of help, but no one saw *anything*."

Shannon marinates on how he could have possibly left the hospital and how the time and energy she expended trying to help him is now quite possibly a waste. Kendra gets up and walks back into the kitchen.

"Mandy! Dinner's ready!" Kendra calls from the kitchen."

* * *

Greg is comfortably nestled in a king-size bed and wrapped in a floral comforter with his head resting against two plump, bright white pillows. The room is dark, and the rainfall outside is vigorous with the occasional crash of thunder. He glances at the hands of the frosted crystal clock that rests on the nightstand next to the bed and the hands display 9:47 p.m. Unable to sleep, he grabs the remote control from the nightstand next to the bed, turns on the television and begins to flip channels until he stops at an antiques program. He slowly drifts away into sleep.

I Don't Want Your Condom or Anything Else You Have to Offer

Greg is dressed in a slim-fit, white dress shirt, a paisley tie, gray slacks, and penny loafers. A gentleman in his early forties, in a gray sweater with a collared shirt and tie underneath, navy blue dress pants, and shiny black shoes sits across him at a small table; the man is an appraiser. A camera faces the both of them. They are at the antiques show. The frosted crystal clock is at the center of the table; it stands at eight inches tall and five inches thick with the timepiece occupying only three inches of the top section.

"So you tell me you found this clock in your late grandmother's house. Do you know how long it's been in your family?"

"No, I just recently found it when I moved back into my grandma's house, and I was just curious to know the history of it."

"That's very understandable, because it *is* a very unique clock. Let me give you a briefing on the history of this particular timepiece. Based on this inscription on the bottom of the clock here, it was produced by the Spence-Zabeth Clock Company. This company was in the business of manufacturing watches and clocks between the years of 1887 to 1932. Around that time, there were many clock companies in the United States, and business was very competitive. Of course, nowadays in the age of cell phones and digital clocks on everything from computers to microwaves, the actual standalone clock and watches are on their way to becoming obsolete. But, of course, it's our custom to want to wear some sort of adornment on our wrists or fingers, so thankfully they won't be going anywhere anytime soon."

The man pauses shortly as he inspects the clock.

"Spence-Zabeth was actually a very well respected company. They made quality products for many years and frosted crystal clocks were one of their most popular sellers. This clock in particular dates back to around 1904 to 1917. It's in very good shape for its age, there is a small chip near this bottom corner, and there's a slight tint to the white color of the clock but other than that—"

The man is interrupted by slight movement of something inside of the clock; Greg notices it also. Whatever it is inside the clock that is moving resembles a very small human, the size of a three and a quarter-inch G.I

Joe action figure.

"Did you see that?" Greg interrupts.

"See what?" the man asks.

They both watch as the object moves again.

"That," Greg says.

"I didn't see anything.".

"You saw it," Greg says. "We looked at each other right after we both saw it."

"Unfortunately, as much as I'd like to give you a full history lesson I do have time constraints," the appraiser says. "So if you would—"

"It's really not a big deal, I just want you to admit that you saw it."

"Look," the appraiser says, "I'll give you $700 for the clock."

"Never mind." Greg grabs the clock and begins to walk away. The appraiser quickly follows and grabs his arm. Greg looks down at his arm and the man removes his hand.

"Wait," the appraiser says. "I'm sorry, I have no idea what came over me. This isn't normally the way I do business. Let's talk."

"You're a liar," Greg says as he lifts the clock, holds it over his head and looks through the bottom. "I know what I saw, and I know you saw it, too."

At a table several feet across the room, two men go over the valuation of a Colt 1911 pistol from the prohibition era. Greg crashes their meeting and grabs the gun. The angry men stand up to confront him in order to retrieve the gun. Greg turns the gun on them and smiles awkwardly.

"I'm sorry," he says, "I'll bring it right back."

"Sure," the owner of the gun says, putting his hands

up. "I'll be over here when you're done. Take your time."

Greg walks to the appraiser and puts the gun to his temple. "Let out whoever that is that's inside the clock," he says.

"Ok, ok" the appraiser says. "Just calm down."

Greg sits. The appraiser shakes the clock, sets it back down, and taps it a few times. A light flickers on, and the frosted crystal becomes clear. Greg recognizes the frail old woman lying at the bottom of the clock as the person that people tell him was his grandmother. She is wearing a kitchen apron and sits, visibly distraught, with her back rested against the wall.

"What is this?" Greg asks. "What's going on?"

"I'll give you $12,000," the appraiser says.

"Ok that's fine," Greg stands up, pointing the gun at the man from across the table. "As long as you let the woman out, you can have it for whatever you want."

The appraiser removes a small, brown leather case from his pocket and hands it to him. "Here, I have a condom from the 1700s made from linen; I bet you didn't know they made these back then. How about an even swap? What d'ya say?"

"I don't want your condom or anything else you have to offer me. Just let the old woman out. Listen, I don't wanna have to kill you."

"But, Greg. That would take all the fun out of it."

Greg cocks the pistol. "Tell me how to get her out or I will blow your brains out."

"Ok," the appraiser says. "It's not easy, I'll tell you that right now."

Greg calmly sits back down. The room goes dark, but

not too dark to to make out the surroundings. The appraiser is still seated across from him; there is no longer anyone else in the room.

"Ok, Greg. This is how it works," the appraiser says. "It's sort of like a game.

"Ok."

"The light in this clock will change colors. I guess you can say the colors only serve as somewhat of a distractor. A tune will play, and after the tune finishes you have to remember it and play it exactly the way you heard it. If you finish playing the song without error, the old lady will be released."

"Why can't we just break it and let her out?"

"Would you really wanna risk that?" the appraiser asks. "If we break it and all of these shards of thick glass fall on her, what do you think will happen to her?"

The clock lights up, accompanied by the sound of a bell ring. The old woman continues to sit against the side of the clock, crying.

"So just repeat the tune like a drum?" Greg asks.

"It won't sound like a drum."

"No, I mean am I supposed to tap on it like a drum?"

"Oh, yeah."

"Can I use both hands?"

"Whatever you have to do."

"Ok, I'm ready," Greg says, nervously, heart racing.

The room goes dark again. The clock plays a tune, which is accompanied by blue, green, red, and yellow lights. Each time a color flashes is the only time the both of them see each other's faces. As the song plays, the old woman assumes what is similar to a tornado drill position and

114

covers her ears due to the blaring noise, which is much louder for her tiny ears. With each flash of the colorful lights, Greg sees the sinister smile on the appraiser's face; he has no idea whether the appetence on the appraiser's face is due to an intense desire to see him fail or just an outward display of the jitters caused by curiosity of what will happen next. The song pauses only to continue shortly thereafter; it seems neverending, playing at least forty notes before it finishes. After it concludes, the light on the inside of the lamp comes back on.

Greg glares at the appraiser, unable to remember any part of the tune.

"Hey, I didn't make the song nor the rules," the appraiser says. The smirk on his face further affirms that he is unapologetically exasperating.

"Can I get another try?"

"No, one try is all you get."

"Well it's impossible to remember that whole song."

"So what?" the appraiser asks. "You're not even going to try? You're just gonna give up?

A minute ago you were ready to execute me, and now you're gonna just quit."

"I mean, I can try but it probably wouldn't do any good."

Greg sits erect in his chair,and tries to recall the tune that played on it a little over a minute ago. He places a hand on the clock.

"Take your time," the appraiser says. "There's no time limit, if that helps. But I'd hurry if I were you, while you can still remember some of it."

Greg pops his knuckles and begins to play. Following

the first tap of the clock, his hands take over and continue to play without the need of help from his brain. The appraiser looks on, eyebrows raised in astonishment. The song concludes. Almost as soon as the tune finishes, a puff of smoke subdues the area. The old woman that was trapped in the clock stands a few feet away from them; she is now of normal size. She looks at Greg, slowly walks up to him and reaches out for him. Greg reaches out to her, trying to grab her hand. His hand goes through her hand as it would a ghost or a hologram. The woman slowly disappears into thin air.

Shortly thereafter, Greg is zapped into the clock. The appraiser laughs sadistically as he places the clock in a black bag made of velvet and tightens the drawstrings of it.

Greg pounds on the transparent walls clamoring to be let out until he realizes that there's not a chance anyone will hear. He sits patiently in a corner until he begins sliding and bouncing across the floor. The appraiser walks outside of the large convention center to a woodgrain station wagon parked in a lot across the street; he places the clock in the passenger seat. Greg is thrown around with every bump and pothole as the car travels down the road. The vehicle stops. Greg feels the clock being lifted and carried before the appraiser removes the clock from the bag and places it back on a small dresser.

An eight-year-old boy and a six-year-old girl stand next to the man. The children both appear to be from late 1970s or early 1980s television commercials, based on their clothing and appearance. The room is decorated with toys, dolls, and decorations that would be a dream to a child from that era. Large letter blocks with both children's initials sit on each side of a large step that leads to another level of the room that is bordered with dolls, ventriloquist dummies, and a large toy chest. A white bunk bed is located across from the dresser where the clock sits.

"Cool!" the boy says, tapping on the outside of the lamp, staring inside.

"I wanted a girl. No fair!" the small girl pouts, folding her arms.

Greg yells from the inside of the clock, demanding to be let out; only a dog would be able to hear a voice so tiny and quiet that it's inaudible to a human ears. The appraiser picks up the small girl, who is his daughter.

"It's ok honey, we'll get you a girl one day," the appraiser says. "But in the meantime you can do whatever you want to him. Just make sure to be very careful with him so that he doesn't run away."

"Can I put him in my dollhouse?" the girl asks.

"You can even put him in your dollhouse," the appraiser says. "But in the meantime we have to feed him. Pete, go get him some food and water. Put them in ramekins."

"Ok dad!" the boy says, before running to the kitchen.

Greg kicks the walls of the clock in a futile attempt to break through.

"What's wrong with him daddy?" the girl asks.

"He's just scared, honey," the appraiser says. "He's in a new home. He'll get used to it."

Pete comes back and hands the ramekins to the appraiser.

"You can do it," the appraiser tells the boy.

"Cool!" Pete says. "Cool" is clearly a favorite word in

his limited vocabulary.

While Greg still tries to devise an escape plan, the boy reaches his hand into the clock and places a ramekin full of meatloaf and mashed potatoes across from him; next, Pete reaches into the lamp to place the small container of water. Just as he sets it down, Greg runs up to the boy's hand and bites his finger as hard as possible. The boy spills the water across the floor of the clock and lets out a high-pitched scream; he panics and snatches his arm from the lamp with Greg still clamped onto his finger.

"Daddy!" Pete cries, trying to shake Greg from his finger. "Get it off! Get it off!"

"Be still, Pete!" the appraiser says. "Calm down, I'll get it."

Greg leaps onto the little girl's shirt and slides down until he reaches her belt loop and falls to the floor. The appraiser, who is slightly distracted by his son's screaming, loses track of Greg's whereabouts. Pete points to the floor.

"There he is daddy!" he yells.

Greg runs as fast as possible, but is unable to cover much ground. The appraiser reaches down to grab him. Just as he reaches down and closes in on him, a short-haired gray cat comes in out of nowhere and swoops him away from the appraiser's reach. The cat darts out of the room with Greg in its mouth as the appraiser and his son chase it. The little girl slowly follows behind. The cat flees into another room and hides under the bed, successfully concealing Greg from danger.

* * *

Greg wakes up abruptly, sweating profusely, heart racing. An infomercial plays on the television and is almost

118

drowned out by the sound of a thunderstorm outside. He climbs into his wheelchair and rolls into the hallway, passing by the room that he slept in for nearly three years. He peeks inside. Life for Greg has been nothing short of tumultuous since the day he woke up in that room. He rolls into the kitchen and stands at the counter trying to keep his balance as he reaches into the cabinet to get a glass. He turns on the sink faucet, fills the glass with water and quickly chugs it. He opens the other cabinets and the fridge to survey their contents: Fish, garlic, cabbage, red peppers, onions, apples, berries, broccoli, celery, white bread, unsalted crackers, rice cakes, egg substitute, and milk. Non-perishable foods are at a minimum. He grabs a few crackers and puts them in the stomach pocket of his shirt and rolls back toward the room.

Greg returns to bed and snacks on the crackers as he switches the channels on the television. He stops at a station airing a replay of an earlier newscast. The news anchor covers a story about the Cascade-Columbia Medical Center; disinterested and unaware that the story is about himself, Greg flips the channel. He stops at a religious program where a preacher sits at a desk similar to a news anchor. The name posted on the screen below him reads: *Billy Gleason*. Gleason, a nationally syndicated preacher, had a well-documented history of chronic alcoholism, D.U.I's, domestic violence, and a penchant for cheap hookers; he resembles someone you would imagine being a regular at a local bar, sitting solitary, reflecting on his afflictions over copious amounts of scotch whiskey. Billy Gleason died a little over two years ago, but the polarizing figure's program is still in syndication during the wee hours of the morning. The man has gray hair so stiff and perfect, that it would be nearly impossible for even a child not to recognize it as a wig. The preacher keeps his freakishly light blue eyes in full contact with the camera through the duration of the telecast. Greg takes little interest in the preacher's message but leaves the television on the station simply by default coupled with the fact that the man's way of speaking offers him a sense of companionship.

Some People Just Never Change

As the sun rises, Greg gets out of bed and climbs into his wheelchair. He grabs an apple and a rice cake from the kitchen and makes his way to the porch. For five hours, he watches the quiet streets as they gradually become active with commuters, joggers and pedestrians. He eventually becomes restless and goes back inside.

Adjacent to the front door sits a foyer table decorated with photographs. A candid snapshot of Linda as a young teen, approximately 14 or 15 years of age, is first in the line of pictures. He lifts the photograph and examines it. She eerily resembles the mother that he remembers from her coarse brown hair, to the broad, gaping smile only to be differentiated by the braces on her teeth and the smoother, more youthful skin. Going down the line of photos, he observes a photo of a male toddler, about four years old, dressed in blue jean overalls and a T-shirt decorated with multi-colored dinosaurs. The smiling boy holds a waffle cone filled with melting, chocolate ice cream trailing down his sticky fingers. The next is a Polaroid of a younger version of the boy sitting on the lap of an older woman whom Greg recognizes as a younger version of the elderly woman that met him following his awakening.

Greg returns to the kitchen, takes a package of ground beef from the freezer, removes it from its packaging and puts it on a plate to defrost. An unexpected, brutal knock at the door startles him. He cruises to the door.

"Who is it?" he asks.

"Hey, Greg, It's me, Andy," the voice says. "Open the door."

Greg opens the door. Andy stands before him, dressed in plainclothes; the clean-shaven appearance from yesterday replaced by stubble and his attire is slightly disheveled. He places his right hand on the doorjamb.

"Hey, man, I was thinking about what we talked about yesterday," Andy says. "So I asked Paul if he had any idea where your mother was, and he told me where I should be able to find her. She's not far from here at all if you want me to take you."

"Yeah, thanks man. I'd appreciate that. Let me get some shoes and I'll be right out."

Greg quickly wheels himself through the halls, returning with an old pair of fluffy, purple, plush-lined slippers. He makes his way to the door and notices Ruth's walker next to the sofa; he wheels himself to the walker and adjusts it to accommodate his height. Andy enters the house; he looks down at Greg's slippers.

"Seriously? You've got to be kidding me," he says, looking down at Greg's feet.

"What?" Greg asks.

"Nothing," Andy laughs. "Let's go."

"They're comfortable. Should I change them?"

"No, don't worry about it. I doubt anybody notices," Andy says. "We live in Portland."

Andrew opens the passenger door of the late model Nissan Sentra and Greg climbs in.

"You've gotta excuse the mess. This is my wife's car. She can keep a house clean, but the car is always a freakin' mess. I'll never understand that."

Andrew travels down the main roads and the highway for approximately five miles routinely disregarding the posted speed limits that he so strictly enforces during his work hours. His road rage-induced dialogue and the silence of his highly anxious passenger makes the drive to their destination anti-social between the two. Andy slows down and scans the area as he passes a strip of old buildings in a revitalized section of the city. An elderly couple in a Buick cruise slowly ahead of them; the driver pumps the brakes frequently.

"What the?" Andy says. "Stop riding your brakes, dumb ass!"

"What's the name of the place we're looking for?" Greg asks.

"There she is," Andy says, immediately stopping the car and backing into a parking space on the curb. A middle-aged woman with long, dark, greasy hair walks along the sidewalk. The woman is dressed in an acid wash jean jacket, a darker blue pair of jeans, and sneakers that were originally white, but are now permanently gray from dirt and wear.

"Linda!" Andy calls out from the window.

The woman turns toward the car and squints, trying to recognize the person calling her name. She rolls her eyes and continues to walk. Andy exits the vehicle and stands outside of the door. He folds his arms and places them on the roof of the car.

Greg takes a look at the woman but doesn't recognize her. "That's not her," he says..

Andy doesn't listen. "Linda, come here. You're not in trouble, I promise. Just come over here for a second."

"If I'm not under arrest I don't have to listen to you!" she says. "I haven't done nothing! Leave me alone."

"I have your son with me and he wants to talk to you!"

Greg exits the vehicle.

"C'mon, man. It's not her," he says, looking at Andrew from across the roof of the car.

Linda turns around and takes a long look at Greg and walks toward the vehicle. Greg watches her, and the closer she gets, the more he realizes that it *is* his mother. She smiles at him. The woman that he remembers from his dreams is somewhere beneath the desiccated, scarred and sunken face. The smile is also the same, with the only difference being her broken, stained and rotting teeth. Greg's stomach turns. The urge to vomit overcomes him, not because of her physical appearance, but from the pain and confusion brewing deep in his soul; he can do nothing but stare.

"Hey, baby," she says, spreading her arms to hug him. "It's so good to see you."

"It's good to see you, too," Greg says, disinclined, not knowing whether his own words are true or not. He hugs her. The musty odor of her clothing reeks as if she hadn't changed them in weeks. He glances at Andrew, who is looking on from about ten feet away. Still discombobulated, he tries to conjure up more words to say. He can't recall a time in his version of the past that he couldn't spark up even a simple conversation with his mother. "How have you been, Mom? I've missed you."

Shocked by his calling her mom, Linda's eyes widen significantly. "Missed you, too," she says, unconvincingly. "Son."

Greg smiles awkwardly, unsure of what else to say. "So they say this rain might clear up at some point today," he says. "I really hope so."

"Yeah, me too."

A short pause follows.

"Well keep in touch, honey," Linda says. "I would talk longer but I got a lot of stuff to do today. I'll see ya."

Greg slowly trudges back to the vehicle while Linda continues in the direction she was initially walking. Greg gets in the car and shuts the door. Andy quickly catches up to Linda.

"Hey!" he softly grabs her arm.

"What?" she says, annoyed.

"Calm down and listen to me for a minute," Andrew says. "Did you know your mother passed away the other day?"

Linda responds with a blank stare, as if to wonder why

he's telling her.

"Yeah, the woman who was taking care of your son for his whole life," he says. "Your son just woke up from a coma. He doesn't remember her, and he doesn't remember any of the heartache you've caused him over the years. Now would be a perfect time to repair the relationship you have with him."

Linda removes a pack of cigarettes and a lighter from her pocket. "First of all, I didn't know the woman died, and second of all, you don't know shit about me and that boy's relationship."

"Oh, trust me, I know all about it, Linda. Everyone who knows you or that man over there sitting in that car knows all about it."

"That boy has disrespected me and treated me like a piece of shit all my life!" she says, her lit cigarette only inches from Andy's face as she emphatically points at him. "I don't owe him a damn thing! And I know it was that bitch telling lies on me, brainwashing him, and turning him against me to make me seem like some kind of...I don't know, but I got nothing to say to him."

"So you're not even gonna try," Andy says. "Is that what you're telling me? He's been looking for you for days. All he could talk about was seeing his mother."

Linda stands silently before responding.

"Nope," she says, looking him directly in the eyes.

"Linda, I've known you for a long time. You've done some horrible things but, this here, this is a low point even for you. I don't see how anyone could be so selfish."

"I'm done. Bye!" she says.

"You might need him one day more than he needs

you," Andy yells to her as she storms off.

She raises her arm and flips him off without so much as turning around.

Andy returns to the car, snatches his seatbelt and buckles it. He watches as Linda aimlessly walks down the busy street. He starts the car.

"I'm sorry man, but you don't need someone like that in your life anyway," he says, still looking out the windshield. "Some people just never change."

"Yeah," Greg says. "You're right."

"Well," Andy says. "That's that. You hungry? Wanna stop somewhere and get something to eat?"

Greg remains silent as he looks out of his window.

"Hey, man," Andy says. "You ok?"

He leans over to look at Greg and notices a single tear roll down his face. He is deeply moved with sympathy and feels awkward at the same time, not knowing how to console the crying man at his side. He pats him on the shoulder. "I know it' difficult," Andy says. "You've been dealing with life without her for this long. I know you're strong enough to push forward."

Andy pulls into the driveway of Greg's house. "Take it easy, man."

"You too. Thanks for the ride. Greg grabs his walker and slowly limps into the house. He sits on the sofa, dejected.

* * *

Shannon stands in the center of the recreational room. A dozen patients in the ward sit in chairs encircling her. There is commotion in the room as the patients interact with each other. Shannon raises a stack of white papers above her head. The techs and nurses quiet the room.

"I have a pretty cool activity for everyone today," Shannon announces. "I know you guys and girls seem to get tired of the same things every day, so I've decided to try something new."

The patients nod their heads and laugh in agreement.

"Well, *excuse me,*" Shannon says gleefully. "I didn't know I was *that* boring."

They laugh again. She hands the stack of papers to an eager patient who distributes them throughout the room.

"I want everyone to take a look at the pictures and the captions below and decide which one best fits their mood for today," Shannon says. "The first picture as you can see, is of a balloon, the next one is of a sailboat, and so on."

Everyone begins to speak at once.

"Ok everyone, settle down for a moment," Shannon says. "Let me explain it for those who may not understand, and I promise I'll give everyone a chance to share their answers."

The patients police each other into being quiet.

"Thank you," Shannon says. "At the top of the list it says 'I feel like' and below that, we have choices. The first says 'a balloon ready to pop at any moment,' then below that you have 'a boat sailing peacefully across the water,' then we have 'like a kitten that just wants to be stroked.'"

The crowd erupts in laughter.

"What is so funny?" Shannon asks. Almost before she finishes her question she realizes what was so amusing. "Oh, stop it. I did *not* mean it like that. I meant stroke as in a kitten wanting to be petted. In other words, do you just need someone to be there for you and comfort you or reassure you that everything is going to be okay? Going down the list, we have 'like a soccer ball being kicked around' or 'like a lion ready to attack it's prey.'"

The patients give a wide range of answers. Madeline predictably chooses a kitten that wants to be stroked. A few others insist on picking more than one answer, while some morph two answers into one, such as, "like a kitten that just wants to be kicked around."

One patient in particular, refuses to answer the question. Mike Amendola, a white male in his late twenties with a short fade haircut, sits silently with his arms in his pockets.

"Is there something wrong, Mike?" Shannon asks. "Is there a reason you don't wanna participate?"

"Ain't nothing wrong with me," Mike replies. "I just don't wanna do it."

"To each his own; I can respect that," Shannon says. "We can talk about it later between ourselves, if you want."

"Why don't you tell us which one *you* feel like," Mike says. "You said everybody was gonna participate." He leans back in his chair.

Caught off guard by the question, Shannon just looks at him.

"Or are you too good to answer?" Mike says.

"Not at all." Shannon looks down at the paper. "You're right, I did say everyone. Let's see."

The room goes painfully silent.

"I think she need that kitten stroked!" Fred Jenkins blurts out. Everyone in the room, including some employees, laugh. A female patient sitting next to Fred scolds him, smacking him on the leg.

"Fred!" says Jimmy the tech, shaking his head.

Even through all of the elapsed time, Shannon has a hard time deciding which option to pick for herself. She has a difficult time choosing not because she doesn't know what suits her, but because she refuses to divulge her inner feelings. In her mind she easily chooses the balloon ready to pop, the kitten wanting to be stroked, *and* the soccer ball being kicked around.

"To answer your question, Mike," she says. "I feel like a boat sailing peacefully across the water, because although there may be storms and heavy waves along the way, no matter what hard times we go through in life they are almost *always* only temporary, and one of the best ways to get through those times are by keeping a level head and striving to remain as optimistic as possible."

Shannon hates lying.

* * *

Greg's feet are planted on an area rug while he lies across the sofa with his head rested on a decorative pillow; he's been in the same position for over two hours. The position puts a significant amount of stress on his back, but he lacks the ambition even to move slightly. All he can think of is how he longs for his old life back and everything in it. The clock ticking on the wall is the only sound in the room until there is a knock on the door. Greg doesn't move. The knocking persists. He grabs his walker, gets up from the sofa and answers the door. Linda stands before him.

"Hey, son," Linda says.

"Hi," Greg says, his response sounding more like a question than a reply.

"Can I come in?" she asks.

Greg steps back and opens the door, just wide enough for her to come in. He closes it. Linda looks at him with a pouty and shameful expression on her face. Her jacket is damp from the rain.

"I just wanted to let you know that I'm very sorry for the way I treated you earlier," she says. "I know I haven't been the best mother, and if it's not too late I wanna change that."

"I don't know what to say," Greg says. "This is all new to me. I don't know how to explain it, but you're not the mother I know."

"I know your grandmother was the only mother you knew," Linda says. "I understand that."

"I'm not talking about that," Greg says. "It's really hard to explain."

"Would you like to take a walk with me?" Linda asks. "I want to hear all about it.

"Sure," Greg says. "I don't have anything better to do."

They exit the front door and Greg closes the door behind them. A bearded man sits in his truck a block away; he watches as they take a stroll down the damp sidewalk. Faded stickers cover the rear of the small, non-matching camper of the banged up, rusted, early Nineties model Toyota Pickup. As they walk, Greg thoroughly explains the bizarre chain of events that led him to where he is now. Linda listens to his words, but unlike the mother of his dreams, she doesn't provide much feedback nor comfort and reassurance. Greg accepts this because even though she doesn't exhibit those qualities, she at least carries a physical resemblance of her.

The scraggly man, who could be easily mistaken for a lumberjack, gets out of his truck and leisurely walks toward Greg's house. He scopes the area to make sure nobody watches as he makes entry. He ransacks the home and makes several trips to the back of his truck with anything he can find of small value. He leaves with the television set, jewelry, and all antiques he perceives as valuable. Before leaving the house, he urinates on the area rug in the middle of the living room.

Just as Greg and his mother step off the curb onto a crosswalk, the old Toyota pickup stops right in front of them. The bearded man reaches over and manually rolls down the passenger side window.

"Get in, Linda," he says.

She climbs into the vehicle and slams the door.

"I have to go, Greg," she smiles. "But it was nice to see you. I love you."

The vehicle takes off in a cloud of black exhaust.

Greg returns home. The front door is left wide open. He notices everything trashed and in disarray before even crossing the threshold. He realizes immediately that his mother was merely a distraction for a simple scheme to rob the house of valuables to support the drug habits of her and her male companion. What Greg doesn't know is that since he was a small child his grandmother was adamant that he was not to, under ANY circumstances, allow Linda into the home when she wasn't there. He walks into the bedroom and finds that the television set is no longer there. Greg is not angered by the burglary, nor is he upset with his mother. Self-pity is his nemesis. Any optimism that he may have had tucked away deep in his subconscious has become virtually non-existent from the moment he stepped back into the home. His arms, shoulders, and legs are sore from the walk, so he lies in bed. A full day passes and he doesn't leave the bedroom. Mental anguish and a heavy mind cause turmoil that prevents him from sleeping.

* * *

In the early hours of the morning, Greg hears creaking of the floors in the hallway. He sits up in bed and grabs his walker to investigate. His walking ability has regressed due to weakness from not eating and physical inactivity. He reaches the door and looks down the hall toward the living room and barely notices a figure walking in the darkness. He writes it off as his imagination and makes his way back to bed.

Before he makes it back to bed, the noises return and he decides to take another look. His eyes have been open long enough to have adjusted to the darkness. He creeps down the hall into the living room and observes televangelist Billy Gleason standing motionless in the corner. Startled, Greg rushes toward a lamp on an end table behind him and falls. He quickly gets back on his feet and turns on the lamp. A mere coat rack stands in the corner; no person, only a coat rack. Greg returns to his bedroom, closes the door and pushes the nightstand in front of it in an attempt to safeguard himself from hallucinations. For the rest of the night, he sits up in bed staring at the wall where the TV used to be.

A total of three days pass that Greg hasn't slept or eaten anything. The more time he spends isolated, the more depressed he becomes. The desire to physically maintain himself has quickly faded. He struggles to come to terms with the realistic possibility that the people and the life he once knew may be gone permanently. As far as he is concerned, his best friend—his mother, is dead. His friends are dead. His co-workers are dead. Being stranded in the purgatory between real life and make believe has taken a toll on him mentally. The confusion between his two worlds have begun to drive him mad. In turn, he just lies there, waiting. He isn't waiting for anything in particular. Although he wouldn't mind if he did, he isn't waiting to die. He isn't waiting for a savior. He isn't waiting to fall sleep. Just waiting.

Mr. Mallet

Shannon lies in her bed at 9 a.m. scrolling through her DVR recordings trying to choose a program to watch. In an effort to relax and clear her mind, she opts not to do anything over the weekend pertaining to work. The idea of a full weekend consisting of lounging around at home seemed ideal, but only two hours into the first morning she already finds herself becoming bored. Her blasé attitude toward the television leads her to the Internet; she makes her rounds on social media, skims random articles on her homepage, and uploads music to her iPod. A documentary style crime show playing on the television behind her catches her attention. The man on the show speaks about being involved in a nearly fatal home invasion that left him lying in a hospital bed, comatose for three days. The television program rekindles her waning interest in Greg.

After dwelling on the pessimism displayed by Dr. Vankman along with Greg's escape from the hospital, Shannon became discouraged. To her credit, the fact that she checked her timidity at the door in the first place was a big stride for her, but unfortunately she was unable to sustain the will and determination to keep going. She types *Greg Mallet* into the search bar and scours the Internet for any new information pertaining to him. The search comes up empty. A figurative light bulb comes on in her head. Shannon grabs her satchel from the closet doorknob and fingers through the folders contained inside. She removes the folder with his name on it and copies his address to a small sheet of scratch paper. She puts her hair up, puts on a pair of sweat pants and running shoes, slides a jacket over her dingy, twelve-year-old, high school graduation tee, and heads out of the door.

The fall season has officially set in, as evidenced by the scattered showers that have immersed the metropolitan area for the past few days. In a matter of seconds, the barely noticeable mist has transformed into a full-fledged thunderstorm. Shannon sits in her car in the driveway trying to decide whether to take a mad dash for the door or wait for the rain to slow. From her vehicle, she looks from end to end of the exterior of the modest, trailer-sized home. The gloomy weather and overcast add to the deserted look of the structure. Shannon wonders if it's worth it to get out and soak herself in the rain when, clearly, no one seems to be home. As she backs out of the driveway, she questions herself as to whether it was even a bright idea to make the visit in the first place. She stops the vehicle and ponders whether she has anything better to do besides sit at home and be bored.

Shannon opens the rickety screen door and knocks. No answer. She turns the doorknob. The door opens and she quietly walks inside.

The rotting stench in the home instantly shocks her nose, prompting her to use her shirt collar to conceal it from the horrible odor. Afraid that the odor may be the result of a dead body, she rushes to the curtains and opens them to let in more light. The dreary overcast disguises the morning as evening, allowing only a small amount of light into the home. She steps over the mess strewn throughout the house expecting, but certainly not hoping, to find an unpleasant surprise. Dreadful scenarios run rampant in her mind. Did Greg resort to suicide because he was unable to cope with his new life? Or will she find an overlooked pet that has starved to death? She feels that she could handle the latter a tad bit easier.

Shannon wanders the hall and into a bedroom. The hospital bed, IV pole, and medical supplies solidify that she has come to the right place. She walks across the hall and attempts to open the door of the other bedroom. The door is blocked and won't budge. She leans on the door using all of her body weight to force the dresser away from it. She squeezes into the room and immediately spots a man lying in bed on his side, facing away from her. She quietly walks to the other side of the bed. Greg slowly turns his head and looks at her, eyes half closed. His lips are severely chapped and skin pale. Shannon touches his arm. His eyes open wider but immediately become low again. Greg recognizes her as someone he's met but his mind can't register who she is. He isn't fully aware of everything that is happening. She shakes him.

"Mr. Mallet," Shannon says, sternly. "Can you hear me? It's Dr. Shannon."

Greg nods his head so slightly that Shannon can't tell whether it was a response to her question or an involuntary movement.

"Can you understand me?" she says.

He grunts.

Shannon rushes to the kitchen and searches for a drinking glass. She finds a mason jar in the dish rack and fills it with tap water. The pungent scent of the rotting ground beef invades her nostrils. She looks down and immediately spots the source of the odor. She cringes at the sight of the maggot-infested raw meat and looks for a trash can to dispose of it but quickly reassesses her priorities. Shannon swiftly returns to the bedroom and sets the glass of water on the broad windowsill. She forcibly tugs at the fitted sheet to sit him up in the bed, then takes the glass of water and slowly pours it into his mouth.

Shannon takes a seat on the edge of the bed and pulls out her phone to dial 911. Instead, she stares down at the screen for a few seconds and drops it back into her jacket pocket. The hospital proved to be a stressful environment for him. Whether the house is a more viable option is yet to be determined. Shannon, however, sees this as an opportunity of having the access to him that she so desired from the time she took interest in him as a patient. She sits with her right hand buried in her pocket, gripping her phone as she mulls over her decision not to send him back to the hospital. She lets go of the phone and removes her hand from her pocket.

The doctor returns to the kitchen in search of something that would adequately nourish him. She initially comes across only expired food and things that would expend too much of his energy to eat. A can of vegetable soup is stashed deep in the top shelf. Shannon uses every centimeter of her reach to blindly grasp the can of soup. She opens the can and grabs a spoon from the dish rack and quickly returns to the bedroom. Greg initially resists her efforts to force feed him, but with little energy to stand his ground, he gives in.

The dreadful odor his body gives off is nearly unbearable. Shannon decides that he'll definitely need a bath if she is to continue being in close proximity to him. She grabs his legs, pivots his feet on the floor, reaches around his torso, and lifts. Greg stumbles and in the process also causes her to fall to the floor. Shannon regains her composure and goes to the living room to get his wheelchair. She physically struggles to get him into the wheelchair and mentally struggles to find a way to cheat the laws of gravity.

"Ok, Mr. Mallet," Shannon says, standing over him, panting. "You're gonna have to help me out a little bit."

Greg makes eye contact with her only when she talks.

Shannon, with all of her strength, finally forces him into the seat of the chair. She rolls the wheelchair into the bathroom and tries to ease him into the tub, limb by limb. She gives him a forceful shove to get him closer to the edge of the chair, but instead he completely falls off. The fully-grown man, dead weight and all, lies awkwardly positioned in the bathtub; after expending so much energy getting him there, she doesn't care. Shannon snatches off his soiled clothing and runs the water. She grabs a bar of soap and a sponge and bathes him. After dressing him in a hospital gown she finds in his bedroom, she starts an IV of normal saline to assist his fluid replenishment.

Shannon thoroughly cleans the house and opens nearly every window. The cool, fresh air combined with the scent of Pine Sol thoroughly replace the home's previous odors. She brings a chair into the room and places it in a corner across from the bed in which Greg rests on his side, still awake but not moving. Exhausted from vigorously exerting herself from the moment she walked in the house, Shannon slouches into the comfy chair and observes him. She begins to fall asleep within an hour. The sound of Greg rustling around in bed awakens her from her light sleep; he looks in her direction.

Shannon quickly gets up from her chair and walks to the bedside.

"Hello, Greg, I'm Dr. Shannon Brewster," she replies. "Do you remember me?"

Greg continues to blankly stare at her without the energy nor the drive to get his thoughts together to speak to her. He raises his arm slightly and begins to take the tape off of his IV.

"You can't take that off," Shannon says, softly grabbing at his wrist, trying to pull it away.

They struggle briefly before he gives in. Shannon stoops down to his ear level.

"I'm here to help you. I know you're not in a condition

to talk right now, and I know you're frustrated," she says. "I just want you to rest for now. All I ask is for you to cooperate with me and give me time to make sure you're fine."

He returns to his side, facing the door.

Shannon has been longing to question him about his thoughts, feelings and most currently, what led him to this point. However, the doctor is aware that she must use patience to fight off her curiosity because the timing isn't appropriate; she doesn't expect it to be long before he gathers himself and asks her questions. The best case scenario is that his inquiries will help her grasp his mental state and find out what he knows about himself, while also setting up a possible quid pro quo of information between the two of them.

Shannon sits in her chair for several hours passing the time by playing games on her cell phone, reading outdated magazines she finds lying around the house, and snoozing every so often. Greg barely moves but remains awake. The sun sets, and night begins to fall. The hours pass, and with nothing else to do, Shannon stays. The house gradually becomes darker and gets much colder as the temperature outside drops seemingly by the minute. She walks around the house closing the windows she opened earlier. A blanket is draped across the back of the sofa, she grabs it and a decorative pillow, and returns to the room. She walks past Greg's bed and glances at him. He is finally asleep. Shannon bundles up in the blanket, nuzzles herself in the comfy chair and falls asleep.

The subtle light of the caliginous morning greets Shannon as removes the blanket from her face. She looks down at her watch and the time reads five past seven. She yawns, stands and stretches. She quietly walks to Greg's bedside. He opens his eyes.

"I have to make a couple of runs," she says. "I'll be back soon. Ok?

Greg looks at her but doesn't respond.

Shannon drives home, showers and gathers some essentials before heading back out. She makes a stop at the supermarket before returning to Greg's place to stock the kitchen with food. The whole weekend consists of much of the same. Shannon makes at least two trips daily back to her place or to run errands, but spends the majority of time tending to her patient. She continues to observe him, assists with his hygiene, encourages him to eat, and for most of the time just keeps him company. Greg continues in his severely depressed state as she consistently reaches for every microscopic hint that could possibly suggest strides in recovery. She records every small detail in her log book.

Progress is a Process

Shannon wakes up early Monday morning to get a head start before going into work. After getting dressed, she goes to the kitchen to prepare a simple breakfast for two. She scrambles a bowl of eggs and boils a saucepan of grits. She returns to the bedroom after several minutes and places two plastic bowls on the dresser. She pushes the large chair to the bedside and grabs both bowls, placing one in her lap and resting the other on the bed next to Greg. She offers him a spoonful of grits and eggs and he opens his mouth. He grimaces almost immediately after taking the initial bite. Shannon laughs uncontrollably.

"I'm sorry," she says. "I should have thought about

that. Not everyone has the same taste as me. It's grits and scrambled eggs, mixed together. Maybe I should have picked something more universally appealing."

Greg smiles.

The smile marks the first time that he has shown any emotion since she found him two days ago. Shannon sings his praises on the inside but contains her excitement by returning a smile his way. She takes the bowl and sets it on the nightstand.

"It's just a quick little country breakfast my grandmother used to make for me all the time as a kid," she says. "I'll make you something else."

Greg takes the bowl from the nightstand. He props himself up by resting his body on his elbow and begins to feed himself. Delighted, Shannon grabs her bowl and also begins to eat. With the exception of their spoons scraping against the plastic bowls, the room is quiet. Silence wasn't the least bit awkward before Greg started to show signs of life. Shannon's poise changes now that she no longer feels like the only person in the room. She doesn't finish her breakfast before getting up from her seat.

"I have to leave for a while," she says, standing near the door, bowl in hand. "I have to go to work. I'll be back here to check on you later on today."

"Okay," Greg quietly says.

Shannon hesitates before completely clearing the door with a feeling that there should be more for her to say. She leaves.

An hour passes, and Greg climbs out of bed and lumbers into the bathroom nearly losing his balance. He stands above the toilet and plants his hands on the wall behind it to hold himself up while he urinates. Greg has an epiphany while standing there peeing, looking ahead at the blank wall ahead of him—he doesn't recall having a single dream for the past two nights.

A note posted on the mirror with medical tape reads: *Dr. Shannon Brewster (503) 555-2880.* Greg sits on the foot of his bed and stares ahead in deep thought. He has gotten accustomed to having the company of someone else and is already reminded of how much more dispirited he felt before the doctor showed up after just a short time of being alone. Not wishing to soak in his feelings, he refuses to lie down in bed. He grabs his walker and roams the house unable to shake his problem-filled psyche. The pacing eventually leads him outside, where he sits on the porch watching the streets for hours.

* * *

Shannon slams the car door and dashes to the porch for shelter against the cold and heavy rain. The hood of her raincoat impedes her peripheral vision, so she isn't aware that Greg is sitting on the porch to her right. She walks into the dark house, turns on the light and is startled as Greg creeps through the door behind her.

"Oh my gosh, you're up," she says, with a completely shocked expression on her face, followed by a smile. "How long have you been up?

"A few hours, I think," he says.

"It's freezing out, come inside" she says, assisting him over the threshold and into the house.

Greg walks toward the sofa. The tennis balls on the feet of the walker leave behind wet streaks in their path. He sits down.

Shannon takes a seat next to him, continuing to look at him like a star-struck fan gazing at her favorite celebrity. "How are you feeling?" she asks.

"I don't know," he quietly replies.

Shannon waits for him to expound on the short statement, but he never does.

"Any different than you have the past couple of days?

"I guess a little different. A little better."

"That's progress," she says. "Progress is good. Progress is a process. You've been through a lot. It doesn't matter how strong the person is, if they were put in your shoes it would take time to recover."

Their conversation consists of the two of them sitting on separate ends of the sofa with

Greg looking forward, speaking monotonously as Shannon looks directly at him.

"How did you find me?" Greg asks.

"I had your address in my records."

"I thought maybe Andy told you."

"Andy?"

Greg nods.

"I'm not sure if I know an Andy. How long have you been here?"

"A few days," he says. "I think."

"How far back can you remember? I want you to tell me what you know about yourself," she says. "As far back as you can remember."

"I remember waking up in that room," he says, pointing down the hall toward his bedroom.

"When was this?" Shannon asks.

"The day the ambulance took me to the hospital."

"Do you remember anything before that?"

"I don't remember an accident if that's what you mean," he answers.

"You don't remember riding your bike and being hit by a vehicle?"

"No."

"Nothing else before waking up that day?"

"Nothing is clear to me," Greg says. "There are some things I remember about my life and it's completely different than what everybody is telling me."

"Like what?" she asks.

Greg takes several moments to gather his thoughts and ultimately chooses to be selective in his disclosure of information. He feels that telling his story would be practically incriminating himself, therefore, setting himself up for another trip to the hospital and a possible rendezvous with the mental ward. How could anyone else listen to this tragic and bizarre chain of events without considering him crazy when he is leaning toward believing *himself* to be insane? He also wonders what Dr. Brewster is to gain by spending her costly time monitoring him.

"Like what?" asks Greg, repeating her question back to her.

"Yeah, you said you have memories of some things but they're different than what you hear from everyone else."

"I'm sorry," says Greg. "That must have come out wrong. What I meant was that I don't remember anything they tell me, which is different than what I remember, which is nothing."

"I see," Shannon realizes from his actions and expression that the questions seem to overwhelm him, so she decides to lay off for a while. All of her questions began spewing from her mouth unconsciously because they had been building up inside of her for so long. "I'm hungry," she says, changing the subject. "What about you?"

Greg nods.

Shannon walks into the kitchen and opens the refrigerator. "I've made myself at home here the past couple of days. I'm sorry if I've gotten too comfortable."

"It's ok," Greg says. "I'm still not comfortable here myself."

Shannon stands in the doorway looking at Greg as he pulls at a loose string on a decorative pillow stuffed between him and the arm of the sofa. "Is there anything you don't like? I have some ideas on what to make. I would suggest something nutritious and pretty easy on your stomach; but I'll let you choose."

Greg shrugs and looks at her as she waits for his response. He watches her for only a few seconds, but to her it feels like more. Shannon awkwardly turns around and returns to the kitchen. She rummages through the freezer and eventually removes two chicken breasts and a bag of frozen mixed vegetables from the freezer, a box of brown rice from the cabinet, and a package of dinner rolls from the top of the refrigerator.

Her telephone rings. "Shannon Brewster," she answers.

"Hello?" a female voice says.

"Hey, Kendra."

"What's up, sexy?" Kendra says. "I haven't heard from you in a few days. Just making sure you weren't dead."

"I appreciate your concern," Shannon says, smiling.

"I've been fine. I've just been *soo* busy the last couple of days with work and everything. What's new with you?"

"Ehh, nothing really," Kendra says. "We went to that comedy show on Saturday; it was ok, nothing special. Not really worth the $35. You didn't miss out on anything."

"Ok good," Shannon laughs. "Who went with you?"

"It was just me, Erica, and Erica's cousin, Julie," Kendra says. "I *really* wish you had showed up. There's only so much of those two that I can take."

"Oh, wow," Shannon says, "I'm sorry, I promise I'll show up next time. I just had a lot of stuff going on this weekend. But, hey, I'm right in the middle of making dinner right now, is there any way I can give you a call a little bit later?"

"I thought doctors were supposed to be the masters of multi-tasking," Kendra says. "You're cooking for a guy aren't you?"

"No," Shannon says. "You are crazy."

"Do not lie to me, young lady," Kendra chides. "You wouldn't keep something like that from me, now would you?"

"No, Kendra." Shannon laughs again. "I wouldn't keep anything like that from you."

"Good," Kendra says, laughing. "But even though I haven't known you long, I can tell when you're lying!"

"I know I'm a horrible liar," she says. "I am cooking for someone but it's not a date.

"Who is it?" Kendra asks.

"Why?" Shannon asks.

"Because I wanna know," Kendra says.

"Greg Mallet," Shannon says quietly.

"Coma guy?" Kendra asks in disbelief. "You have got to be shitting me. Is he at your house? Where did you find him?"

"At his house," Shannon answers. "I came here the other day, and he was here."

"I guess that wasn't too hard to figure out," Kendra replies. "How is he?"

"He was in bad shape when I got here, but he actually seems like he's doing really well now; he's talking, eating."

"That's awesome," Kendra says.

"Well, I'm going to finish up here and I'll call you as soon as I get home," says Shannon.

"Ok, don't you dare forget."

"I won't."

Shannon finishes cooking and prepares both plates before setting them on the table. She goes to the living room where Greg stands before a mantle, admiring the polished brass decorations. He turns and looks at her.

"Dinners ready," she says. "No rush, just letting you know."

"Thank you," he says as he sets down a brass merry-go-round horse knick knack.

Shannon returns to the kitchen and begins eating. Greg slowly enters the room. She glances up at him and gives her mouth a single swipe with a napkin. Greg takes a seat in front of his plate and picks at his food. Shannon notices him doing this, but decides to mind her business and pay attention to her own meal until she can't bear but say something.

"I'm not much of a cook, but I swear it's not as bland as it looks."

"There's nothing wrong with it," Greg says. "I just don't have much of an appetite lately."

"Oh. I figured it may have been a while since you had eaten anything when I got here."

Another sequence of silence ensues.

"It's good that you don't have to use your walker as much as you did before," Shannon says, trying to break the silence.

Greg nods and takes a bite of his food. "You're a psychiatrist, aren't you?"

"Yes I am."

"Do you like it?"

"I love it," she says. "But just like everything else, sometimes it has its disadvantages."

Shannon holds her hand over her mouth when she talks so as not to expose her food while speaking. She puts her hand down after she finishes chewing. "I *would* ask you what you do, but instead I'll ask you what interests you."

"I wish I could say," he replies.

"It'll come back to you, I'm sure" she says, not so confident in her own reassurance.

"What did you do today?" she asks.

"Sat around, thinking about things," he answers.

"You know you can feel totally comfortable talking to me about anything," she says. "Everything stays between you and me. I won't judge you based on anything you tell me. Even if you bash me I won't get upset, trust me, I've probably heard it all."

"Thank you," he says. "I'll keep that in mind."

They both start to eat again.

"It must have been hard," Greg says. "And expensive, going to school to become a doctor."

"Hard? Yes. Expensive? Yes, but thankfully I didn't have to pay for it.

"That definitely makes it a little easier," Greg says.

"I guess you can say that," Shannon responds, using her hand to cover her full mouth.

"How much do you know about me?" Greg asks. "Me and my life before."

Shannon takes a sip of iced tea from her glass. "Honestly," she says. "Not a lot about *you* per se. Most of what I *do* know about you comes from what I've read in your medical records. There were complications with your health when you were born, you spent a couple of weeks in neonatal intensive care. Your grandmother was your guardian who took care of you from the time you were an infant. You were an avid skateboarder and biker from the time you were an adolescent and made *lots* of trips to the ER to show for it. You also apparently had a couple of stints in the county jail on misdemeanor charges. And of course, most recently, I know about the latest accident which you're still recovering from."

"Wow," Greg says.

"Don't remember any of that?" Shannon asks.

"No," he says. "I'm learning new things about myself every day, it seems."

"How does that make you feel?" she asks.

"I don't know. I honestly don't know. It just feels like something I have to deal with. I'm stuck in this life now so I feel like I have no choice but to, like, piece the puzzle together, I guess."

"Well you have me to help you piece it together, if need be," Shannon says.

"Is someone paying you to take care of me?" Greg asks.

"No, I'm here of my own free will. I love helping people. It's my job."

"So you're one of those free doctors?" he asks. "For the homeless or low-income?"

"No. Not that either."

"You just feel that I'm so crazy that you'll treat me for free," he says, with a dead serious look on his face.

"No," she laughs. "Not at all, there's no such thing as a crazy person. Just crazy situations we all go through, and if we were to judge crazy off of that, we'd all be considered crazy."

Shannon finishes her food and takes her plate to the sink and washes it. Greg's plate is pushed away from him and his face tells that his mind is elsewhere.

"You look tired," Shannon says, drying her hands on a dishtowel hanging on the oven door handle. She walks back to the table. "That all you're gonna eat?" she asks. "I'll put it in the fridge for you in case you wanna eat it tomorrow."

"Ok, thanks," Greg says.

A violent crash of thunder startles them both; the lights in the house flicker.

Shannon puts the food in a Tupperware container and stores it in the refrigerator. She walks down the hall and returns several minutes later with both arms full with several bags of an assortment of clothes, hair supplies, toiletries, books, and other random items. She places everything on the sofa.

"Do you need help?" Greg asks.

"No," she says. "You can barely even walk on your own yet. I'll be fine. It should only take a couple of trips."

Shannon goes into the living room and lifts her jacket from the coat hook. She walks back to the kitchen and stops near the doorway. She zips up her jacket and puts the hood over her head. The hood partially covers her eyes just as she starts to speak. Slightly embarrassed, she quickly removes the hood and laughs.

"Well," she says, "I'm gonna get out of here. If you need anything, my phone number is posted on the bathroom mirror. I'm gonna continue to check on you periodically, if that's okay with you."

"I appreciate it."

"I'm serious," she says. "Anything at all. Take care of yourself. And get some sleep."

She leaves the kitchen and walks toward the sofa. She puts her hair back and covers her head with the jacket hood. Greg turns around in his seat and watches as she miraculously grabs the heap of personal items and makes her way to the front door. She turns the knob and faces the violent thunderstorm. When the door is opened it amplifies the sound of the heavy rainfall similar to the loud static after powering on an old television set on a channel with no reception.

"Oh my goodness," Shannon says. "Maybe I should wait a little while to see if it slows down, if you don't mind."

"I don't mind," Greg says, pushing against the surface of the table to keep balance as he stands.

Shannon lets the baggage slide from her arms and drop to the floor. She sits on the sofa as Greg goes to his bedroom. Shannon fiddles with her telephone to pass the time, and the thunderstorm doesn't show any signs of slowing down. With her elbow placed on the arm of the sofa she rests her head in her palm, eventually dozing off.

* * *

Shannon wakes up and immediately looks at her watch. The time is 2:32 a.m. She decides that she might as well stay. She turns off the lights, lies on the sofa, pulls the throw blanket draped across the back of the couch over her, and returns to sleep.

Honestly, Terrified

Searching for a selection of clean clothes is the activity of the morning for Greg. They don't have to match, neither do they have to be stylish; the only requirement is that they fit. He shuffles through the items in the closet, and it's only filled with towels, rags and bed linens. He walks over to the dresser in front of the light switch that he so vividly remembers being his nemesis the day he woke up from his long sleep and opens the top drawer. The drawer is stuffed with folded shirts and several hospital gowns. He grabs a red and black flannel shirt and finds a pair of frayed jeans in a drawer below. Spending so many hours cooped up in the house does nothing positive for his mood. He gets dressed and leaves the house.

Greg walks down the damp sidewalk in the direction of a strip of old, independently owned businesses. He left his walker behind purposely so that he can get used to not relying on it. He quickly regrets the idea because it doesn't take long for his legs to tire and nearly give out. Just over a mile into his walk, he stops and takes a seat on the curb. Not even thirty seconds pass and a car pulls up and honks for his attention and commences to parallel park next to where he's sitting. Greg stands and brushes the debris from the back of his damp jeans. He walks another block and the muscles in his legs feel like they're in flames. He limps down the sidewalk in search of the closest establishment with a place for him to rest. He wanders into a small empty bar.

Greg takes a seat at the bar and focuses his attention on the closed-captions on the muted television set on the wall. The raunchy talk show playing on the TV is based on the typical subject of infidelity. Just as the woman onscreen slaps the defenseless man with a mullet as he sits in his chair pleading his case to her, the bartender comes from the kitchen located behind the bar. Greg doesn't notice him.

"Ohhh," the bartender says, "that hurt! She should have slapped him like that when he came home with that haircut."

Greg turns around and notices the man staring up at the screen while drying his hands with a dishtowel. The bartender snatches up the remote control and switches the channel to sports highlights.

"What can I get for you, buddy?" the bartender asks. "You need a menu?"

"Nothing, I'm cool," he says. "Just needed to sit down

for a couple minutes if that's okay."

"You're fine, dude, no worries," the bartender says. "Want a glass of water or something?"

"Yeah, thanks," Greg says.

"No problem."

The bartender is an average-sized man in his early thirties with a full sleeve of tattoos on his left arm and a neatly trimmed goatee. He wears a faded dark gray tee that reads *Toast* on the left breast pocket with the words *Beer and Spirits* beneath it in a smaller font. The bartender grabs a clear plastic tumbler from beneath the bar, and scoops the ice with it. He fills the the cup with water.

"Doing pretty good today?" the bartender asks as he slides the cup toward Greg.

"Not too bad. What about you?" Greg takes a swig of water.

"I with ya' man, doing ok so far. *Juuust* getting started," the bartender says. "You from around here?"

"Yeah, kind of," Greg says. "I was gone for a couple years but I'm back now."

"What brought you back?"

"It's a long story," Greg smirks. He puts his elbows on the bar and takes another drink of water.

"Look around us, man," the bartender says, looking around the empty bar. "I've got time if you've got it. It's my job. I don't just make drinks, I'm like a part-time therapist. You pour your heart out while I pour the liquor."

"My grandmother recently passed," Greg asks.

"Oh, man I'm sorry to hear that," the bartender says.

There is a short silence.

The bartender pours a generous glass of gin and places

it in front of Greg.

"Sorry, I don't have any money," Greg says.

The bartender frowns and shakes his head as if to say it's ok. "I'm Conrad, by the way."

"I'm Greg."

A cordless phone near the corner of the bar starts to ring. Conrad looks at the display and answers. "Hello." A minute goes by without him saying anything else. "This is like the fifth time this month, we can't keep going through the same thing over and over."

There is a pause.

"I'm not accusing you of lying," Conrad continues, " that's not the point. The point is that you're calling out *after* the time you were supposed to be here again, *knowing* we can't cover you."

Pause.

"Dude, how many times have we had this exact conversation? You might as well be speaking to the wall. Eventually, he's gonna get fed up with it and think its not worth it to keep you onboard."

Pause.

"I'm just saying, bro...Ultimately, it's not my decision."

Conrad walks into the kitchen to make his conversation private. Greg finishes his glass of gin and watches television. Conrad returns, shaking his head and sets the phone on the bar.

"You need a job?" Conrad asks, facetiously.

Greg takes his eyes off of the TV and directs them at Conrad as if he's taken aback by the question.

"I'm just fucking around man," Conrad laughs. "You looked at me like you wanted to jump the bar and wring my neck."

"No," Greg answers. "I wasn't sure if I heard you right. Did you ask if I needed a job?

"Yeah."

"I could use a job."

"You could *use* a job?" Conrad laughs. "I think that's what was wrong with the guy I was on the phone with. He could *use* a job. He just didn't want or feel like he *needed* a job."

"I really don't have anything better to do," Greg says, hoisting the last swallow of liquor.

"I guess that's a little better," Conrad laughs again. "Where'd you move here from?"

"Move from?" Greg asks.

"Yeah, you said you just got back from somewhere," Conrad asks. "Where from?"

Greg opens his mouth and begins to answer but realizes that he has no response for the question. His throat gets dry and he reaches for his cup of water.

"Sorry, man. You don't have to answer. It's none of my business." Conrad folds the dishtowel he had previously and goes into the kitchen for a few minutes. He returns with a bowl of sliced lemons and limes and drops them in containers at the bar.

"Do you follow the news?" Greg asks him.

"We keep the front page framed in front of a urinal in the bathroom, that's about it,"

Conrad says. "If that counts as following the news, yes."

"Did you hear about a guy waking up after three years of being in a coma?"

"Yeah, I remember that," Conrad replies. "Everybody was talking about it. It's like

something out of a movie. I thought it was bullshit. They said the guy was awake and talking like nothing happened. I don't know if I believe it."

"It was real," Greg says.

"I don't know," Conrad says. "I just don't think so. I saw a special on TV about this guy who woke up from a coma years later, and he was a vegetable. They had to feed him like a baby, change his diapers, and he had the mind of a two year old. Then the show went on to talk about how a lot of people who wake up from comas don't live long after they wake up because of complications. Then this guy comes along out of nowhere like 'Hey everybody, I just woke up from a coma, and I'm perfectly fine. Feel good story of the year! Oprah, Barbara Walters, *Good Morning, America* come interview me!' I just think he's trying to get paid, but hey, if it works I can't blame him. He's going for the gusto, which is much more worth it than these people that stand on every corner out here twenty four hours a day begging for money. Personally, I just think it's kind of odd that he's just coming out with this after his grandmother he lived with died since he obviously can't live off of her anymore."

Conrad's rant slowly fades off. Even a legally blind person in darkness could easily read the "Oh shit" expression on his face.

"You're that guy," Conrad says.

"Yeah," Greg says in a low, timid voice.

"You're dead serious," Conrad says. "Now that I met you I don't feel that way at all. I really didn't mean to offend you, man."

"No offense taken," Greg says as he shakes Conrad's hand. "I should probably get out of here. It was nice meeting you. Thanks again for the drink."

"Yeah, bro," Conrad replies, embarrassment still written on his face. "Take care."

Greg shuffles to the door.

"Hey, man," Conrad says. "If you're really interested in the job, the owner will be in later today. I'll talk to him about it. It doesn't pay great, but it's something."

"Thanks, man. I really appreciate it," Greg says. "I'll see you around."

* * *

Shannon pulls into the driveway and notices Greg sitting on the porch below the old, rusty light fixture. She grabs the two-liter soda and large box of pizza she bought on the way and closes her car door with her hip. She gets to the porch and smiles.

"We've *got* to get you a TV or something," she says. "You're like somebody's grandpa out here sitting on the porch all day. Don't you get bored?"

"Sometimes, yeah," he answers. "It's not so bad though. It could be worse."

"Tell me about it," she says. "You could have *my* job."

"I thought you liked your job."

"I do. I guess you can say I'm a glutton for punishment." She sits in the chair next to him and doubles over in an attempt to warm herself.

"Speaking of a job, I was offered one today," Greg says.

"What? Where?" Shannon asks with a puzzled

expression on her face, laughing.

"A bar a couple miles down the road.

"What bar?" she asks, with a huge grin on her face. "And when and how did this happen?"

"A bar a few blocks away called *Toast*. What's so funny? You don't think I'm capable of having a job?"

"No, no. Well, yeah. This is coming out wrong. Hold on." She gathers her thoughts. "No that's not what I'm saying and *yes* I think you're capable of having a job. I'm just sort of confused. I didn't know you left the house today. You went there yourself?"

"Yeah," he answers. "I had to get out of the house for a while, so I went down the street and sat in this bar and the guy asked me if I wanted a job."

"That's great! What would you be doing?"

"I'm not sure, he didn't say."

"Well I guess since it's a bar there couldn't be too many things. Maybe working in the kitchen or something. Are you gonna take it? It'll be a good way to get your mind off of things and move forward."

"I don't know. The guy said he was gonna talk to his boss today about it. I may go back in tomorrow."

"Well I think it's a good idea. You should consider it." Shannon gets up from her seat. "It's really cold out here and this pizza's getting cold. You ready to go inside?"

Greg slowly removes himself from the chair.

"I'll carry that," he says as he takes the box of pizza from her.

The both of them go inside the house and Greg places the box of pizza on the coffee table in front of the sofa.

"You want to eat in here?" Shannon asks.

"I don't mind it," Greg says.

"Fine with me," Shannon says. "A little change of scenery never hurt anyone."

Shannon walks into the kitchen and removes two glass plates from the cabinet and brings them, along with a few napkins, back to the table. She opens the box of pizza.

"I wanted to call you and ask you what you liked on your pizza, but I don't have the phone number here," she says. "I couldn't decide whether to go with the pepperoni or just plain cheese, but then I remembered a survey I read online a while back that said that 65 percent of people in the U.S. chose pepperoni as their favorite topping, so I figured I probably couldn't go wrong with pepperoni. You come across so many trivial and quite possibly skewed statistics online, but I tend to believe this one may be pretty accurate.

"Don't judge me," she says. "I know I'm a nerd. I research *everything.*"

Shannon puts three slices of pizza on Greg's plate and two on her own.

"Cups, cups," Shannon says as she gets up from her seat.

She brings back two plastic cups from the dish rack and sits back down on the sofa. They begin eating.

Shannon laughs. Greg looks at her.

"I was just thinking," she says. "Did you ever watch the *Teenage Mutant Ninja Turtles* as a kid?"

"Teenage mutant turtles?"

"I thought everybody knew about the ninja turtles," she says. "Oh, I'm sorry. You probably don't remember. Well they were four turtles that lived in a sewer. Some green, radioactive ooze transformed them into anthropomorphic turtles that were taught by their rodent karate master to be ninjas. I used to love it as a kid. The pizza just reminded me of it because their favorite food was pizza and the pizza they had used to look so good to me that every time I'd watch it I'd literally *beg* my parents for pizza. My dad loved pizza, too, so even if my mom said no he'd usually give in."

"This was a movie?" Greg asks.

"Yeah, I think it started out as a comic book series and went on to become a cartoon series and a movie trilogy."

"That's funny," Greg says.

They continue eating.

Greg takes a deep breath. "You told me not to judge you for being a nerd."

Shannon looks up at him.

"I won't judge you if you don't judge me," he says.

"I won't judge you, I promise," she says, wondering where the conversation is headed.

"Well, you mentioned turtles living in the sewer," he said. "I met mermaids who lived in the sewer the other day."

"Oh, now that would be an interesting movie," she says, laughing.

Looking directly into his eyes, Shannon recognizes the blank expression on his face.

"I tend to think I'm pretty good at reading facial expressions, but I swear it's such a challenge with you, and your face right now tells me you're serious."

She wipes her hands with a paper towel and interlocks her fingers. "Tell me about it."

Greg has been waiting patiently for someone to talk to and confide in for so long that when he finally starts talking, the words flow with no interruption. He explains everything that happened in his life from that fateful morning that he opened his eyes to the present day. Shannon listens intently, barely even blinking, as he recants every minute detail of every dream down to the physical descriptions of the characters, environments, and events that an average person wouldn't even remember about if they were awake. Greg concludes after nearly speaking a half an hour straight without interruption.

Shannon comes to, and her reaction can be likened to someone being snapped out of a hypnotism. "Wow. Um, you recognize these events as dreams, am I correct? And I'm only assuming that because you said you woke up immediately after each one of them."

"Every day is a struggle for me recognizing what's real or not," Greg says. "I know that sounds like it doesn't make sense but that's the only way I can explain it. I know that I wake up after each of the *dreams,* but sometimes I wonder if I'm dreaming right *now*. I feel trapped. There's no other way to explain it. Those people I just talked about, my mother, my co-workers, my friends, my job, I have memories of them. I miss them, but it seems like lately every time I go back something bad happens. Of course I want my mom back, I want my friends back. I want peace of mind. I don't have memories of this here but I guess I'm getting used to it. I don't know, maybe this is just a big dream I'm gonna wake up from at any minute."

"When you say 'whenever I go back' how exactly do you go back?" Shannon asks.

"Just by sleeping," Greg says.

"So whenever you sleep you go back to that life?"

"Not lately," he says. "Since you've been here I've slept, but I haven't went back."

"How does going back make you feel?"

"Honestly," Greg says, "terrified. I wanted to be there because it's all I know, but now only crazy shit happens there. If I could go back to the way things were before I woke up in that room over there, I would."

"How does being here make you feel?"

"Like I said—I'm getting used to it. Imagine everyone and everything being taken away from you and having to deal with it on your own. That's basically what it feels like."

"I can't sit here and tell you that I know exactly what's going on with you, but I can certainly try to help you cope and understand where your feelings are coming from," she says.

"We'll try our hardest to figure this thing out one way or another."

"Yeah," he says. "One way or another."

"You think you'll be ok here tonight by yourself?" she asks.

"Yeah," he says. "I'll be okay."

"You sure?" she says. "I don't mind. This is actually closer to work for me anyway."

"I'll be fine.

"That didn't sound very convincing," she says. "I'll stick around."

Shannon gets up from the sofa and takes her things into Ruth's former bedroom.

* * *

Greg wakes up at 10:00 a.m. and walks into the bathroom and turns on the shower. He grabs his toothbrush and clenches it in the side of his mouth with his molars. He reads a note taped to the mirror that says: *"Good luck with the job, Greg* :)." He grabs the tube of toothpaste and climbs into the shower.

* * *

Greg ditched his walker again, and his legs hurt as much as the last time. The regret of going without it is becoming customary, but he recognizes the pain that comes along with regaining his muscle strength is a necessary evil. He enters the bar and notices Conrad talking to a gentleman, approximately in his late fifties or early sixties with gray hair and a thick gray mustache. The man is wearing a faded, long-sleeve, cotton Budweiser shirt with the sleeves rolled up, a pair of blue jeans, and a pair of all-white sneakers that look like they were manufactured in the early Nineties, but are almost as clean as a brand new pair. They seem to be discussing the seating arrangement of the dining area. They both turn around as Greg walks into the bar. Greg takes a seat at the bar next to a skinny middle-aged man with an unlit cigarette behind his ear. The patron is holding a loud, gossip-filled conversation on his cellular phone as he slides his empty shot glass across the surface of the bar from one hand to the other. Conrad and the man in the Budweiser shirt continue to talk as Greg waits patiently at the bar. They approach him from behind.

"Dan, this is the guy I was telling you about who came in yesterday about the job," Conrad says.

"Hi, Greg, I'm Dan Winston," the man says in a loud, gruff voice as he shakes Greg's hand.

"I'm doing okay," Greg says. "How's it going?"

"I'm here," Dan says. "I woke up this morning. The

wife and daughter's out of town for a few days so I get the house to myself. Couldn't be better."

"Well that's good," Greg replies, smiling.

"Hell, you're telling me," Dan says. "So Conrad tells me you're looking for a job. You have any experience as a line cook?"

"No," Greg says.

"Any experience in a restaurant type of environment at all?"

"Not that I know of," Greg says.

"Oh," "We were looking for someone with some sort of experience working in a kitchen." The inflection of Dan's voice signals disappointment.

"I can understand that," Greg replies.

"I think he could handle it," Conrad interjects. "I could show him a few things."

Dan hesitates. "The pay starts at $10 an hour, is that something that'll work for you?"

"That works for me," Greg says.

"When is the earliest you can start?"

"Whenever is fine with me," Greg says. "I can start now."

"Okay," Dan says. "We're gonna keep you for a couple days and see how it shakes out. Conrad's going to show you around the kitchen and go over how things work, and if it's a good fit we'll keep you around. Sound good to you?"

"Sounds good," Greg says.

Conrad takes Greg through the swinging door behind the bar. He opens the door to a small office in a rear corner of the kitchen. The room resembles a recycling facility with all the stacks of paper, trash, and empty bottles scattered throughout. The office is packed with a collection of at least fifteen years of unsorted clutter with barely enough room to maneuver around.

"You can put your jacket in here if you want," Conrad says.

Greg takes off his jacket and hangs it on the inside doorknob of the office.

Conrad looks around the kitchen trying to decide what to show him first. "There's really not that much to learn here once you know where everything is," he says as he walks to the freezer and opens it. "Pretty much everything on the menu is precooked, all you've gotta do is drop it in the grease or pop it in the microwave."

Conrad taps each item with his hand as he names them off.

"Fries, chicken tenders, onion rings, mozzarella sticks, jalapeno poppers. Then we have hamburger patties, chicken breast cuts for grilled chicken sandwiches or salad, but those are easy; just shake a little seasoning salt on them, sometimes I add a little pepper. Then you have the veggies here on the other side. Mayo, butter, salad dressing over here. Tortilla chips, cheese sauce, seasonings, mustard, ketchup, hot sauce, and other non-refrigerated condiments over in the pantry over there. There's not really much to it, I think you'll be okay. People that come here don't usually come for the food anyway."

Dan pokes his head in the door. "You've got somebody out here waiting on you, Conrad."

"We'll go over the rest later," Conrad says as he leaves the kitchen. "If you have any questions just give me a holler."

"Greg, while he's out there taking care of the customer do a little cleaning back here, will ya?" Dan says. "It needs it bad."

As soon as Dan says this, Greg is immediately reminded of the trashed office. He wanted to something to keep him busy. He got his wish.

I'll get right on that," Greg replies.

Pickle Salsa/Raspberry Beret

It's not difficult to notice when nobody's home in a small house like the one that Greg grew up in. The squeak from a mouse or a penny drop from any room in the house with an open door would probably be heard throughout the place if listening close enough. Shannon enters the home after a tedious day of work. Not a sound can be heard. Not a light in the house is on. Shannon removes the knit beret from her head and the cashmere scarf from her neck. She roams the house looking for Greg before realizing that he's not home.

A half an hour passes, and Shannon is preparing dinner when Greg comes home. She turns around to open the refrigerator and is startled when she notices him standing near the kitchen door.

"You really have to stop doing that," she says, panting. "I get scared very easily if you haven't already noticed."

Greg smiles and sits down at the table.

"Why are your clothes so dirty? What happ—" she asks. "The job! You started, didn't you?"

"Yeah."

"Congrats!" she says as she puts her hand up for a high five.

Greg smiles and taps her hand.

"What did they have you doing?" she asks. "Do you think you'll like it?"

"They had me doing a little of everything," he replies. "Cleaning, cooking, stocking. It was okay."

"That's good. I'm happy for you," she says. "If I had known you got the job I would have let you pick dinner; Oh well, I hope you like chili."

"Who doesn't like chili?"

"I, for one, *love* chili," she says as she removes a pair of bowls from the cabinet. "I think anyone who doesn't like chili, especially in this weather, is crazy."

"I thought there wasn't such a thing as crazy people," Greg says.

She looks at him with a confused expression until she realizes that he's referencing a previous statement made by her the other day. "Clever!" she says, laughing, pointing at him. "You're in a sassy mood today, aren't you? I think you know what I meant, Sir."

"I know what you meant," Greg says.

They both take a seat at the table. Greg puts a

generous dollop of sour cream into his bowl of chili and mixes it until the dark red chili becomes a shade of light tan.

"Do you want some of this?" Greg asks.

"Yeah," she says, sliding her bowl toward him. I *love* sour cream."

"I don't know how much you want."

"Just give me a spoonful."

He drops a small amount in her bowl.

"A little more," she says.

He scoops a larger amount.

"Not that much," she says.

He dips the spoon back in and gets a smaller scoop.

"A little bit more than that," she says.

He laughs and shakes his head as he drops the spoon back into the tub of sour cream and reaches across the table, setting it in front of her. His smile quickly dissipates. Her mood quickly follows suit.

"I'm sorry," she says. "Am I annoying you?"

"No," he says, he smiles again but only to let her know that no offense was taken. "It's just that my mom used to do things like that all the time."

"Oh, okay," Shannon says. She slowly begins to eat her chili.

"Yeah," he says, his facial expression as spiritless as a statue as he stares down at his meal.

"Are you sure you're okay?" she asks.

He nods.

Shannon removes herself from the chair and without hesitation wraps her arms around his neck. Greg buries his face in her shoulder and cries for several minutes, neither of them saying anything, only embracing one another.

* * *

The next morning, Greg walks the entire way to work through the pouring rain. He enters the bar with his clothes drenched, face dripping with water, and the sides of his shoes covered in mud. Conrad turns his attention away from the television program that he was so absorbed in when he feels the cold breeze from the outside when the door swings open. Conrad contains his amusement up until the moment he hears the soles of Greg's shoes squeaking against the floor with each step.

"That's sad man," Conrad says, his face beaming. "Did you walk all the way here?"

"All the way," Greg says, smiling like a good sport. "It wasn't that far, though."

"Wasn't that far, yeah," Conrad says. "But too far to walk in this rain and at the same time too close to hop on the bus. You got the shit end of the stick this morning didn't you?"

Dan emerges from of the kitchen area with his arms raised, rejoicing Greg's arrival with an emphatic smile spread across his face. His attire today completely contrasts that of the day before. His pale blue dress shirt and gray slacks are stiff as a board, heavily starched, apparently fresh from the dry cleaners. He interrupts whatever conversation was about to begin with his two employees.

"There he is!" Dan says. "What's up, Greg?"

"Nothing much at all," Greg says. "Same old, same old." He smiles awkwardly, caught off guard by his boss's excitement.

Dan extends his arms and grabs Greg's shoulders firmly.

"I just want you to know that was a great job you did yesterday," Dan exclaims. "I walked into the kitchen this morning and I was speechless. Ask Conrad, tell him Conrad, I honestly didn't even know what to say."

Conrad nods in agreement.

"The kitchen is spotless, the floors were waxed like I had never seen them before, I could actually move around in my office without climbing over anything, among other things," Dan says. "How are things going back there? You picking up things pretty quickly?"

"Oh, yeah," Conrad interjects. "I only have to tell him everything one time and he's got it. It's like clockwork."

"Well that's good," Dan says. "You've impressed the hell out me so far, keep up the good work." He steps back and sizes him up. "Did you walk here?" he asks, grimacing.

"Yes, sir," Greg answers.

"Good God. Do we have any extra shirts back there?"

"No, we need to order more," Conrad answers, "But I brought a couple of mine from home that he can use."

"Okay," Dan says. "Let's get you changed out of that shirt. Conrad, let's just do pretty much the same as yesterday getting him acclimated. I'll be in the office, then I have to go meet an electrician at one of my houses in a couple hours."

"Sure," Conrad says.

* * *

The inclement weather contributes to the already slow business, causing the hours to creep by. A large portion of the day consists of Greg trying to stay busy in the kitchen and occasional small talk between he and Conrad. 2 p.m. rolls around, and Conrad walks into the kitchen and approaches his restless co-worker who is busy using a butter knife to scrape grease from the inner corners of the stove hood.

"You don't have to do that," Conrad says.

"I was just trying to stay busy. Kind of feeling like I'm running out of shit to do."

"Oh," Conrad says. "That's gonna happen. You'll run out of shit to do here. This place never really gets busy."

"Never?" Greg asks.

"I've been working here for six years, and the only time I've seen this place more than half-full was when Dan's niece got married and they had the reception here two years ago."

"So how does—?"

"How do we stay in business?"

"Yeah," Greg says.

"Dan is loaded. He owns *tons* of property, and his favorite TV show is *Cheers*, which is why he wanted to own a bar; which is exactly why this place is called *Toast*. This bar is his baby. He literally makes no money off of this place. As a matter of fact, I'm quite sure this place *loses* money. My dad told me that about 25 or 30 years ago, that this bar used to be the place to be, especially on the weekends; not anymore. Dan's a great guy, I admire his passion, but I don't think he recognizes that he's getting too old for all of this. Handling all of that property he owns, this restaurant. He's 63, his wife is 34, and they have a thirteen-year-old daughter. I don't see how he does it all, but he wouldn't have it any other way."

"It seems like it," Greg says. "It seems like he's always running around, always has somewhere to go."

"Because he is," Conrad laughs. "Always running

around, always has somewhere to go. But anyway—you hungry? I'm fucking starving."

"I thought you'd never ask," Greg says.

"Ok," Conrad says, putting his hands together. "Since there's literally like seven things on the menu, and I've been eating all seven of those things for five or more days a week for six years, I just started making my own shit back here," Conrad says. "Yesterday I made a grilled cheese burger."

"A grilled cheeseburger?" Greg says.

"No," Conrad says. "Not a grilled cheeseburger. A grilled cheese burger. I took a hamburger patty, two slices of white bread, and about four slices of American cheese and made it just like a grilled cheese sandwich. That might be considered a melt, but I think a melt is supposed to have bacon and we were out of it, but it was still awesome."

"I can do that?" Greg says. "Make myself whatever I want back here?"

"Yeah. Dan doesn't care. As long as the work gets done and we don't have customers, I could stand out there and watch porn on one of the TVs, and he wouldn't say a thing. Plus, so much of this stuff back here goes to waste because we don't use it. But there is one rule I have for the kitchen."

"What's that?" Greg says.

"You've gotta be creative. We've got almost everything in this kitchen that you can name, so there are *no* excuses."

"Except for bacon," Greg says.

"Except for bacon," Conrad laughs. "So if you want a BLT that's too bad, it's gonna have to be an LT today and that is definitely out of the question, because there's nothing less creative than a lettuce and tomato sandwich. Even though it does fit your personality."

"What's that supposed to mean?" Greg laughs.

"I'm just fucking with you, man, calm down," Conrad says. "But seriously, I act like you when I get up in the morning. And it takes me three hours to fully wake up. You were asleep for three years; I'd be the same way."

Greg starts by looking at the freezer, then over to the pantry.

"So what are you thinking?" Conrad says.

Greg walks into the fridge and grabs two individually wrapped chicken breasts.

"And he chooses what's behind door number one," Conrad says. "And what's behind door number one? *Two* boneless chicken breasts."

Greg removes both chicken breasts from their wrappers.

Conrad tries to speak as if he's on a television cooking program, but instead, the quiet voice he uses sounds more like a golf announcer. "First we'll start off with two average sized breasts of a chicken. Female chicken breasts or male chicken breasts, also known as man boobs of chicken, aka rooster boobs, it doesn't matter, whatever your preference."

Greg laughs as he slices the breasts into strips.

"What's he gonna do next?" Conrad says.

Greg walks back into the fridge and comes out with a carton of eggs.

"He's a man of mystery, he only reveals one ingredient at a time in order to keep you on your toes."

Greg places the carton of eggs next to a large mixing bowl.

"Why don't you just get everything you need first so

you don't have to keep walking back and forth the whole time?" Conrad asks.

"Because I don't know what I'm gonna need next unless I'm standing there looking at everything," Greg says.

Oh no," Conrad says. "You're not gonna do what I think you're gonna do."

Greg cracks several eggs and beats them in a bowl and coats the chicken breasts with egg.

"Nooo," Conrad says. "That's not right, man. Coating mom with her baby. I knew there was something wrong with you. So sadistic. Put the chicken away now. You've traumatized me. I'm vegan now."

Greg walks into the pantry. "I guess you're right, I can just grab everything I think *might* sound good and just decide what to use when I get over there."

"Good idea," Conrad says. "What are you making?"

"Chicken tenders," Greg says.

"Chicken tenders?" Conrad says. "Did you forget the rule already?"

"What about a chicken tender taco?" Greg says.

"Now we're getting somewhere," Conrad says. "But still not creative enough. I think I've had one of those somewhere before."

"Not creative?" Greg laughs. "It's more creative than your cheeseburger with extra cheese."

"Hey, you're in violation of rule number two."

"What's rule number two?"

"Never insult another's creativity."

"I'm not insulting your creativity," Greg says, snickering. "You insulted mine. And you said there was only one rule for the kitchen."

"It wasn't an insult," Conrad says. "It was constructive criticism."

"Well mine was constructive criticism, too," Greg says.

"Rule number three," Conrad says. "A person with less seniority in the kitchen is prohibited from doling out any type of criticism, constructive or *destructive,* to the chef with higher seniority than him."

"You're full of shit," Greg says. "What about a chicken tender burrito?"

"Cop out," Conrad says. "Same thing as the taco, except rolled up."

"With onion rings?" Greg says.

"Are you asking me or telling me?"

"I'm telling you," Greg says.

"Okay, okay," Conrad says. "We're making strides."

"With salsa," Greg says.

"What about some pickles? Let's throw a few pickles in there."

"Whoa there, buddy," Greg says. "Whose recipe is this?"

"Hey, just being the Mr. Miyagi to your Daniel-san. You seemed like you needed a little guidance."

"I want salsa," Greg says. "You want pickles."

"Yeah?" Conrad says.

"Go get me some ingredients for pickle salsa."

"Oh!" Conrad says. "Now, that's what I'm talking about!"

* * *

The song "Flashing Lights" by Kanye West streams in Shannon's headphones. She loudly sings along while stirring a large pot of rice simmering on the stove. Greg walks into the warm house and immediately smells the aroma of chicken broth. As he gets closer to the kitchen the sound of Shannon belting out the lyrics to the song gradually becomes louder. He quietly pulls a chair from under the table and holds in laughter while watching her unknowingly embarrass herself. She reaches for a glass of wine on the counter beside her and spots Greg in her peripheral. Startled, she jumps and the wine from the glass nearly spills. Shannon snatches the earbuds from her ears.

"Oh my God," she says. "You did that on purpose!"

"That's two days in a row," he laughs. "You really need to be more aware of your surroundings.

"How long have you been sitting there?" she asks.

"Long enough to know why you chose to be a doctor over being a singer," he says, laughing.

"Shut your mouth," she says. "You did *not* see that. And if you ever tell anybody about this I'm gonna kill you...and them."

"I can't make any promises," he says. "What are you cooking?"

"Well, I was trying to make a chicken and rice soup but I added too much rice."

"So now it's just a huge pot of rice with a little bit of chicken, celery and carrots in it."

"It might still be good."

"That's what I'm hoping," she says. "How was the bar today?"

"It was cool," Greg says. "Slow, but good. Conrad told me he had an old bike he could sell me for 75 bucks. I think I'm gonna take him up on the offer when I get paid. It's better than walking every day."

"Oh yeah, definitely," Shannon says as she stirs the rice. "I really hope this stuff turns out ok. 75? That's cheap. I guess if it's a decent bike and it rides well, that's a good deal."

"Yeah, I think so, too."

"Do you need some money?" she asks.

"No, it's ok," Greg replies. "I can wait until I get paid."

"Don't worry, it's only $75. If you feel bad about it you can pay me back later."

"It's ok."

"Okay. Suit yourself." She removes the pot from the stove. "Now for the moment of truth. Can you grab a couple of bowls and spoons for me?"

"Sure," Greg says.

The room is completely quiet as they both begin to eat the bland, fluffy rice. Shannon stops eating and watches Greg as he grabs the pepper shaker and mixes a considerable amount into his rice. He continues to eat.

"It's not good at all," Shannon says.

"It's not *bad*," Greg says. "I'm sure it would be a great soup with the carrots and celery it has in it and all."

"Eat out tonight?" she asks.

"You said it, not me," Greg says, smiling.

* * *

The open seating section of the restaurant is occupied with mostly sports enthusiasts watching the Thursday night football game. Greg and Shannon find a vacant booth in the corner, the table still damp just seconds from being wiped down. Shannon removes her scarf and jacket and stuffs it between the wall and her purse. Greg slides his hands in his jacket pockets and leans back on the wooden bench seat. A waitress dressed in all black approaches the table; her dark, full hair pulled back in a ponytail. The young woman points at Shannon's gray sweater with her ink pen.

"That is such a cute sweater," the waitress says. "I love it."

"Thank you so much," Shannon says. "It's my favorite."

"Where did you get it? If you don't mind me asking."

"I can't remember, I got it a couple of years ago" Shannon says. "TJ Maxx or Marshall's,

I think. Or maybe Ross. One of those stores."

"Yeah," the waitress says. "It's kind of hard to remember with those stores, they're all pretty much the same."

"Exactly."

"Are you both over 21?" the waitress asks.

"Yes," Shannon says as she opens her purse.

"You don't have to take it out. I'll take your word for it, I just had to ask. First off I'd like to let you two know that Tuesday through Thursday we have an all-day happy hour. Do you guys know what you'd like to drink tonight?"

"Let me get a lemonade," Shannon says.

"I'll just take a water," Greg answers.

"Do you guys know what you want or do you want me to give you some time?"

"I know what I want," Shannon says. "What about you?"

Greg looks up from the menu. "I'll get whatever you're getting. I'm not picky."

"Ok," Shannon says. "We'll have an order of the

pulled pork sliders, the spinach and artichoke dip, and the mozzarella sticks for now."

"Will that be all?" the waitress asks.

"Yes, thank you," Shannon says.

Shannon smiles, shaking her head.

"What's wrong?" Greg asks.

"I was just thinking about it," she says. "I can't believe you let me stand there making a fool of myself in the kitchen, singing. I'm still embarrassed about that."

"Oh," he laughs. "If I had come up behind you and tapped you, you would have gotten just as scared, so either way I was gonna surprise you."

"Trust me," she said. "That would have been much less embarrassing."

"Well, you're lucky because it's not like I really have anybody to tell."

"That's right, I guess I am. And it's not like it's the first time I've made a complete fool out of myself singing, either."

"When was the last time?" Greg asks.

"It's so embarrassing. I don't even wanna tell you."

"You brought it up," he says. "So now you have to tell me."

"Okay, well since you have nobody to tell...When I was a freshman in college, I didn't really have any friends. I just hung out with my roommate sometimes and she was one of those girls that would do just about anything to fit in. I didn't trust her at all. But anyway, this one night I went along with her to this karaoke bar that a lot of people from the school used to hang out. You know, typical small college town, not a whole lot to do so pretty much everyone hung out at the same few places. I was antisocial like you wouldn't believe. I was unable to associate with *anyone*. I wasn't even *willing* to get to know anyone, that's how much of an introvert I was. But this one night I decided 'You know what? I'm not happy with the way I am and if I'm gonna have any chance of changing that, I've gotta start now.' Lydia encouraged me to go out, that was my roommate's name, Lydia. So we got dressed, left the dorm and went to the karaoke bar. I wasn't a drinker, but like I said, that night was gonna be the night that I was gonna shed the old me. Well, I drank, I think, three drinks. They were all cranberry juice and vodka. I was totally trashed. I don't remember anything after the drinks but apparently I got on stage that night and sang "Raspberry Beret" by Prince.

"I woke up the next morning on a bench in the middle of a courtyard. Lydia left me out there all night. Didn't help me get home or anything. She was jealous because of the attention I got from everyone. A couple of weeks passed and Valentine's Day came around, and I was in one of my classes and a few of my classmates chipped in and gave me a card and this raspberry colored knit beret that I'm wearing on my head right now. I really made a fool of myself that night, so I didn't know whether they were mocking me or whether it was all in good fun but I didn't care. I was just happy to be noticed."

"So how was the college life after that?" Greg asks.

"It never really changed," she says. "I was still reserved, an introvert, but I became okay with it. I accepted that it was who I was, and if anybody didn't like it, oh well."

"I agree," Greg says. "I've noticed that sometimes you seem a little shy but I never knew it was really on that level."

"It's gotten better over the years, thank God," she says. "I don't know how I'd be able to have the career that I have if I wasn't able to interact with people. On a personal level though, outside of work, it does take me a while to get totally comfortable around most people."

"What about me?" Greg asks. "Are you comfortable around me?"

"Yeah," she smiles. "I'm pretty comfortable around you. You're easy to talk to."

"I guess it's not hard to be comfortable around someone after you've seen their ass, right?" Greg asks, laughing.

The waitress comes back to the table with the food, overhearing Greg's last statement.

"Did I come at a bad time?" the waitress asks with a huge grin on her face.

"No, no," Shannon says, laughing. "That's awkward, I'm sorry you'll have to excuse him."

"It's okay, I'm kidding," the waitress says. "If there's anything else you need just let me know."

The waitress walks away.

"Oh!" Shannon says excitedly before pausing to finish chewing. "I did some reading today about what we talked about the other night. You know, when you were explaining your dreams to me and everything."

"Yeah," Greg says, listening intently.

"So what I read is that there are two areas of the brain that scientists have said are known to be involved in distinguishing fantasy and reality, the amPFC and the PCC. They used a test called functional magnetic resonance imaging to compare the brain's response when processing real and fictional characters. They reached the conclusion that our brains may be able to distinguish between the two because real things tend to have a higher degree of personal relevance to us than fictional things."

"Ok," he says.

"During the experiment they showed a group of subjects the names of friends, family, and people they know personally. They put the names of those people on cards. They also added cards with the names of famous people or celebrities that the subjects have never actually seen or met but we all know exist, such as the president of the United States or a famous celebrity. They also showed them the names of fictional characters, you know, from movies or whatnot. The conclusion they came up with was that the people the subjects knew in real life were more *real* to them than the celebrities were, while the celebrities were more real to them than the fictional characters. You're probably wondering where I'm going with this. I'm gonna tell you what my theory is based on the things you told me about your life and the things that you remember."

Greg continues to listen.

"While you were in a coma you were living another life," she says. "The whole time."

"How could that even be possible?" Greg asks, skeptically

"When you got into the accident that put you in a coma, you suffered brain trauma and whatever section or *sections* of your brain that were affected caused you to have a very long, continuous dream the whole time that you were sleeping. Living a totally different life than the one before the accident, which probably explains why you have such an extensive memory of those people. This isn't exactly my field of expertise and I'm basing this strictly off of someone else's research, but I'm inclined to think that's the reason that your brain is so much sharper than other people who have been in comas as long as you have. Your brain was never totally dormant. Your vivid dreams kept your brain active."

"I know you may be skeptical about the whole thing but listen to my explanation." Shannon looks down at her watch. "Right now we're aware that its 7:32 p.m., right? When we dream, not only are we totally unaware of the time but it's totally immeasurable, abysmal. When we dream we can go through what may seem like a whole days span in five, ten, fifteen minutes, an hour. We can be asleep for twenty minutes and wake up and it feels like we've been sleeping for an hour. Well, you were asleep for three years. If we can dream about waking up for work, going to work, eating lunch and coming home all in a span of fifteen minutes, imagine what all can happen if we were asleep for three years. You could have very well lived what seems like hundreds of years in your dreamlike state."

"You're saying that everything in my mind, everything that I remember is fake. That it was all one huge dream. Everything. If you're saying that, I can go back to the research you were just explaining to me; based on the *research* the only thing separating reality and fiction is actually our state of mind. So how do I know this isn't all just one big dream that I'm living right now?"

"That's exactly what I'm saying," Shannon says. "Those people in your dreams have high personal relevance to you because they're all you remember. It's like they're *real* to you. That's why it's so hard for you to accept. Even your mother. I think the relationship that you had with your mother in your dreams was actually the way you wished your relationship was with her in real life. The reason I feel your dreams are so different than the norm is because of how vivid they are, how much you remember the small details, how much you remember the people in them. That's not typical."

"So this is all you could come up with?" Greg asks. "You told me you'd help me figure things out and you come to me with theories and research you probably found on Google?"

"I'm sorry," she replies. "I just thought it was interesting and figured you would have liked to hear what I thought."

"Why? What does it really matter at this point? Apparently we both knew I was crazy and now you're trying to solidify it even more. What's the point? I don't know why you even waste your time on me."

"Well, like I said, I just thought you'd like to know."

"Not really. Not at all."

Through the course of the night, Greg is visibly irritated but has no loss of appetite and continues to work on his portion of the food. Shannon, on the other hand, picks over her food and passively watches the football game on a TV in the distance to quell the awkward tension that is amplified by their silence. Greg is oblivious to her change in mood. The dullness continues throughout the drive back to Greg's house. Shannon parks her car in the driveway and immediately gets out of the vehicle, swiftly walking ahead of him.

"Man, it's freezing. The temperature dropped really fast tonight," Greg says as they walk toward the house.

Shannon pretends not to hear his statement as she opens the front door. Greg follows her inside. She immediately walks through the hall en route to the bedroom she sleeps in and collects her belongings on the bed. Greg goes into his bedroom and lies down in his bed unaware of what she is doing. Shannon opens the bathroom door and flips on the light switch. What starts off as the lone sound of the old, rickety bathroom fan is followed by the loud, clattering of objects in the bathroom. Curious as to what the commotion is, Greg pokes his head out of the bedroom.

"What's wrong?" he asks. "Are you leaving?"

She ignores him and begins to stuff her tote bag more aggressively. Greg approaches the doorway and watches her for a few moments.

"Excuse me," she says quietly as she squeezes between him and the doorway to leading into the hallway.

Greg moves to the side and continues to watch as she bundles her items together on the bed. She gathers her belongings and quickly walks down the hallway toward the living room.

"You're ignoring me now?" Greg asks.

"Nothing's wrong," she says. "I just think it's about time I left. I'm sure you're probably getting tired of me." She cracks the front door.

"I'm not getting tired of you," Greg says as he walks toward the door. "If this is about what I said at the restaurant, I'm sorry. It's just hard for me to think about those things and not be put in a bad mood. It's one of those things where you're happy when you're not thinking about it, and when you're reminded of it, it depresses you again. And it's not your fault. It's not your fault at all. Trust me, I appreciate everything you've done for me."

Shannon turns to him and looks into his eyes to measure the extent of his sincerity. She then puts her head down to conceal the tears streaming from her eyes.

Greg hugs her; she doesn't hug him back. "Don't cry," he says. "I'm the only one who's allowed to cry around here."

Shannon can't resist but to laugh at his statement because even though the comment was meant to be funny, his expression stayed serious. He smiles. Shannon gazes at him through her tears with a smile. Their eyes lock in on one another's, and with what feels like an out of body experience, their lips meet. Greg softly places his hand on the base of her neck. Her heart begins to race and her body is overcome with weakness. Her bags drop to the floor. The passion of the moment quickly escalates, almost reaching the point of no return. Shannon suddenly releases herself from the embrace and steps back, avoiding eye contact. She blushes and wipes the residual tears from her eyes.

"Excuse me," she says. Ashamed, she walks to the bathroom and closes the door.

As Shannon looks at her reflection in the mirror, she immediately thinks back on the ineptitude of her actions but regret doesn't once cross her mind.

Shannon chooses not to leave that night. Clashing judgment and common sense make it difficult for her to sleep. Even though her thoughts and feelings are in shambles, one aspect of the experience is as clear as day. For the mere three seconds that their eyes met preceding the kiss, it was as if all time had stopped. Those brief moments felt like eternity; time wasn't relevant and nothing else even mattered. Everyone and everything else in her life was non-existent. She falls asleep with one question lingering in her mind. How could she ever fault Greg for not wanting to let go of his dreams if they ever felt like this?

Top Five, Maybe Three

The face of Andrew Jackson is wedged between the dingy laces of Greg's right shoe. He hooks the shoelaces with his index finger to loosen them and pulls out the folded wad of money ; seventy-five dollars. Shannon left him the money anyway. He stuffs the money into his pocket and leaves the house for the especially long walk to work today. The prospect of not having to travel to work on foot prematurely spoils him.

Greg enters the building and walks past the bar en route to the kitchen. He takes his jacket off and hangs it on the doorknob inside the office. A dark red bike is leaned against the door that leads outside to the alley behind the restaurant; Greg closes in for a better look. The dried rubber on the handlebars and the light rust show evidence of its age and history of outside storage. Several minor abrasions and a loose kickstand show signs of neglect. Greg wheels the bike back and forth across the small area in the rear of the kitchen. Conrad quietly enters the kitchen and watches from a short distance.

"So what do you think?" Conrad asks. "Did you feel how light that shit is? You can pick it up with one finger."

Greg lifts it and sets in back down.

"I was thinking about selling it on Craigslist a while back but I just didn't wanna let it go," Conrad says. "I always say I'm gonna start riding every summer but I never end up actually doing it. You'll get more use out of it in the first week than I have in the eight years I've had it."

Greg reaches in his pocket, and hands Conrad the wad of cash.

"You wanna test ride it?" Conrad asks. "I've gotta get it out of here anyway; I'm not sure, but it's gotta be some type of health code violation to have this back here and that *would* be something Dan would kill both of us over."

"Sure," Greg says.

"Ok," Conrad says. "I've gotta go find the key for the padlock on the back door, I always leave it in the lock but Dan takes it out thinking that somehow if it stays in the lock it'll make it easier to break in here. He loses it every time."

Greg gets down on his knees and tinkers with the loose kickstand while Conrad rustles through the drawers in the office. Greg hears footsteps behind him. "Did you find it?" he asks without turning around.

When Greg gets no answer, he stands and slowly turns

around. Dan stands before him; he doesn't look infuriated, but the serious expression on his face when enraged has an air of intimidation and unpredictability that can make one wish that he was frowning instead. He stands, hands in his pockets, and looks at the bicycle, then at Conrad who is now walking out of the office, and finally at Greg again. He massages the wrinkles on his forehead.

"Hey, Dan. Have you seen the key to the back door?" Conrad asks, trying to diffuse his boss's anger by pointing out his proactivity.

Dan disregards the question. "I don't care whose it is, but somebody get this piece of shit bike out of my fucking kitchen, right now," Dan says without so much as raising his voice.

"That's why I was looking for the key to the padlock," Conrad says.

Dan gives him the stare and emphatically points to the door leading to the bar.

Greg walks the bike toward the door.

"Pick it up off of the floor and carry it out so you don't track dirt in my kitchen" Dan says, in a loud, stern voice.

Greg lifts the bike and carries it out of the main entrance of the bar. He waits near the door for Conrad, who is following closely behind. Conrad exits the bar, snickering as the door swings closed behind him. Greg wastes no time before asking questions.

"Why didn't you tell me he came in?" Greg asks.

"I didn't see him either," Conrad says, laughing.

"I'm gonna get fired, and I haven't even been here a week."

"Trust me, it's not a big deal" Conrad says. "Don't take it personal. He's not gonna fire you. He'll probably forget anything ever happened by the time we go back in. I used to get pissed at the way he talks sometimes, but he doesn't mean anything by it, and he never does anything."

"Oh ok," Greg says. "I turned around thinking it was you behind me and when I saw him

I was like 'Oh shit.'"

"I know, I saw you," Conrad says, still amused. "I looked down at your shoes because I thought I'd see piss leaking out of the bottom of your jeans."

"Get the hell outta here, man," Greg says, laughing.

They walk down the narrow, damp and littered alley behind the bar. Conrad reaches out for the bike. Greg hands it off to him.

"We've gotta hide it somewhere so the tweakers don't get to it," Conrad says, scoping out the area.

"You don't have a lock for it?" Greg asks.

"I do somewhere at home, but I couldn't find it," Conrad says as he rolls the bicycle behind the large trash dumpster behind the building. "If I find it I'll sell it to you."

"Sell it?" Greg says. "Can't you just throw it in?"

"No I can't just throw it in," Conrad says.

"How much did you pay for it?" Greg asks.

"Forty bucks."

"Forty dollars?"

"Yeah, this is the West Coast," Conrad says. "We have no shortage of meth, crack and bicycles. So what does that make the junkies? Part-time bicycle locksmiths. You gotta have a good lock."

"So how much will you sell me yours for?" Greg says.

"Thirty," Conrad says.

"Thirty?" Greg says. "That's more than a third of what I paid for the bike!"

"I'll see what I can do," Conrad says.

"If my bike gets stolen from behind this dumpster, I want a refund," Greg says.

"Sorry, no refunds," Conrad says. "I only give credits. If your bike gets stolen, I'll *give* you the lock."

Greg playfully wraps his hands around the back of Conrad's neck. They both laugh as

Conrad tries to escape his grasp.

* * *

An extended work day and a short visit to her apartment causes Shannon to arrive at Greg's house later than usual. She walks into the house and notices Greg's bicycle leaned against the wall below the coat hooks. She gives it the once-over and hangs her coat on the hook, stuffing her hat in the pocket. Shannon proceeds down the creaky floors of the hall and stops at the doorway of Greg's room. He quietly sleeps in prone position still fully dressed in his working clothes. She removes his shoes and leaves the room.

At 2 a.m. Shannon wakes up to go to the bathroom. She notices the dim light shining from the lamp in the living room. After leaving the bathroom, she peeks into Greg's room and finds that he's no longer there. She walks to the living room where he quietly sits on the sofa looking down at a bulky photo album resting on his lap.

"Having trouble sleeping?" she asks.

Greg turns his attention toward her. He was aware of her presence but so heavily entranced by the photos that it didn't register in his mind. Greg is only five pages into the album nearly two hours after opening it.

"Yeah," he says. "Sort of, I woke up at around ten and my mind has been all over the place since then."

Shannon walks over and looks down at the photo album. A candid photo of a middle-aged woman with a child on her lap catches her attention. The woman in the photo has one arm wrapped around the midsection of the child and holds a fork in the other hand while trying to block her face from the camera at the same time.

"That must be your grandmother," Shannon says. "She's beautiful."

"This is the woman who found me when I woke up."

At a loss for words, Shannon nods her head. She sits on the ottoman across the room.

"I can see the love. I can feel the love that she had for me but I can't remember her," Greg says. "I can feel it when I look at her pictures. I was so lost and afraid when I woke up and she was the first person to let me know that everything was okay, and I couldn't even thank her for it. I miss her and I don't even know her; I don't even know how that's possible?"

"Greg, this is only the beginning," Shannon says. "I'm confident that these things will come back to you. Even if it doesn't, she'll always be with you. You didn't have to thank her; she knew. She knew how much you appreciated her. You woke up and she was able to see it and that, I'm sure, was her greatest gift of all besides you, yourself."

"I just feel like I don't have closure," Greg says. "I'm stuck between two lives and there won't be closure for either. Two lives. One of them I can't remember, and slowly but surely I'm losing the other."

"I know how you feel," Shannon says. "I can't say I've been through what you're going through but I've experienced the loss of loved ones too. If you're looking for closure it may not come in the form that you want it to. Closure is a state of mind. It comes from within ourselves and sometimes it takes time. It's different for everyone."

"What happened with you?" Greg asks. "Who did you lose?"

"When I was twelve my father died in a freak accident at the factory he worked in. From that day on, my life changed drastically. My mother became severely depressed and turned to alcoholism. Unfortunately, she was also pregnant with my younger brother at the time. Within a month I was living with my grandparents. My grades dropped, and I went into a shell that I never completely got out of. It was like I suddenly lost two people out of nowhere."

"I'm sorry to hear that," Greg says.

"My younger brother has numerous health and behavioral problems that doctors attribute to my mother's excessive drinking. I wanted to help her, I tried my hardest to get her to stop drinking. It didn't work. No one knows how it feels to be completely powerless until they're in the shoes of a child with an alcoholic or drug-addicted parent. In order to gain closure I had to learn to pick out the positives of every situation. I was fortunate to have grandparents there to care for me and to steer me in the right direction. The money that put me through med school was the settlement money from my father's death. I wanted to use my past experiences and the things I've been through in life to help others. That's why I became a psychiatrist. To think that before all of that stuff happened I wanted to be a model. Life has a strange way of throwing us curveballs, it's all about knowing how to adjust."

She smiles.

"That's true," Greg says. "Maybe not remembering isn't such a bad thing. There are always people that have it worse than you."

"I wouldn't exactly say that," Shannon says. "It's impossible to compare problems, because if you really think about it, everyone has someone worse off than them. And one person's problem may not be a problem for another person. It's all relative. We just have to accept that we all have problems and that they're a part of life, they make us stronger. Each problem no matter how big or small makes us more resilient. It's all about learning to deal with them."

"That helped me out a lot," Greg says. "I wish I could say more but it's not as easy for me to think of words to say than it is for you. I know you were close to your dad, and I'm sure he would be really proud of the person that you became. I would be."

"Thank you," Shannon says, smiling. "That does mean a lot to me. More than you know."

* * *

Greg tightly wraps a clear, plastic container of sliced tomatoes in plastic wrap and places it on a shelf in the fridge. Conrad slightly opens the kitchen door and squeezes the top half of his body through the opening. He looks around.

"Greg!" he calls out, seeing no one. "Greg!"

He walks out of the fridge.

"Come out here for a minute," Conrad says.

Greg walks out to the bar. A slender man approximately in his early thirties sits at the bar. He's wearing a pair of glasses, a green, mesh Portland Timbers cap and dressed in what looks to be second-hand clothing. His dark blue wool sweater with brown faux leather epaulette-like shoulder straps doesn't match the faded gray pants, the pants don't match his tan suede shoes, and none of it matches the ponderosa green cap with the yellow axe logo displayed in the middle of it, but somehow the arrangement fits very well together.

"This guy doesn't believe me," Conrad says. "Tell him who you are."

"What?" Greg says.

"He doesn't believe who you are," Conrad says. "Tell him.

Greg turns around and goes back into the kitchen.

Conrad follows him into the kitchen. "What's wrong?"

"What's wrong?" Greg says, in a loud and angry whisper. "I don't want everyone knowing my business. I don't know that guy."

"I'm sorry, man," Conrad says. "I didn't know you really cared that much. I knew you didn't like talking about it, but I didn't know you were keeping it a secret."

"It's cool," Greg replies after calming himself. "You didn't know, I probably should have told you instead of assuming. That's my fault."

"No, it's all me," Conrad says. "I should have just kept my big mouth shut. If it's worth anything, that guy comes in quite a bit, and he's pretty cool. I don't think he'll tell anyone. I didn't tell him much, but if I do tell him not to say anything I'm sure he'll listen. And I'm sure whipping up one of those burgers you made earlier wouldn't hurt either."

Greg is annoyed by the situation but is somewhat excited to have the opportunity to break out his cooking skills for someone other than his co-worker. He prepares the burger and a side of hand-cut fries and delivers the plate to the gentleman at the bar.

The man shakes Greg's hand. "Greg?" the man says. "I'm Stephen."

"Nice to meet you," Greg says.

"I'm not gonna say this'll be the best burger you've ever tasted; that's too bold of a statement," Conrad says. "But I will tell you it *will* be in your top five, maybe three."

"I don't know," Stephen says. "That's still a pretty bold statement. I've had some *good* cheeseburgers in my life."

"I'll let you judge for yourself," Conrad says.

Stephen takes a large bite out of the massive burger. He takes another bite before setting it back on his plate. He nods his head in approval, snatches a napkin from its holder and wipes his mouth. "*That's* a damn good burger," he says.

"I told you," Conrad said. "You thought I was bull-shitting you."

"Definitely better than the one I had the last time I was here," Stephen says. "What's different?"

"We created a maple syrup and Coke-based marinade with chili pepper and—" Greg begins.

"Whoa, stop, hold it right there," Conrad interrupts. "Don't give him the recipe."

"I'm not going to steal it," Stephen says, laughing. "I

can't cook nor do I have a desire to learn."

"So if your girlfriend chooses your clothes for you and your mom does all the cooking, what do you do?" Conrad says, laughing.

"You know what?" Stephen says, pointing at Conrad, laughing. "Kiss my ass." Their amusement fades away, and he looks at Greg. "So how are you adjusting to life after the coma?"

Conrad gestures for Stephen to stop. "Hey, man," Conrad says. "I told you not to bring it up. Respect the man's wishes. He doesn't want to discuss it."

"What?" Stephen says. "It's just a simple question. I don't plan on interrogating him.

There's nothing wrong with initiating friendly conversation."

"It's okay," Greg says to Conrad. He then directs his attention to Stephen.

"It took a little time to get adjusted at first but it's getting better," he answers.

"What was the hardest thing you had to get adjusted to?" Stephen asks.

"Probably just connecting with people," Greg says. "Not feeling like an alien around other people."

"You don't have to answer those questions, man" Conrad says. "Why don't you go back in the kitchen and finish up what you were doing. "

Greg walks back into the kitchen and begins to wash and put away dishes. He keeps busy and the hours pass by quickly. Conrad approaches him.

"I'll take care of everything else if you wanna go home early.".

"You sure?" Greg says. "I don't mind staying."

"It's all good, man," Conrad says. "Go home and enjoy your weekend."

"Thanks," Greg replies as he unties his apron. "You too."

Greg gets on his bike and coasts through the light traffic on his way home. The sky is clear and the weather is surprisingly warm for a mid-fall day. A perfect breeze sways the leafless trees that line the street back and forth in the wind. He glides through the quiet neighborhood and hops off of his bicycle just as it crosses his driveway. A blue compact vehicle slowly pulls up to the curb on the opposite side of the street. The driver of the vehicle is Stephen Hughes, the patron from the bar. He captures several photographs of Greg as he walks into the house.

Welcome to My World

"Ok," Shannon says. "Set in a totalitarian society in the year 2017, a man who was wrongly convicted of being responsible for a deadly massacre of hundreds of innocent victims must try to survive a public execution staged as a game show. Starring Arnold Schwarzenegger,

Jesse Ventura, Jim Brown, and the late Richard Dawson as game show host Damon Killian."

"Which one is that?" Greg asks.

"The Running Man," Shannon says. "It's an old movie."

"Let's watch that one," Greg says.

"Really?" Shannon says. "You are aware that we could

probably *buy* this movie on DVD somewhere for three dollars instead of paying to watch it at the movies."

"You asked me to choose, so I chose," Greg says. "The other ones didn't sound interesting.

"I guess I did say that," Shannon says. "And it's always funny to watch the Eighties' version of the future. It starts at 8:15, we should probably leave now if we wanna make it on time."

* * *

The marvelous lights and the classic 1920s architecture on the exterior of the historic cinema elicits in fine detail the former glory of what movie theaters used to be. A young, heavyset male with a full beard wearing a pair of eyeglasses that are small in relation to his face is seated behind the thick glass. He slides the two movie tickets through the small opening at the bottom of the window. Greg and Shannon walk through the door into the theater's main lobby. Many years of usage and transformations inside of the building are evident through its many layers of paint and a faint smell similar to that of an old elementary school. The thin dark red carpet shows signs of wear and slight fading in areas of heavy foot traffic. Witnessing the fading beauty of the movie theater is akin to looking at the photo of an outwardly beautiful woman in her younger days only to see her allure wilting away with age and infirmity.

"I love places like this," Shannon says. "It gives me a feeling of nostalgia. I know I wasn't alive when typical movie theaters were actually like this, but when I walk into a place this old or through a museum I can imagine myself there. It's just a weird feeling I can't explain."

"Weird feelings you can't explain. Welcome to my world," Greg says with a smile. "Do you go to museums a lot? Is that a hobby of yours?"

"I haven't been to any since the school field trips when I was younger, actually" she says.

"My adult life has just been school and work. I always plan on doing things like that but I never get around to it."

"We should go to a museum one day," Greg says.

"That sounds like a good idea to me," she says. "Since I'm taking you out to a movie, you have to take me to a museum."

"Deal," he says.

"I'm holding you to that. You'd better not forget," Shannon says.

"I won't forget," he says.

"Ok. You can find us a seat," Shannon says. "I think the movie should be about to start.

I'll get the popcorn."

"You sure?" he says.

"Yeah," she says, smiling. "I'm sure I won't lose sleep if I miss the beginning of *The Running Man.*"

The movie is just beginning as Shannon makes her way into the dark theater. The audience for the movie is sparse and she quickly spots Greg seated in a center row. She places a large Coke in the cup holder, hands him the popcorn and takes a seat next to him. The movie keeps the both of their interest more than expected. Somewhere near the midpoint of the movie, Greg reaches over, and Shannon, assuming that he's reaching for the popcorn, blindly offers him the bag. Instead of taking the popcorn, he reaches for her hand. Surprised, she hesitates at first, looking at him to see if he's actually reaching for her hand. She takes his hand and locks her fingers in his. Shannon feels contentment, an emotion that she hasn't felt in a very long time.

The music of the ending credits plays loudly as they make their exit from the theater.

Greg holds the door open for Shannon and a few others trailing behind them. He yawns.

"Were you sleeping?" Shannon asks.

"Just dozed off for a few seconds," he says.

"I thought I'd be the one sleeping, but it really wasn't too bad of a movie," she says. "It seems like whenever I have low expectations for a movie it turns out better than I thought it would be."

"Yeah," Greg says. "I liked it a lot."

"I wouldn't say I liked it a *lot*," Shannon says. "It *was* kind of creepy."

"I don't think it was meant to be scary," Greg laughs.

"Yeah, I know," Shannon says. "But sometimes sci-fi and horror should be classified as the same thing."

They walk outside and get into Shannon's car, which is parked on the curb directly in front of the main entrance. Shannon starts the car and begins to drive.

"What do you think was creepy about it?" Greg says.

"Well, a lot of things—the violence, the music, the whole premise of the movie, the cinematography," she says. "It was just creepy, not scary, but definitely something that could give someone bad dreams."

"Someone meaning...you?" Greg says sarcastically.

"Of course not *me,* " she says, with a sly smirk on her face. "Never."

Shannon slows to a stop at the red light. She powers on the car's radio as they both watch a group of at least a half dozen pedestrian hipsters trot down the crosswalk. A couple walking in the opposite direction through the crosswalk pass by them, hands intertwined, simultaneously turn around as if sharing their opinions to one another about the group.

"Are you hungry?" Shannon asks.

"No," Greg says. "Not right now anyway."

"Yup, I feel the same," she says. "Too much popcorn." Shannon freezes in her motion and concentrates on the barely audible music coming from the speakers. "Gypsy" by *Fleetwood Mac* plays on the radio station. Shannon raises the volume and begins to quietly sing along. "I love this song," she says.

Greg watches and listens as she gradually sings louder and with more enthusiasm as the song goes on. She isn't conscious of Greg's undivided attention until she notices him looking through her peripheral vision. They both begin to laugh, Greg at her, and she at his amusement. Unable to think of another way to play off her embarrassment, she continues singing as if not to care that he's watching.

Shannon's exaggerated emotion and off-key tune of her performance would probably make most any other person cringe. Greg is fully aware of her lack of musical talent, but seeing the smile on her face that is directed toward him as she sings causes his heart to sink into his stomach. He is captivated by the way her large green eyes sparkle whenever she smiles, a smile so genuine that it is highly infectious. Greg doesn't know whether she is singing her heart out for him or if she's merely entertaining him, but either way, the feelings that she provokes in him helps him achieve peace of mind, which has been elusive until this moment.

The hours are getting late and upon entering the house they both go their separate ways. Shannon prepares for bed to get rest before another long day of work. Greg drinks a glass of water and turns off the lights before going to his room.

The bedroom becomes pitch black after Shannon turns off the lights. She opens the curtains to let in the moonlight. She climbs into bed and stares out of the window. She can't sleep; certain disturbing scenes of the movie play back in her mind. It doesn't help that periodic noises of the old heating system beneath the window mildly startle her each time it sounds. Shannon steps out of bed, taking the comforter and a pillow along with her into the hall. She peeks into the other bedroom to see if Greg is sleeping. He is facing the door with his eyes closed. Shannon tiptoes into the room and spreads her comforter on the floor, folding it in half into the shape of a sleeping bag and drops her pillow on top. Greg is awakened and notices her in the room.

"What's wrong?" he asks.

Shannon reflexively turns to him, surprised by him being awake.

"Nightmares?" he asks.

"I haven't even fallen asleep yet," she replies quietly, smiling.

"You don't have to sleep down there," he says. "I will."

211

"No," she whispers. "I'm not kicking you out of your bed."

"I don't mind," he says. "You can sleep next to me, there's enough room for the both of us. I'll try not to snore in your ear."

Shannon walks over to the side of the bed. "It's big enough for the both of us," she says. "Just scoot over a little bit."

Greg slides over and stuffs a pillow beneath his head. Shannon places her pillow on the bed and wraps herself in his blanket; she faces the door and he is turned facing the window. Several quiet minutes pass, and Shannon turns her head to see if Greg is still awake. Feeling her movement, he also turns around. Their eyes meet. Shannon turns back around and Greg reaches out, resting his arm on her midsection while she inches back closer to him. Their bodies remain in contact with one another in somewhat of a loose embrace. Greg adjusts his body slightly in an attempt to control his arousal while she involuntarily squirms because of her sexual impulses. Shannon feels the inconspicuous pulsations of his penis against her body, it makes her wetter; she holds his arm tighter against her body as it lay across her slightly exposed midriff.

Greg places her hair behind her ear and tenderly kisses the back of her neck, immediately giving her the chills. Shannon reaches back and softly grabs the back of his neck as she rubs her lower body against his hard member. Heart racing, she unknowingly holds her breath as his hand caresses her body until it reaches the bottom of her cut-off gym shorts. Shannon exhales. She turns to face him, and they begin to kiss so aggressively that their teeth collide; so caught up in the moment, they continue as if nothing happened. Shannon hooks her thumbs at her waistline and takes her panties down to her ankles, removing them the rest of the way with her bare feet. Greg slides his hand between her warm thighs, and his finger easing effortlessly into her immensely wet vagina. She vigorously kisses on his neck and reaches into his black briefs and grabs his hard cock. He pulls off his underwear and she immediately lies on her back.

Greg climbs over the top of her as she lies there with her eyes closed, puffy nipples exposed, as she anxiously awaits for him to enter. She spreads her long legs, and Greg eases inside of her. She pants heavily in his ear, initially trying her hardest not to moan until she can no longer hold it in as he slides in and out of her. Greg slowly pulls out, turns her around and enters her from behind while she is flat on her stomach. Shannon tightly clenches the fitted sheet, removing it from the mattress as he grinds deeply inside of her.

"I want you to cum," she says, returning to missionary position.

She wraps her legs around the back of his thighs, and holds him tightly around the waist as he thrusts in and out.

"Don't stop," she says. "Please don't stop, baby."

Greg feels a warm flush out of Shannon's vagina as she reaches orgasm. He senses his climax and attempts to pull out of her.

"Don't stop," she says. "Please don't stop, baby."

They kiss as Greg finishes inside of her. They both roll over, exhausted.

Can't Help Your Feelings

The librarian seated behind the desk resembles the stereotypical middle-aged woman who curls up in her large recliner, homemade quilt spread across the back, reading a novel, cats resting on her lap, while sipping coffee from her favorite novelty mug; a real-life, slimmer version of Annie Wilkes in glasses. The librarian corrals the tall stack of cooking recipe books to her side of the counter.

"Do you have a library card?" the librarian asks.

"I don't think so," Greg says.

"Would you like to get one?"

"Yes," Greg says. "What do I need to get one?"

"Just an approved photo I.D. Do you have a driver's license?"

"No."

"Picture Identification or Passport?" she asks.

"No."

"I'm so sorry," she says. "But we can't give you a library card without a valid form of

I.D. Do you have a friend that might be able to check them out for you?"

"Could you check to see if I have a card?" Greg asks.

"I sure can," she says. "What's your name?"

"Greg Mallet."

"I have one Greg Mallet here," she says. "Can you verify your address or date of birth?"

"4471 NE Ivy St."

"Ok, that's good enough for me," she says as she scrolls down the monitor.

"My, it's been a while since you've checked out any books," the librarian says. "February 25, 1999, to be exact."

The librarian scans the books and hands him a receipt. Greg thanks her and walks to a large unoccupied table and skims through the books, looking at recipes that interest him. After several hours at the library he stuffs his books into his backpack, leaves the table and heads for the main entrance. On his way out of the lobby, he slowly passes by and glances at a bulletin board tacked with numerous flyers and notes. One flyer in particular garners his attention, it reads: *Dream Interpretation and Therapy Group, Every Saturday from 2:30-4:30 pm, All Are*

Welcome. Greg makes a mental note of the address and continues out of the door.

* * *

A petite woman in her mid-twenties is sprawled across a large brown sectional flipping though channels on the television set. Her blonde hair is set in a ponytail and she wears an oversized sweater, a pair of yoga pants, and dingy red socks. Stephen sits at the small, glass dining room table some feet behind the couch typing away on his laptop.

"I'm hungry," the woman says. Without waiting an adequate amount of time for a response, she repeats her statement. "Did you hear me, Stephen? I'm hungry," she says, without removing her eyes from the TV, continuing to flip through the channels, eyes squinted.

"Yes, Katie, I heard you," Stephen says. "Just give me a few minutes to finish this."

"Don't we have leftover Thai in the fridge from Thursday night?" he asks.

"Gross," she says. "That's from two days ago."

"Two days is fine," he says. "I've seen you eat leftovers older than two days before."

"Well, I don't want it, ok?" she pouts.

"What do you want baby?" he says, continuing to look at his computer screen.

"I want something good," she says. "How about that place in Northwest that we went to for my cousin's birthday?"

"The Italian restaurant?" he says. "I don't think we can afford that right now. All the money I have in my checking account is for the rent."

"I feel like you don't care about me anymore," Katie says. "You barely buy me anything anymore, you don't take me out. I feel like you're not even proud of me anymore."

"What do you mean I don't buy you anything? I gave you my credit card Saturday, and you had to make about three separate trips to bring all of the stuff you bought into the house.

Plus, we've already went out about three or four times this week," he says. "I just think we

need to start cutting expenses a little bit so I don't have to keep pulling from my savings. That's why I went grocery shopping yesterday. We've discussed this, remember?"

"But you can go to the bar and spend money," she says.

"One time. That's how many times I've been to the bar this past month."

Katie starts to sniffle. Stephen immediately removes himself from the table and sits next to her. Her knees are pressed against her chest as she wipes her eyes with the sleeves of her sweater. He tries to hug her. She pushes him away.

"Come here," he says.

She pushes him away again.

"Okay," Stephen says. "You win. Let me finish this up and we'll go."

Katie stops crying. "When are you going to be finished?"

"Really soon," he says.

"Why does it have to take so long?" she asks.

"It's a big story I'm doing. You remember the guy from the news who woke up from the coma?" he asks.

"No."

"The guy who woke up from the coma after three years? It was all over the news."

"No," she says. "Get to the point."

"Well he works at a bar in Northeast," he answers. "Nobody knew where he was, nobody ever even got a chance to interview him, nobody even really knew what he looked like. Until now."

"And...," she says.

"And? Do you know what this means for me? I can go from neighborhood newspaper freelance journalist getting paid shit, to being a writer for *The New York Times, USA Today*, maybe even *Time* magazine. Point is, something like this can be huge for my career. It gives me options, leverage that I could have never dreamed of. I have an exclusive story that I'm working on and I'm trying to make this story a masterpiece. And that means I'll be able to take you out every night if you wanted it, because that's what you deserve."

"Only a few more minutes," Katie says.

"Okay," he says. "Let me just finish up this one paragraph on my rough draft and we can leave."

She pulls his shirt as he starts to walk away. He turns and looks at her.

"Who's the most beautiful girl in the world?" she asks.

"You are," he says. "That's why I love you more than anything in the world."

"What else do you love me more than?" she asks.

"Freshly baked chocolate chip cookies straight out of the oven," he says.

"More than your mom?" she asks.

"Yes, I love you more than I love my mom."

"I love hearing you say that," she says. "Come here."

She puckers her lips, and he leans over and kisses them.

* * *

The silence in Shannon's office is broken by a series of solid knocks on the door. "Come in!" she exclaims.

Kendra bursts in, stopping right past the doorway. She shakes her head.

"Why are you shaking your head?" Shannon says, returning a smile.

"I have been calling you and calling you, I've even sent you a voicemail and I *never* leave voicemails, only to be ignored, so I decided to pay you a visit," Kendra says. "What's new, stranger?"

Shannon opens her mouth to begin to speak.

"I'm sorry, *Dr*. Stranger," Kendra says.

"Shush," she says. "I've really been meaning to call you back, but I've just been so busy.

What's new with you?"

"No, no, no, we're not talking about me right now," Kendra says, smiling as she takes a seat across from Shannon's desk. "I'm not done with you yet, young lady. I want details."

Shannon laughs. "What are you talking about?"

"Oh, I think you know exactly what I'm talking about," Kendra replies. "Who is he?"

"Who?"

"I'm not stupid, Shannon," Kendra says with a sly expression draped across her face.

"We hung out regularly then it just stopped out of nowhere; You're neglecting me. I think I know what that means."

"I don't know what you're talking about," Shannon says, quickly glancing at her friend, looking away to avoid eye contact.

"You met a guy," Kendra says.

Shannon tries hard not to smile but her efforts are futile.

"You did!" Kendra says. "When are you going to learn that you can't hide these things from me? Go ahead and cough up the details. Who is he?"

"I told you it's nothing," Shannon says.

Kendra watches Shannon use her computer monitor as a decoy to take the attention away from her. The room goes silent for several moments.

"Dr. Brewster," Kendra says.

"What?" Shannon says defensively.

Kendra's eyes get bigger and the smile on her face seemingly grows in slow motion.

"Greg Mallet," Kendra says, her eyes now widened intensely.

"What?" Shannon says. "*Nooo.* You don't think? *Nooo.*"

"You fucked him didn't you?" Kendra asks accusingly.

"Kendra!" Shannon blushes.

"Why didn't I know?" Kendra exclaims.

"Shhhh," Shannon says.

"Oh, I'm sorry," Kendra whispers. She scoots her chair closer to the desk.

"I know it was a huge mistake," Shannon says. "I shouldn't have done it."

"Was liquor involved?" Kendra asks.

"No," Shannon replies.

"Well it wasn't a mistake," Kendra says, jokingly.

"It wasn't supposed to happen," Shannon says, frantically. "We were lying there and one thing led to another and—"

"Calm down, Shannon," Kendra says. "You don't have to explain it to me. I'm not judging you. He *is* pretty cute. You know me, I just wanna know if it was good or not."

"You're silly," Shannon says.

"I'm kidding. But seriously, what are you going to do? Are you dating him? What's he like? I have *sooo* many questions."

"He's really sweet," Shannon says. "He's respectful, I have fun when I'm around him and most importantly, he listens to me."

Kendra continues to watch her as if waiting for more.

"I don't know what I'm going to do," Shannon says. "I don't want to just desert him. I think he needs me, and I'm starting to get used to having him around."

"Well I'm sure you know what I'm going to say," Kendra says. "Do what you feel is best for *you*, you can't help your feelings. You sound like this guy makes you happy but you *do* have to be smart about it. Everything you say is safe with me but if certain people find out about this, you and I both know what could happen."

"I know," Shannon says.

* * *

Greg walks into the building where the dream group therapy is being held. A group of fourteen people of various types are congregated in the spacious conference room in the otherwise vacant old office building. Nearly everyone in the room takes turns staring at Greg within his first two minutes of being there. They are not accustomed to seeing new attendees. There are no chairs, only pillows forming a circle in the center of the office carpeted room. A plastic foldable table is propped in the corner of the room with a coffee pot of a yellowish-colored tea next to a tall stack of 8-oz. paper cups.

A middle-aged woman in a light purple, quilted vest and blue jeans approaches Greg. She puts her hand out to shake his hand, he obliges. "Hi, I'm Janine," she says.

"I'm Greg."

"It's nice to meet you." Janine is the type of person that looks at those she speaks to with an expression that makes you think there is something on your face.

"It's nice to meet you too," Greg says.

"I haven't seen you around," Janine says. "First time here?"

"Yes, ma'am."

"Well, make yourself comfortable. We're happy to have you. Help yourself to some tea."

Greg walks over to the table and fills a cup of the hot tea and takes a sip. He scowls and looks down into his cup as if trying to look for the source of the unpleasant taste.

"It's not for everyone," an older gentleman with snow white hair says as he approaches.

Greg begins to set the tea back on the table. The old man smiles.

"I'm sorry," he says. "I should rephrase that. The tea *is* for everyone, but not everyone likes it. It's an herbal tea. It's an acquired taste for most people. It's Ashwaganda Tea. It promotes a sense of well-being and it helps to clear your mind from stress and exhaustion. By the way, I'm Arthur."

"I'm Greg, it's nice to meet you."

A thin man with glasses and long, dark hair tucked behind his ears stands at the center of the perimeter of pillows. The man has a cordless headpiece with a microphone attached that is wirelessly connected to a small speaker in the corner of the room. The room is small and there aren't many people to warrant a microphone, but the object displays his control. He raises one of his arms, his sleeves rolled up beyond his elbow.

"It's time to start," Arthur pats Greg on the bicep and quickly finds a pillow to sit on.

Greg walks to the circle of pillows and waits for everyone to sit down before finding a spot. The thin man looks at him and greets him with a smile and a nod of the head.

"You can sit anywhere," the man says. "We don't have assigned seats."

Everyone takes a seat.

"For all who don't know," the thin man says, "well actually, I'm sure I recognize all of you except one. I'm Eugene Singler, and I'm a clinical social worker. I've been studying dream analysis and interpretation for eleven years and have spent the last several years working on my tried and true method of dream therapy. The goal of this form of dream therapy is to teach you to take your dreams, or nightmares, and transform them into positive energy that will help you in your daily life. Mental health, emotional health, spiritual health, and physical health are all one, and the positive energy from this therapy will change your life for the better. Take Arthur, for example. Before today's session, Arthur was explaining to me how it's helped his quality of life. Arthur, how has dream therapy helped *you* recently?"

"Well," Arthur says. "Three months ago, my doctor told me that my hypertension had become nearly uncontrollable. I was taking a water pill and two blood pressure pills along with a prescription for high cholesterol, and my blood pressure and my LDL were still through the roof. When I started coming here and taking walks every day, my blood pressure and my cholesterol went down significantly, and now I'm only taking water pills."

"Perfect example," Eugene says. "Why don't we all give Arthur a hand?"

A woman utters "good job" as all give him a round

225

of applause.

"Ok," Eugene says. "Does anyone want to go first today?"

No one volunteers.

"No one?" Eugene says. "Surely *someone* has a dream they'd like to share today."

"I will," says a slim young woman who slightly raises her hand while twirling her long, braided ponytail with her other hand.

"Ok, Beth," Eugene says. "You're up."

"Wednesday and Friday night," Beth says. "No, Tuesday and Friday I think it was, I dreamed that I was being chased. I don't know what or who was chasing me, but whatever it was had me horrified. It was a weird feeling. It was like I was running in place like I was on a treadmill but whatever was chasing me couldn't catch up to me. I had the exact same dream twice. I think it *has* to mean *something*."

"Well, Beth, dreams of being chased often symbolize the avoidance of heavy emotions, challenging situations, or problems," Eugene replies. "The origin of your dreams may be found in your personal life, your boyfriend or girlfriend, family, bills, your job or even yourself."

She nods.

"Everyone join hands for Beth," Eugene says.

Everyone joins hands. Greg looks around and notices everyone bowing their heads, their eyes shut. He does the same. Eugene passes sheets of paper around the room, placing a sheet in everyone's lap.

"Ok," Eugene says. "Beth, I want you to think of

everything it is that you think might be chasing you in your dreams. Everything. Everyone join in; let's all do this together because we all, undoubtedly, have something in pursuit of our inner peace just like our friend Beth does. I want you to turn around and face whatever is that is chasing you because it has no power over you. Empower yourself. Regain control of your mind. I now want you to take the sheet of paper in front of you, keep your eyes closed, and pretend it's whatever it is that's chasing you and crumble it up into a little ball as small as you can make it."

Everyone crumbles their paper.

"Now toss it as far as you can. Just get rid of it. It's like a little mouse that's infiltrated our home—it doesn't belong."

Paper balls rain down in the center of the room.

"Now let's everyone take a deep breath," Eugene says." Slowly release... And open your eyes."

Everyone opens their eyes and look around the room as if they'd just been awakened in a foreign environment..

"I want you to do that whenever you feel something is weighing down your mind. It's a form of empowering yourself."

"That felt good," Beth says. "I feel relieved."

"Who's next?" Eugene asks.

No one volunteers.

"I'm going to pick on the new guy," he says, looking at Greg. "I didn't get your name."

"Greg Mallet," he answers.

"Okay, Greg, we're glad to have you join us today,"

Eugene says. "Would you like to share a dream with us?"

"Well, I haven't really had any in a few weeks," he says.

"It's okay, I don't care if it's twenty years old and it has a longing effect on your life,"

Eugene says. "If you want to share it, feel free. And remember, we don't judge here."

Greg senses the group's eyes burning a hole into him, curious to hear his response.

"Well, a little over a month ago I started having dreams of everyone I care about dying, and I feel like I'm somewhat responsible for it," Greg says, reluctantly.

"Who in your dreams died and how did they die?" Eugene asks.

"First, my grandmother died, that was in this life, she died while she was lying in the bed next to me. Then my boss died, I know it sounds weird, but his head exploded in front of me. My friend, I followed him into the sewer, and he was killed there. And not long after that, my mother also died in front of me."

"Over what time span did you have these dreams?" Eugene asks.

"Over the span of a few days," Greg says. "And the weird thing is that I couldn't tell what was real and what was a dream. I now know that my grandmother's death was real, at least that's what I believe now. I'm just still kind of confused because the dreams were so realistic that I feel like if they weren't real that they have to at least *mean* something."

"Was there any tension in your relationships with

these people who die in your dreams?"

Eugene asks.

"Not that I know of," Greg says. "I don't remember much about them before the point that they died. I just know that I knew them and that we were close. And each day that goes by I forget them more and more."

"You just said that they were people you cared about," Eugene says. "How do you care about people you can't remember much about? I'm sorry, I'm just a little confused."

"It's a long story," Greg says. "I have a condition where my brain has trouble with reality perception.

A heavyset woman speaks up from across the room. "So what you're saying is you don't know whether these people are really dead or alive? That's a little disturbing. Have you talked to the authorities about any of this?"

Greg is at a loss for words. He regrets saying anything and at the same time doesn't want to go into the details of the coma because more questions would be sure to follow. Several people in the room look at each other exchanging mixed signals.

"In any event," Eugene says. "Greg, we know you're going through a rough time. Sometimes dreams can seem so real that they feel like a harbinger of things to come, but in reality, many of our bad dreams stem from stressors in our day-to-day life. Your body language and the pain that I see on your face tells me how much you *do*, or *did* care about these people. Your dreams tell me that you're probably a protector of those that you love and these dreams make you feel powerless because you can't always be there to save them. Whether the dreams foreshadow anything or not, try to take pressure off of yourself and understand that you can't control everything. Cherish those that you love every day and make it count."

Greg continues to vaguely listen to the rest of the meeting but the words directed at him resonate in his head. Cherishing the memories of those he dreamed about and people he met in real life that have helped him along the way occupy his thoughts.

* * *

Shannon sits in her car as it idles in Greg's driveway. She is still strapped in her seatbelt, her hands resting on the bottom of the steering wheel. Eighteen minutes have passed since she parked. Her brain has been going in circles since her brief conversation with Kendra earlier in the day. Before the conversation, her time spent with Greg was considered unethical in her mind, but the guilt would pass so quickly that it never left an impression on her conscience. Hearing her reservations validated by another person single-handedly brings the issue to the forefront of her mind. The time spent dwelling on everything has not gotten her anywhere closer to a resolution.

Greg crosses the driveway on his bike and knocks on her window. She rolls it down.

"What's wrong?" he says, noting her glum expression.

Shannon forces a smile. "Nothing. Just a little exhausted."

"Oh ok," he says. "I guess I'll give you a break and cook tonight. I saw a recipe with

Grilled Chicken stuffed with Italian sausage."

"Sounds delicious," Shannon says as she slowly gets out of the car.

"Need help?" Greg asks.

"Yes," she answers, smiling through her tired expression.

Greg drapes her arm across the back of his neck and begins to walk. Their legs become slightly entangled. She screams as she nearly trips as they walk across the front lawn. "Ok, stop!" she laughs. "I'm falling!"

Their legs become fully entangled and she tumbles to the grass accidentally pulling him down with her. Greg lands on top of her.

"Shit," he says, laughing. "You okay?"

"Yes, I'm ok," Shannon says, laughing as she reaches for his outreached hand to help her up.

"I guess you're better at helping people walk than I am," he says.

"Yes," she says. "You suck at it. You have to be patient, don't walk so fast. Let me show you. Put your arm across my shoulders."

He puts his arm around her shoulders.

"Now move your feet," she says. "One at a time. Slowly, give the other person time to catch up. Where you go, I go."

Greg starts off slowly but begins to walk faster.

"Stop!" she says. "You're messing it up on purpose!"

"What?" he laughs. "I didn't do anything. I was just walking."

"Whatever. You sabotaged it because you're jealous

that I'm better than you."

"Jealous of *you*?" he says. "Never.

They walk into the house leaving all the stress of the day behind.

* * *

Dan hovers over the top of the large waste container in the kitchen with his head cocked to one side before taking the initial bite of an oversized burrito. Juice from the salsa and ranch dressing drips from the bottom of the burrito into the trash can. Greg and Conrad stand nearby watching.

"Somebody needs to learn how to roll a burrito," Dan says. "Everything's gonna fall out before I take the first bite."

"Well you asked for the ranch inside," Conrad says. "That's why it's leaking. You're supposed to dip it."

"Doesn't matter. The burrito's still not supposed to leak." They quietly watch as he takes a huge bite of the burrito. "Oh yeah," he says with his mouth full. "This is awesome. Hand me one of those paper towels."

Greg rips a sheet from the paper towel dispenser and hands it to him. Dan wipes his mouth and hands before dropping the paper towel in the trash.

"What do you think?" Conrad asks.

"I said it was good," Dan says, walking toward the office.

"Good enough to put on the menu?" Conrad asks.

"Conrad, I told you the last time—"

"No, no hear me out," Conrad says.

Dan stops in his tracks and rolls his eyes.

"Happy hour," Conrad says. "Pretty much every bar in the city has one except for us. Let us come up with a small menu and see how it does for a couple months, and if it doesn't work, you can take a dollar from my hourly."

Dan looks at Greg and shakes his head. "Newbie, you on this bandwagon now too?" he asks.

Greg nods.

"We need a change," Conrad says. "We can only rearrange the place so many times."

"Shoot me some ideas and let me think about it," Dan says, walking to his office. "I'll tell you boys one thing. That burrito is too big to be on a happy hour menu, cut it into threes, turn it into a taco or something. I don't like to lose money." He closes the office door.

Greg raises his eyebrows and shrugs. Conrad smiles big and puts his fist out for a dap, Greg gives him a pound.

"He just said he'd think about it," Greg says.

"You don't understand. I've never gotten a response *close* to that," Conrad says. "I'll come up with the cheap cocktails, and you work on the menu."

"Sounds good to me," Greg says.

"I'm telling you man," Conrad says. "One day we'll have our own bar. We make a fucking awesome team."

* * *

Shannon and Greg make their way to her apartment for the evening. She opens the door and turns the lights on and Greg follows her in.

"So this is my place," Shannon says.

Greg looks around the apartment and immediately

233

walks over to the large window overlooking the city. She stands beside him and also looks out of the window.

"This is why I chose this place," she says. "I didn't care what the apartment looked like or how small it was, as soon as I saw the window I was sold. I probably could have been more patient and chosen something better or more spacious, but I have a problem with making quick and irrational decisions."

"I don't blame you," Greg says. "The view is amazing."

"Yeah," she says. "You know what's crazy?"

"What?"

"I look at all the cars that pass through every day and I can't think of a time that I've ever seen the same one more than once. I'm sure I have because I know a lot of the same people take the same route every day. It reminds me of how big this world is, how many people there are in this city alone and how irrelevant it makes us all seem individually. It kind of puts things into perspective. The world stops for nobody."

"Trust me, I understand the feeling," Greg says. Shannon walks behind him and wraps her arms around his waist. He turns around and kisses her.

What's Wrong

Shannon walks into the office of Dr. Cindy Kern, chief of staff at the hospital. Just thirty minutes prior, on this gloomy Monday morning, Shannon received an e-mail from her marked as urgent. Her nerves go into disarray, because in the past she has rarely had contact with the COS at all, being able to count on one hand the number of times that she has ever even interacted with her at all. Dr. Kern opens the door to the office and invites Shannon to take a seat. The COS is known as a notoriously impersonal and intimidating woman that who takes her job very seriously. She's the type of person that you couldn't imagine ever being married or having a family, couldn't imagine taking a vacation, or having a single hobby outside of work.

A male staff member knocks on the door, and Dr. Kern apologizes and excuses herself from the office. The room is exceptionally chilly, but Shannon accepts it as her present nerves are taking a toll on her physical body, therefore, making it feel colder than it really is. She soon gains a little bit of comfort when she hears the doctor's seemingly good mood as she has a light-hearted conversation with the fellow staff-member in the hall. Cindy re-enters the room and closes the door. She takes a seat at her desk.

"I'm sorry to keep you waiting, Dr. Brewster," Cindy says. "You know how Monday's are."

"Oh yeah, definitely," Shannon replies, with a smile.

"Do you know why I called this meeting with you so early in the morning?"

"I can't say that I do," Shannon replies.

Dr. Kern moves her disposable coffee cup from one side to the other and slides a newspaper across the desk to Shannon. Shannon looks at Dr. Kern and notices her lips are smiling but the rest of her face is as serious as a chess player contemplating his next move.

"Turn to page 3-A," Dr. Kern says.

Shannon takes the newspaper in her lap and turns to page 3-A, and the first thing she notices is a photograph of Greg holding her and the two of them smiling as he helps her off of the lawn. The photo was apparently taken when they were helping each other walk into the house, which was more than two weeks ago. Her stomach is immediately turned in knots. After her initial shock, she begins to skim over the article impatiently.

"Greg spends quality time with his girlfriend on the front lawn of his Northeast Portland home," Cindy says, reciting the caption underneath the photo.

Shannon looks at Dr. Kern, whose half smile has dissipated.

"Yeah," Dr. Kern says, "I've memorized that caption because I read it over and over again yesterday morning. I was so shocked when I saw the photo that I forgot my coffee was scalding hot and I took a big sip of it and burnt my tongue. But do you know what hurt me more than my burnt tongue, Dr. Shannon? Dr. Brewster, I'm sorry."

She doesn't give Shannon sufficient time to give an answer.

"How a smart young woman like you can just toss her career in the trash like yesterday's newspaper; no pun intended. I've been watching your career since you were hired here. You've been involved in more volunteer work in your teenage and adult life than I've ever seen in my nearly twenty-five years as doctor, and you graduated Summa Cum Laude. You have so much going for you but you don't carry yourself like it. If I looked at your CV and looked at you, do you know what the first thought that came to my mind would be?"

"No, ma'am," Shannon says.

"That's not her on this sheet of paper," Dr. Kern says. "I would say 'there's no way that's the same woman.'" Dr. Kern pauses to let her statement sink in. "I'm not saying that you don't have it in you because I know you do, but in case you didn't know, I see everything. I have eyes everywhere. You can't hold my position successfully without utilizing all resources. Three things stick out to me about you, one thing good and two not so good." Dr. Kern holds up three fingers and brings each of them down as she goes through her list. "One, you let people walk all over you. Two, you have no confidence in yourself, and three, excuse my language, but you've got a shitload of potential. You had two things going against you, now you have three; you're reckless. That's one for four. Tell me what's going on with this guy."

"I took it upon myself to—" Shannon begins.

"Wait, before you start I want to tell you one thing. If there's one thing I can't stand, it's being lied to. I can be your number one ally, but if you lie to me there is absolutely nothing I can do for you."

"I took a personal interest in Mr. Mallet from the time I initially saw his story on the news. A personal interest, professionally, that is. I thought my expertise could be integral in his recovery. I wasn't granted the time nor the support in my pursuit so I took matters into my own hands. After he left the hospital, I made a visit to his house and found him in bad shape physically and mentally, and I took advantage of the opportunity to assist him in his rehabilitation the way I saw fit."

"When you couldn't get access to him while he was a patient here, it never crossed your mind to approach me about seeing what we could do about giving you more time with him?" Dr. Kern asks. "I've been associated with this hospital for over twenty years, I can't control everything, but I *can* make *some* things happen around here."

"No, ma'am," Shannon answers. "It didn't cross my mind. I didn't want to rub anyone the wrong way."

"Didn't want to rub anyone the wrong way?" Dr. Kern says. "You've got to pick and choose your battles wisely, honey. You're not wanting to rub one or two people the wrong way could quite possibly rub a lot more people the wrong way when word about this paper gets around. The people who could actually have an effect on your livelihood. You ever heard the phrase 'shit rolls downhill'? Well it'll start all the way at the top and come crashing down to us and the higher it starts, the faster it comes down and the harder it crashes when it reaches the bottom."

Shannon nods.

"Did you assist or encourage him in any way to leave the hospital?" Dr. Kern asks.

"No, ma'am," Shannon says. "I had no idea he left the hospital until it was brought to my attention a couple of days afterward."

"Do you have any type of relationship with him that would be constituted as unprofessional or unethical by the American Medical Association standards?"

Shannon takes a deep breath.

"Do you have a romantic relationship with him, Shannon?" Dr. Kern asks.

"Yes," Shannon says.

Dr. Kern is obviously perturbed by her answer but

she composes herself calmly. "Have you had sexual intercourse with the patient?

"Yes I have," she answers, reluctantly.

Dr. Kern sighs. "Dr. Brewster, you do recognize how serious this is, don't you?"

"Yes," Shannon says. "I'm ashamed, and I had no intentions of this happening."

"This could put your job in jeopardy and more importantly your licensure, especially considering the nature of his medical problem, and the degree of emotional dependence he probably has on you. This is serious. I understand that you feel like you're helping him, but you could be hindering his progress. Think about it, if you were on the outside looking in, what would you think about the relationship between a psychiatrist and a patient with his history?"

"I would think it was totally unprofessional and inappropriate," Shannon says.

"It's in the newspaper, Shannon," Dr. Kern says. "Definitely soon to be on the news, nationally, and covered all over the Internet. The board will make an example out of you. This isn't a love story or a movie where everything ends happily ever after. You need to break all ties. End it."

Shannon nods.

"Look at me," Dr. Kern says. "You might love him or the sex might be great, but whatever it is that attracts you to him, if you care anything about your career, reputation, the hard work you put into it, or even *him*, you need to end it. I'll take care of any questions people might have about the photo. I'll e-mail you a statement for anyone who asks you anything about it. If it makes it any easier, once he gets through everything and moves on with his life you may no longer be in it. And you'll get over it. And one day you'll find the man of your dreams and have plenty children. You may be a stepping stone for Mr. Mallet right now. He'll be happy and you'll be searching for a new career. Is it worth it?"

"No, Dr. Kern," Shannon says. "You're right, it's not worth it."

* * *

The telephone on the kitchen wall rings, interrupting Greg as he spreads peanut butter on a slice of bread. The ring comes unexpectedly, since the phone rarely rings. He walks to the phone and answers, butter knife still in hand.

"Greg, what's up?" Conrad says on the other end of the phone. "Hey, can you come in early?"

"Yeah, what's wrong?" Greg says. "I thought Jay was working this morning."

"He is, just get here as soon as you can. I gotta go," Conrad says before abruptly hanging up the phone.

Greg rushes to his bedroom and changes into a work shirt and walks swiftly to the door. He turns around and grabs the slice of peanut butter bread, folds it in half and stuffs it in his mouth before getting on his bike and heading to work.

From a quarter of a mile away, Greg notices the small parking lot of the bar packed with vehicles. All attention is directed at him when he enters the building. Most of the customers smile at him while a few pull out phones and snap pictures. He looks over at the bar and is surprised to see Dan bartending. Dan looks up and smiles at him for all of two seconds before going back to work hustling drinks. Andy Lambere is seated at the bar, he looks at Greg and nods, greeting him. Greg goes into the kitchen to see Conrad and another employee, Jay, preparing food in the kitchen. Conrad looks at Greg.

"Thank God," Conrad says. "It took you long enough."

"I came as soon as possible," Greg says. "What's going on? Why is it so crowded?"

"It's you, man," Conrad says as he mixes a large metal bowl of onion rings in batter. "You were in the newspaper yesterday, they did a story on you and the bar."

Dan bursts through the door. "Conrad," he says. "Go take care of the bar for me."

"I think you were handling it well out there for someone who hasn't done it in over fifteen years," Conrad says as he rinses his hands in the sink.

"Told ya' I still got it," he says. "I'm gonna make a run to the store, did you write down everything we need?"

"Yeah," Conrad says. "It's on your desk."

"Ok, hurry up and get out there, the customers are waiting," Dan says. "Jay, go and check on the tables. You've been back here long enough."

Everyone but Greg leaves the room; He looks at the orders and begins to prepare the food. Dan re-enters the kitchen.

"I know it's a lot, but do the best you can," Dan says.

"No problem," Greg says as he puts a clean but dingy white apron over his head.

"Oh," Dan says, turning around before walking back into his office. He walks up to Greg and puts out his hand. "Thank you."

"For what?" Greg asks, shaking Dan's hand.

"This place hasn't been this busy in years," Dan says, choked up. "We've gained new customers and old regulars I didn't even know were still alive are out there catching up on old times. This means a lot to me, and it's all because of you."

Dan returns to the office. Greg stops and reflects for a moment, touched by the statement. He ties his apron and continues his work.

* * *

At 10 p.m, Greg enters the house and leans his bike on the wall. He removes his coat and walks into the kitchen. Shannon is seated at the kitchen table still wearing her coat and scarf. Her hat is lying on the table in front of her. Sunday's newspaper is placed beside it. Greg begins to speak before making it to the kitchen.

"You would not believe what happened today," he says. "Work was crazy. All I need to say is everything we worked on was a huge success."

"That's great," Shannon says, glumly.

"What's wrong?" Greg asks.

Shannon places her hand on the newspaper. "Have you read this?"

"Is that yesterday's paper? Not yet," Greg says. "I was going to read it earlier, but I didn't have the time because I didn't really get any breaks today. What's up?"

"*What's up?* Greg, there's a picture of us in it."

"Let me see."

She hands him the newspaper without looking in his direction. He observes a photograph of he and Conrad on the front page smiling as they converse behind the bar. He assumes that the photo was more than likely taken via camera phone the day he met Stephen. He turns to page 3-A.

"What's wrong with it?" he asks.

"It's inappropriate," she says. "You're the patient, and I'm the psychiatrist. It's not ethical. I'm not supposed to be with you."

"But I'm not a patient anymore." Greg looks down at the photo. "And we're not doing anything inappropriate in the picture."

"You were a patient in the hospital, where I'm employed, who left suddenly before the termination of treatment, and now they have a photo in the newspaper portraying us as lovers. People will have questions."

"Who cares if they have questions?" Greg says. "The relationship between you and I has nothing to do with them."

"Greg, it could put my career in jeopardy. I could lose everything I worked so hard to get, and if this is syndicated nationally I can kiss my career goodbye. And if I don't lose my license no one will ever hire me anyway. Yes, the story helped you, the bar, and I'm happy for you that it did, but it's detrimental for me."

"I don't care about how the article helps me; I care about *us*."

"I just wish you hadn't spoken to the reporter who

wrote this article," Shannon says.

"I didn't know he was a reporter, and I barely even said anything to him. Two or three sentences, max."

"They can use a few sentences and write a whole article on it and spin it however they want," Shannon says. "Everyone knows that."

"I'm sorry. I'll figure out how to fix this. Next time I see the guy I'll make sure he clears it up."

"It's not your fault," Shannon says. "It's mine; I should have known better. The damage is already done and there's only one way we can fix it. We can't do this anymore, Greg. It has to be over between us." Shannon rises from the chair without making eye contact with him and puts her hat on. She leaves the kitchen. Stunned by her words, it takes a few seconds for them to register in Greg's mind.

"You don't mean that," he says, following her to the door. "Let's wait a couple days to figure out something else."

"Greg, I'm sorry that it has to be this way," she says before walking out. "In the long run I'm sure this decision is best for us. You're a great person, and I'm sure you'll find a great woman who can appreciate that. I just can't be the one; it's just not meant to be. I'm sorry."

Greg watches as she swiftly walks to her car.

Of all of the trying times in her life, even the death of her father, holding back all of these tears has to be the hardest, which is why she tried to make the goodbye as quick and painless as possible; like ripping off a Band-Aid. As soon as she slams the car door, she breaks down in tears. Shannon allows her emotion to pour out because the darkness outside won't allow him to see her cry. She so desperately wanted to hug him before leaving but knew it would make her emotional, forcing her to change her mind about leaving.

Greg watches the until her car is no longer in sight. Just like that, she's gone.

* * *

The large spray nozzle discharges hot water leaving a large cloud of steam in front of Greg's face. He stands at the stainless steel sink full of dirty pots and pans holding a wad of steel wool, staring into space. A new female employee, a recent high school graduate, approaches him from behind.

"I can wash those if you want me to," she says, snapping him out of the trance.

"I got it," he answers.

"Conrad told me to keep busy, and the lunch rush is over and I can't cook, so..." she says.

Greg walks to the office without saying anything. The girl watches as he walks away, looks at him oddly, and begins to wash the dishes. Shortly afterward, Conrad wanders into the kitchen and notices Greg seated in the office with his head buried in his palms.

"You ok, man?" Conrad asks. "You don't seem like yourself today?"

Greg looks up. "Just not really feeling it today. That's all. I'll be okay."

"Is this about the newspaper article?"

"No," Greg says, unconvincingly. "We got what we

wanted didn't we? A little notoriety, more business, raises."

"Yeah," Conrad says. "I just know you didn't want the exposure and you still don't want to take calls from the media, which means your stand hasn't totally changed. I know I fucked up telling Stephen all of that stuff, man.

Greg gets up from the chair and smiles between his otherwise drained facial expression. "You're fine, Conrad. Stop apologizing. I'm just tired, I didn't get much sleep last night."

"Your girlfriend keep you up too long last night?" Conrad says. "The girl from the picture in the paper, she's pretty cute; you never told me about her."

"No," Greg says, with a smile that quickly fades away. They walk out of the office and get back to work.

Shannon's mind is on a fritz for the duration of the workday. She tries to occupy her mind with other things, but can't shake the image of Greg standing on the porch watching her leave. Looking back at the way she handled the situation and the way she completely tuned him out when he tried to tell her about his day makes her feel guilty and insensitive. She never knew she had it in her character to be so rigid. She tries to convince herself repeatedly that it was something that had to be done, that it was only a fling and her fragile emotions had gotten the best of her. That Greg was only leaning on her because he had no one else; that *she* had forced him into dependence on her in a way similar to Stockholm's Syndrome. If any one of her thoughts that she has to make her feel better about the situation proves successful, it only helps briefly before the negative thoughts creep back into her mind.

For the first time in several weeks, Shannon has nothing to look forward to when she gets off of work.

Greg enters the home and hangs up his jacket and goes into the bathroom. He takes the Post-it note with Shannon's hand-written phone number on it and attempts to drop it in the trash; it floats away from the brim of the trash can like a falling feather and instead lands on the floor. He reaches down to grab it and instead of trying to put it back in the trash, he places it on the counter. The smallest things remind him of her, such as the loose strands of her hair that he finds on the counters, the bed, and stuck in his clothes from their laundry being washed together. Those small remnants of her remind him of her goofy laugh when she was caught off guard and unable to conceal it in time; the concentrated face she would make when he would play with her hair because she liked it. Greg goes into his room and waits up for hours in hopes that she would change her mind about everything and come back or even for the phone to ring. It never does. The next several days consist of sleepless nights and thoughts of hopelessness.

On a morning that he doesn't have to work, Greg makes a trip to the doctor's office to seek help for his sleep deprivation. A male doctor with a salt and pepper beard faces a computer in the examination room and scrolls down the computer screen. Aside from the lab coat, sharply creased slacks and the shiny, expensive dress shoes, he more closely resembles a home improvement guru or an expert of the outdoors than a medical doctor.

The doctor rolls his small, wheeled stool toward Greg.

"Ok, we're going to start you on a prescription of 10mg of Ambien once daily," he says. "It acts pretty quickly, so take it right before you go to bed. Make sure you have time for at least seven or eight hours of sleep before taking the drug and, obviously, you don't want to operate heavy machinery after taking it." The doctor hands him the prescription sheet. "Ok, Mr. Mallet, I hope this helps you get some sleep. Stop at the front desk before you leave so we can schedule you for a follow-up appointment."

"Thank you," Greg says.

Greg stops at the drug store immediately following his visit to urgent care. As he waits for his prescription to be filled, he watches as people enter and exit the store seemingly all in good moods. He compares his mood with theirs and finds himself wishing that he was someone else; almost anyone else. The prescription takes longer than expected, but he has to kill time before meeting up with the dream group anyway. He glances at his watch and realizes that the time has passed by quickly. He walks up to the counter to check on the status of his medicine. The pharmacy tech advises him that they called his name twenty minutes ago. He pays for his prescription and rushes out of the door.

Greg makes it to his destination just a couple minutes late. He walks into the old office building and almost immediately hears the microphoned voice of Eugene resonating throughout the 1st floor. Greg attempts to turn the doorknob where the meetings are held. It doesn't turn. The door is locked. He knocks on the door; no answer. Knocks again; still no response. The parking lot is nearly as full as it was last week, so surely there's no shortage of people to answer. Assuming they don't allow latecomers, he begins to walk away.

Eugene opens the door partially and squeezes out of the crack, closing the door behind him.

Greg turns around and smiles. "I thought you guys weren't going to let me in. Sorry I'm late. I had to pick up a prescription and it took longer than expected."

"Fred?" Eugene asks.

"Greg."

"Greg, I think you'd be better served finding help somewhere else," Eugene says.

"Somewhere more structured where they can help you and work with you on a more personal level. I wish I could be the one to do that, but there are people that are more qualified than me to carry that out."

Greg nods. "I totally understand," he says. "I'm working on that right now. I've been seeing a psychiatrist and things are getting better. It took a little time at first but I'm getting there."

"I understand that, but—," he pauses. "Greg, you made a lot of the group members uncomfortable the last time you came," Eugene says, speaking in a slight whisper while closing his eyes briefly. He holds his head down in shame, yet relieved with his admission.

Greg squints, confused and mildly embarrassed. "But you said there would be no judgment. I didn't even want to share anything at first."

"I understand that, and it's my fault, I'm sorry. If it were up to me I'd let you sit in with us, but the group trumps me. And again, I'm very sorry, I hope everything works out for you."

Eugene abruptly goes back into the room and shuts the door behind him. Greg stands at the closed door for several moments. Faint voices heard through the door suggests that the session continues, barely missing a beat.

* * *

Shannon makes a rare visit to the gym in an effort to free her mind. She changes into her workout clothes and immediately starts on the treadmill. She inserts her earphones and begins to run, watching the television in front of her but paying no attention to the program. After running for nearly two hours she eventually slows her pace to a fast walk. The people on the machines surrounding her have all been replaced by others, and the gym has become deserted compared to how crowded it was when she first arrived. A song begins to play in her earphones, a song that reminds her of Greg, *Flashing Lights* by Kanye West.

There is a brief turn in her stomach the moment she hears it, but the bittersweet sentiment of it prevents her from changing the song.

Shannon gets off the treadmill and with tired, heavy legs, walks toward the locker room. She removes her earphones and sits on the bench in front of her locker and cries. Grabbing her towel, she pretends to wipe sweat from her face to hide the tears. An observant middle-aged woman notices her crying; the woman's clothes are clean and she seems to be in a rush to leave but instead sits next to Shannon and gives her a much needed embrace.

* * *

Greg turns on the sink and lets it run before reaching in the cabinet for a glass. He fills the glass with water and carries it to the table. He sits, crosses his arms on the table, and buries his head in them. A couple minutes pass, he lifts his head and reaches into his pocket and pulls out the bottle of sleeping pills. He opens it, drops a pill on his tongue, and swallows. The dim light barely shines through the kitchen window as the sun sets and no lights are on in the house; the house is eerily quiet. Greg re-opens the bottle of pills and finishes off the remainder of its contents.

* * *

Shannon enters her home and immediately plops down on the sofa. She stares out of her window at the night view of the city. Without motivation to move, she sits there for what ends up being nearly half an hour before dressing down and going to bed early. Not even a minute passes after lying down before she hops out of bed and puts her shoes back on. Still in her sleep garb, she retrieves her coat and storms out of her apartment. She takes the elevator to the parking garage, gets in her car and drives directly to Greg's house without a second thought.

As she pulls up next to the driveway, she realizes that all of the lights are out and the home looks vacant. She continues down the street to the bar to see if he is working. His bicycle is not parked outside on the rack. She crookedly parks the car on the street and walks into the bar. The building is at nearly maximum occupancy with no sign of

Greg. Shannon squeezes past customers socializing near the door who don't acknowledge her. She walks around the bar frantically, even trying to peek through the window of the kitchen door. Her plight draws the attention of several patrons, particularly the seated ones that she brushes up against as she walks past.

Conrad approaches her. "Ma'am, can I help you with something?"

"Yes. Have you seen Greg? Is he working today?"

"No, he's off today," Conrad answers. "Why? What's wrong?"

She storms out of the bar. Conrad chases after her, apologizing to customers as he pushes past them. Just as he makes it out of the door her car drives off.

Shannon's intuition tells her that things aren't quite right and although he is only a few blocks away, she rushes back to his home as quickly as possible.

Once there, Shannon gets out of her car, leaving the engine running. She enters the house and turns on the lights. "Greg!" she calls. "Greg!

She looks into the kitchen, notices the empty pill bottle on the table and runs to his bedroom. He lies in bed on his back, eyes closed. Adrenaline gives her more strength than normal as she grips his shirt with both hands, vigorously shaking his limp body. She checks his carotid pulse for circulation and watches his chest to check for breathing.

"Greg, Wake up," Shannon pleads. "Wake up now. Please."

Her voice trails off.

A late news program plays on the muted television set in the ICU waiting room. Conrad paces the floor, tightly clenching a rolled up magazine in one hand. Dan is seated, leaning forward on the teal blue couch next to his wife who is rubbing his thigh consolingly. Shannon sits alone in a chair in a corner of the room, wiping tears from her grief stricken face. Kendra enters the room from the hallway.

"I convinced them to let us back," Kendra says, glumly, "but they said they could only allow one person at a time."

Everyone looks at Shannon. Her head nodded, elbows rested on her thighs and fingers buried in her hair.

"Shannon?" Dan says.

Shannon is slightly startled by the call of her name. With her state of mind in shambles, everything else going on around her is involuntarily tuned out. "Yes?" she says as she looks up, her face flushed.

"They're allowing us to see him," Dan says. "You go first."

Shannon slowly gets up from her seat, grabs her purse from the floor and walks toward the door leading into the hall. Dan's wife reaches out and grabs Shannon's hand, briefly caressing it.

"I'll hold that," the woman says, reaching for Shannon's purse.

"Thank you," Shannon says as she hands it to her.

"You're welcome, honey," the woman replies.

Shannon leaves the room.

Smitten by a combination of anger and sadness, Conrad hurls the magazine he was holding to the floor with full force. His expression of anger soon gives way to tears that profusely stream down his face.

Dan immediately approaches Conrad and puts his arm

around his shoulder. "It's okay, Conrad," Dan says. "Take it easy, we need to be strong for him. He's a strong fella he's pulled through something like this before. He can do it again."

"It's my fault," Conrad says, through his abundance of tears. "How could I be so fucking stupid? If it wasn't for me opening my big mouth this would have never happened."

"It's not your fault, honey," Dan's wife says. "You can't blame yourself."

"He's such a good guy," Conrad says "He doesn't deserve this. He just wanted peace of mind, happiness. He was getting better every day and what I did changed it."

Kendra rubs his back to console him.

"The last thing he'd want us to do is blame ourselves, Conrad," Dan says. "He had...he *has* pain inside of him that we probably don't even know about. Let's take this time to think positive, pray and come together for him."

I'm Not Scared Anymore

Greg slides full speed down a tunnel surrounded by L.E.D. lights with neck-stiffening momentum. The cage-like capsule he is seated in eventually crashes onto the concrete landing with incredible force accompanied by the sparks of the metal grinding the concrete. He shakes the initial shock and minor pain and looks around at his surroundings of what appears to be an underground city. It's dark outside and the only light that shines on the scenery are the scarce amount of working street lights. The streets are deserted and surrounded by abandoned and dilapidated buildings. Vehicles that appear to be implanted from a junkyard randomly line the curbs. He climbs out of the top of the capsule. The tunnel that the capsule came out of is no longer there. Greg has no choice but to to walk and hope to find something or someone harmless in order to ease his tension. He periodically looks over his shoulder as he blindly explores the city in search of life or occupancy. Every street he peers down appears endless with the dim and creepy street lights towering over the structures standing on the far ends of the streets.

Greg soon hears the bass of dance music playing somewhere in the near distance. He looks around and frantically runs nearly a block in every direction seeking out the source of the music. The music plays for a while before stopping for a brief period and starting again. Frustrated and exhausted, he doubles over and rests his hands on his knees. The music plays again, this time louder before suddenly stopping. Every lit street light blows out simultaneously. Greg turns around, still panting, and notices an old, brown, two-story brick building covered in moonlight. It's the only building that light is shining on.

Suspiciously paranoid, Greg slowly walks toward the old building. He meticulously scans the area while slowly approaching the door; he pushes it open. The interior of the building is pitch black. He sweeps the wall with his hand in search of a light switch as the door closes behind him. He finds the switch and flips it on.

"Surprise!" a party of at least fifty people dressed in business casual attire exclaim when the light comes on. The announcement is followed by a round of applause. The happiness on the faces of the wine glass and hors d'oeuvres-wielding guests show just how excited they are to see him. The building is a banquet hall that is much larger and nicer than it appeared from its exterior. A banner hanging from on the back wall reads *Welcome Home*. Greg recognizes a number of friends and co-workers from his old job. He walks through the middle of the crowd, relieved and no longer scared. Wearing a huge grin, he exchanges handshakes and embraces from one guest after another.

The night continues with dancing, drinking, and festivities. Several people pass out in their chairs from intoxication while some even dance on tables. Greg finds a spot in the corner alone and watches everyone enjoy themselves in celebration. His smile disappears as he senses that something about the environment doesn't feel quite natural. Thoughts of his waking life flash before his eyes.

Confetti rains down from the ceiling. He looks up and notices that the confetti is falling from nowhere, simply appearing out of thin air.

"Turn off the music," Greg announces in a loud voice. He looks around for the origin of the music but there isn't a DJ, sound system or speakers in the room.

The room goes completely quiet and everyone focuses their attention on him. Even those that were passed out drunk wake up appearing to be completely sober. Greg walks to the head of the room.

"I just wanna make an announcement," he says, before pausing and looking around at everyone. Greg notices the body of his former boss, Bill Elson, whose head previously exploded, seated in a chair next to the door. The crowd watches him, intent upon hearing what he has to say.

"I appreciate everything that you've done here for me," he continues. "You all are a part of me and I can't change that, nor would I ever want to. If it weren't for everyone here and this life I probably wouldn't be where I am now; all things happen for a reason. This is hard for me to do but, none of you are real people. Just concocted in my imagination. And it's time for me to move on."

Greg walks off the stage. All of the guests of the party become as wax figures, frozen in their positions. He walks through the maze of a crowd without looking back and exits the front door.

When Greg goes outside, the dark, desolate city is no longer there. It's daylight, and he finds himself walking out of the front door of a convenience store standing next to two boys whose ages range between 11 and 13. Greg is suddenly his 12 year old self.

"Greg, let me see your skateboard," the oldest boy says.

"See," Greg says as he lifts his skateboard from the ground, showing it to the older kid.

"Come on, man. I'll give it right back."

"My grandma told me not to let anyone else ride it but me," Greg says.

"You're such a pussy," the boy says. "What is she gonna do? Spank you?"

"Shut up, Andy," Greg says. "My grandma hasn't spanked me since I was a like six. She said since you guys are always breaking my stuff that only I can ride it, so when it gets broken she'll know who to blame."

"Let me see the skateboard," Andy says. "Just for a minute. I wanna show you a trick. I won't break it."

"Okay," Greg says, handing him the skateboard. "What's the trick?"

"I'm gonna make a skateboard disappear," Andy says.

He drops it on the ground and skates down the sidewalk at full speed. Greg chases him.

Andy stops and picks up the skateboard and runs away with it. Andy's younger brother, Paul, follows behind them, laughing.

The three boys run two blocks before Andy decides to run into the alley behind a Chinese restaurant to hide. The other two boys catch up and find Andy exhausted, breathing heavily, leaning on the old building near a large, rusty, green trash receptacle. The Dumpster is surrounded by discarded beer bottles, cardboard boxes, and other loose trash and debris.

"Ok, ok," Andy says. "I quit." He returns Greg's skateboard.

Paul is still hysterically laughing. Greg socks him on the shoulder.

"Ow," Paul says, rubbing his shoulder. "That hurt like a motherfucker. *I* didn't take your skateboard."

Andy stares at a large disposable aluminum roast pan near the emergency exit of the restaurant.

"What are you looking at?" Greg asks.

"That pan over there," Andy says. "Is that dog food?"

Paul walks to the pan to get a closer look.

"It is dog food," Paul exclaims. "Or cat food, I don't know."

"So it's true," Andy says. "They do cook dogs!"

"Maybe they're feeding them because they don't want them going in and out of the trash," Greg says.

"You're stupid," Andy says. "They're feeding 'em so they can trap 'em and feed 'em to their customers, dumb ass."

Greg walks closer to get a better view.

The boys suddenly hear rustling behind the Dumpster. Greg takes a peak to see what it is. A man jumps out from behind the trash fastening his belt, swiftly walking away trying to partially hide his face. Greg backs up slowly, his eyes still fixated behind the Dumpster.

"What's wrong?" Andy asks. "What is it?"

Greg runs away from the alley without looking back.

"Greg! Where ya' going?!" Paul calls out as Greg turns the corner of the buildings, out of their view.

Andy walks closer to the trash to find out what it was that had his friend so distraught. Linda, Greg's mother, is seated behind the Dumpster on top of a flattened cardboard box pulling up her tight, faded blue jeans. She looks up at Andy, shamelessly.

* * *

Greg makes it all the way home and slams the door on his way in. He walks down the narrow hall into his room and also slams that door. Ruth, who is preparing dinner, peeks around the corner curious to see what the commotion is.

Fuming with anger, Greg throws himself onto the bed, lies on his back, and stares at the ceiling. He closes his eyes and tears fall from the corners of his eyes. Ruth dries her hands and walks to his room. She knocks on the door.

"Greg," she says, "are you ok, sweetheart?

"I'm fine!" he yells back.

"Is there something you want to talk about?"

"No."

"Did you want to help me make dinner?" she asks.

"That's ok. I just want a little time to myself,

Grandma."

"I know there's something bothering you because you always want to help me cook," she says. "I'll leave you alone right now but we're going to talk about what happened over dinner, ok?"

"Ok."

"I love you," Ruth says.

"I love you too, Grandma."

* * *

Shannon walks into the hospital room where Greg lies on the table with his eyes shut, unconscious. She pulls up a chair next to the bed and takes a long look at him before sitting down. She takes his hand.

"There are so many things I want to say to you that I don't know where to start. I hope you can hear me right now. If you can't, I know I'll get the chance to tell you later, because you're gonna make it through this, ok?"

Shannon pauses and begins to smile through her tears.

"Me sitting right here next to you like this reminds me of the days I used to force feed you, the grits and scrambled eggs that I knew you didn't like but you ate to make me feel better."

Her smile dissipates. She sighs and the tears begin to fall profusely as she puts her head down and continues speaking to him.

"I'm sorry, Greg, I'm so sorry I did this to you. I left when you needed me the most. What you didn't realize is that you don't need me as much as you thought you needed me, you're strong. You're much stronger than I could ever be." She wipes her eyes and beneath her nose with a Kleenex and continues. "I need you much more than you need me and I regret not being able to see it. In the short time we've known each other I have never felt as comfortable around anyone else like I am with you. My life has never been happier. Not being around you is like torture for me and regardless of what anyone says, I want to be with you." She raises her head and looks at him. "It was the worst decision I have or will ever make for me to choose something else over someone so special to me. If I could go back I promise I'd pick you. I don't care what I have to do as long as I have you. I would give anything to have you back in my life. We made plans together; you're supposed to take me to the museum. I can't do those things with anyone else, but even if it's not with me, you deserve to be happy. You deserve to be here. Ever since you showed up, you've changed all of our lives. Please pull through because we love you. I love you so much." Unable to continue speaking through the tears, Shannon buries her face in the bed sheets and cries.

* * *

An adult Greg sits at the kitchen table while his grandmother chops vegetables for dinner.

"What have I told you about wearing your hat inside the house?" Ruth says.

"I'm not gonna be here long, Grandma," he says. "The quicker you give me that money, the quicker I get out of here."

"I gave you $30 yesterday," she says. "Where does all of this money go?"

"I'm about to head out and make a few runs and I just need a little spending money. You know I'll get it back to you."

"I'll think about it," Ruth answers.

Ruth quits chopping the vegetables, sets her knife down on the cutting board and hangs her head.

"Grandma," Greg says.

She doesn't acknowledge him.

"Grandma," he repeats. "What's wrong?"

"When you were a little boy you used to tell me 'Grandma, when I grow up I'm going to get a job and take care of you like you take care of me.' You said that you wanted to wear a suit and work in a tall building like the people on TV do *and* you wanted to be a chef. I said "Sweetheart, whatever you do I'll be proud of you,' and I'm *still* proud of you. But I must say that at this moment, for the first time in my life, I'm disappointed in you."

"Oh, come on, Grandma," Greg says. "It's a few bucks."

"It's not about the money," she says. "But boy do I wish it was only about the money."

Ruth turns around and looks at her grandson with an expression of sorrow and disappointment. A grievous look that resembles crying, minus the tears.

"What, Grandma?" he says. "Why are you looking at me like that?"

"Greg, I know what you do with the money I give you."

Greg frowns intensely, accompanied by a light shake of his head.

"What? What are you talking about?"

"I've been in denial for a long time," Ruth says. "When your mother started, I was naive; I knew nothing about drugs. But after so many years of seeing it, I can see the signs without even trying. You know your own children—and grandchildren—and you know when something's not right."

"Grandma," Greg says, defensively. "Stop it. You know I don't do any of that stuff."

She walks over to him and holds both sides of his face with her hands. She looks directly into his eyes.

He tries to keep eye contact with her but his conscious won't let his lying eyes do it.

"Greg," she says, still looking into his eyes. "I love you more than anything in this world.

Whatever you're doing, stop it. Please, I'm begging you. My heart can't bear to lose another one to drugs."

She walks back to the counter and continues chopping the vegetables.

"Grandma," Greg says. "I'm—"

Without even turning to him, she raises her hand to stop him from talking. "If you're going to lie to me, don't say anything."

"You're not even letting me say anything," he replies.

Ruth takes off her apron and sets it on the counter. She walks into her bedroom and sits on the bed, facing the window leading to the dreary outdoor weather.

Greg follows her and stops in the doorway. "Grandma, talk to me."

She ignores him.

Greg walks out of the room. He grabs his jacket and leaves, riding his bicycle in the drizzling rain en route to his apartment he shares with Paul and two other guys. The rain progresses from scattered sprinkles to a steady shower just as he reaches his destination.

The apartment is a converted garage attached to the back of an old convenience store that provides little room for four tenants. The garage is conducive to their lifestyle because the owner is indifferent to what goes on within the confines of the apartment as long as he receives his monthly $400 rent. Greg leans his bike against the peeling, painted tan brick building and opens the man door located next to the bay door that hasn't been opened in years.

He walks into the dark, musty room where his roommates are gathered. Paul and one of his other roommates are seated on the floor at a small rain-damaged wooden coffee table across from each other. Paul rolls an empty beer bottle on its side across a bag of roughly two grams of cocaine, crushing it. The roommate seated across from him reaches in his jacket and pulls out a pair of brand new syringes and two small bags of heroin and places them on the table. The fourth roommate is lazily sprawled across the worn-out futon.

"It's about fucking time," Paul says, glancing at Greg. "You were about to miss out, bro. You got your money?"

"No," Greg says.

"No? You've been gone long enough," Paul replies. "No IOUs today. I paid good money for this shit."

"I'm done," Greg says.

"Done with what?" Paul says, turning his attention away from the coffee table. Everyone looks at Greg.

"I can't do it anymore," Greg says. "I did some thinking and reflecting on my life on the way here."

They wait for him to expound on his statement.

"Have you guys ever thought about it? We're not far from thirty and so many years of our lives have been wasted doing the same shit every day. There's probably nothing we haven't done known to man to get high. What are we looking for? It's like a never-ending circle that's almost impossible to get out of. I don't wanna be like my mom. I just can't fucking do it anymore. None of you ever feel that way?"

"Not really," Paul says. "Good speech, though."

The others join Paul in laughter.

"First of all," Paul says. "You're nothing like your mom. Even though it's the most bang for your buck, you don't smoke meth. But as great as it is, it's not natural. Cocaine-natural, heroin-natural, LSD- comes from natural shit, Oxycontin-legal. Doctors use this shit. It's no worse than the chemically-altered food we eat every day. We've talked about this. The onlything we're guilty of is self-medication. Now come here, if it feels better, think of this as an early birthday gift."

"No, man," Greg says. "I'm done. I gotta leave."

"This shit is pearly white and as moist as your grandma's brownies, just like you like it.

At least try a little bit and see how you like it," Mike says. "My guy let me do a free test line and you know he doesn't give anything out free, trust me...it's some of the best I've ever had. No lie."

Greg puts his hand on the door knob. "No offense, fellas. I'm sorry, I decided I'm gonna move back in with my grandma until I get back on my feet. I'll be back to get my stuff later."

"You do hear that rain, don't you?" Paul points to the ceiling. Everyone remains quiet as they listen to the sound of the vigorous rain shower outside. "You might as well wait for it to die down before you leave."

Greg looks outside of the window and back at his friends. They no longer acknowledge his presence as they are now all sitting on the floor around the table as if preparing to eat a long awaited supper. Greg resists the temptation to join them. He thinks about his grandmother and how he had never seen her so sad in his life. He opens the door.

The bleak weather matches his dreary mood. He covers his head with his hood and walks outside, closing the door behind him. A short-haired, gray feral cat that he sometimes feeds rubs against his leg. He bends over and scratches her behind the ears. He stands up and grabs his bicycle and watches the heavy rain fall as he mentally preps himself for the trek through the dismal weather.

* * *

Shannon stares out of the rain-spattered window trying her hardest to cherish the short time that she has with Greg. She lies next to him on the cramped bed in a loose embrace with her arm draped across his body, her head resting lightly on his chest. She reminisces of the times they spent together and tries her hardest to forge future moments between the two of them in her mind. She looks at her watch and realizes that fifteen minutes have quickly passed and removes herself from the bed. She watches him for several seconds in hopes that he'll suddenly open his eyes. When he doesn't, she leans over him, lies upon his chest, closes her eyes and gives him one last hug. She stands up from the bed and gives him one more long stare before backing away toward the door.

"I'll be back later. I promise" she says. "I have to let

the others see you now. I love you."

She slowly walks out of the room, crying profusely, and closes the door behind her.

* * *

A five-year-old Greg lies in his twin size bed with his grandmother, his head rested on her warm body as she reads him a story. The huge smile of enthusiasm on her face are a telling sign that she enjoys these small moments as much as he does. Greg looks up and watches her facial expressions while listening to her voice the characters of his favorite childhood book about a man and a mermaid. She finishes the book and closes it.

"Ok, sweetheart," Ruth says. "Goodnight and—"

"Noooo," Greg says. "I don't *wanna* go to sleep."

"You want to grow up to be a big boy, don't you?" she says. "Do you want to be five years old forever?"

"No."

"Well if you don't sleep you won't grow up to be big and strong. But it's okay. I want you to be five forever so I can keep you here and hug you and kiss you forever." She hugs him and plants about five kisses on his face.

"Ok, ok, ok," he says, laughing hysterically, pushing her away. "Stop, Grandma!"

"Goodnight," she says. "I love you."

"I love you, too, Grandma," he says.

She walks to the door.

"Grandma," he says.

"Yes, sweetheart?" she asks.

"You can turn the light off. I'm not scared anymore."

She smiles at him and turns off the light.

* * *

A physician stands at the foot of the bed as the cardiac arrest resuscitation team awaits his orders after several failed, aggressive attempts to restart Greg's heart. The electrocardiogram displays asystole, a flat line.

"That's all we've got, lets call it. Time of death is 2214 hours," the doctor says.